ANSWERING THE CALL

Praise for *Answering The Call*

"Let gifted author Parris Afton Bonds be your guide as you join Lauren on this captivating adventure of a lifetime!"
—Cynthia Wright, NY Times and
USA Today Bestselling author

"Bonds' latest work is strengthened by her vividly descriptive prose and brisk pacing."
—*Kirkus Reviews* on *When the Heart is Right*

ANSWERING THE CALL

PARRIS
AFTON BONDS

Other Books by
Parris Afton Bonds

Reluctant Rebel

THE TEXICANS
*The Brigands • The Barons
The Bravados • The Betrayers
The Banshees*

*Blue Bayou • Blue Moon
The Calling of the Clan • The Captive
Dancing with Crazy Woman • Dancing with Wild Woman
Deep Purple • Dream Keeper • Dream Time • Dust Devil
The Flash of the Firefly • For All Time
Kingdom Come: Temptation • Kingdom Come: Trespass
Lavender Blue • Love Tide
Made For Each Other • Midsummer Midnight
Mood Indigo • No Telling
Renegade Man • Run To Me
Savage Enchantment • The Savage
Snow And Ice • Spinster's Song
Stardust • Sweet Enchantress
Sweet Golden Sun • The Wildest Heart
Wanted Woman • Widow Woman
Windsong • When the Heart is Right*

This is a work of fiction. No part of the publication may be reproduced, distributed, or transmitted in any form or by any means, or stored in a database or retrieval system, without the prior written permission of the publisher.

Text copyright © 2023 by Parris Afton Bonds
All Rights Reserved. Printed in the United States of America
Published by Motina Books, LLC, Van Alstyne, Texas
www.MotinaBooks.com

Library of Congress Cataloguing-in-Publication Data:

Names: Afton Bonds, Parris
Title: Answering the Call
Description: First Edition. | Van Alstyne: Motina Books, 2023

Identifiers:

LCCN: 2023934415

ISBN-13: 979-8-88784-013-0 (paperback)
ISBN-13: 979-8-88784-012-3 (e-book)

Subjects: BISAC:

Fiction > Romance > Suspense
Cover and Interior Design: Diane Windsor

It's always the friends we encounter, and not the sights, in our life's travels who make the difference.

For Linda Cudd, Sandy Bazinet, and Murray Pura
You have made a difference in my life's travels.

AUTHOR'S NOTE

I do not think I would deem this novel even semi-autobiographical; however, it does encapsulate a phase in this last part of my life, when, at seventy-eight and fifty novels more or less under my belt, I decided to answer the call to adventure and move to Mexico. I sold my household furniture and my car and kept only enough clothing to pack into two suitcases. A third one contained my laptop and miscellaneous financial documents. The items in my purse included the requisite passport and my COVID vaccinations card.

During this year in Querétaro, Mexico, I wrote *Answering the Call*. I hope my novel enlightens and entertains—that it enlightens somewhat, at least, my approach to the aging process, as well as, living in a foreign country, but even more importantly I fervently hope it entertains the reader.

CHAPTER 1

There has to be an easier way.
 The words slipped unbidden and aloud over Lauren Hillard's lips. Each morning as she showered . . . or sometimes earlier, when groping to shut off the alarm . . . the phrase audaciously intruded. Still its daily surfacing never failed to take her by surprise.

Naturally, her mind would be fixated on that day's demands. They centered around a monotonous routine, dominated by her older daughter's psychotherapist practice which Lauren managed: wake, go to work, return home, go to bed and read a while, go to sleep—or not, as was more often the case these days. Occasionally, lunch or an outing with friends or family interrupted the regimen.

For how long now had the words *There has to be an easier way* leaked in and out of her consciousness first thing in the morning? Two or three years? Something within her insisted there had to be more meaning to life.

She was aware that life was continuing around her; yet participate though she did, she in no way felt part of life.

She was not clinically depressed, as her daughter Renita might label it, just apathetic.

She tried Meetup's book clubs, Spanish classes, hiking expeditions, choral groups, and more. Nevertheless, she invariably felt as if she did not belong . . . did not belong anywhere anymore.

For over a year, she had volunteered a couple of evenings or weekends at Houston's MD Anderson Cancer Center. In observing the magnitude of suffering and only occasional relief or remission for the patients, rather than feel fortunate for her circumstances, she felt burdened by guilt. Guilt, because she had so much—yet felt so alone, so bereft. This despite her good health at nearly seventy, her family and friends, and her relatively stable financial security.

"Relatively stable financial security" only for so long as she continued to work for Renita. Lauren's Social Security benefits were only one bump above being a bag lady. Her funds, frugally saved over the years, were overseen by Renita's latest partner, a financial planner who successfully managed other people's money.

Of course, Lauren's younger daughter Sylvie had offered recently for Lauren to live with her and her husband, to which Lauren amiably but adamantly refused. Her stomach knotted with the thought of her daughters tucking her away like a precious heirloom on a shelf.

Yet, if she wished to live off her social security benefits and abstain from dipping into her savings, her options were zero. Her condo lease would expire in two months. Either she renewed the lease now and continued working for yet another year—or give her two-month notice to vacate, resign herself to shelf life with Sylvie and her husband, and tell Renita that she would be retiring from Behavioral Health Solutions.

Naturally, Renita would go off into one of her fits. Her authoritarian approach to muddled patients was mollified by Lauren's coddling them before and after appointments.

Renita and Lauren's polar but complimenting personalities were probably the reason the clinic's balance sheet stayed in the black over the years, although just barely. Nineteen years before, Lauren had quit her lucrative position as advertising manager for Pepsico International to help jumpstart her daughter's burgeoning psychotherapist practice.

Lauren toweled off, swiftly dressed in appropriate muted colors with low heels, and for a more subdued appearance clipped up her dark, shoulder-length hair, shot full with gray. Lastly, she lightly swiped on the requisite makeup for the working woman of a certain age—mascara, a deft brushing of rouge, and a smudge of pale matte lipstick.

Nothing vivid to attract awareness to her frame, no longer sleek; nor to the faint wrinkles amassing around her eyes, the marionette lines recently evidencing at either side of her mouth, and the faltering flesh at her once firm jawline. A furtive glance in the mirror confirmed her dismal reality . . . she was gradually fading from view.

But then that was one good thing about her aging appearance—she was not terribly disappointed by its deterioration, as she had never really felt pretty anyway.

By the time her daughter arrived at Behavioral Health Solutions, promptly at fifteen minutes before eight, Lauren had already started the coffee, turned on Echo's soothing music background, opened her computer, and was reviewing the day's patient schedule.

Renita cast a brief smile for Lauren. "Morning, Mother." Striding briskly toward her office, her forty-seven-year-old sturdy physique was still indicative of her college track scholarship.

She out-topped Lauren's five feet, two inches by another good eight inches. Then, too, Lauren suspected her advancing years had robbed her of a precious inch despite her sporadic efforts at yoga, Pilates, and tennis. "Morning, babe."

That early morning exchange was the only time they addressed one another personally within the office confines. Thereafter throughout the work hours, they addressed each other as Dr. Hillard and Lauren.

Emerging from her office, Renita shrugged into one of her starched white coats with its ID tag. She felt the white coat instilled the sense of a professional practice. Her auburn hair, cut short for efficiency, looked untidy lately. And she seemed cranky.

Lauren had to wonder if her daughter and partner Rick were having domestic problems; or maybe Renita was experiencing her excruciating migraines more often. Or just maybe she was on the verge of menopause, which could trigger psychotic behavior in even a sainted abbess.

She came up behind Lauren's desk. "You didn't forget Rick's birthday party tonight at our house, did you, Mother?"

In Renita's tone was a barely perceptible note of disparagement. While mentally counting to five before answering, Lauren watched the provider insurance info app open on her computer screen. "Of course not. I bought Rick his favorite cologne. And already gift wrapped it. Just need to sign the card." She could feel the usual morning tension gathering taut her shoulder blades, like Velcro tugging on them.

Normally, Andi Lyons, the front-desk eighteen-year old, hotfooted it in anywhere between eight-twenty and eight twenty-nine. Instead, she called, wailing, "The alarm didn't go off!" She would be forty-five minutes late.

The Velcro tugged even closer on Lauren's shoulder blades. That meant double duty for her, covering the telephone and checking-in the first patient, in addition to performing her own tasks—medical billing, coding insurance claims, and collecting on past due accounts.

Still, how could she be annoyed with Andi? The pudgy lilliputian girl exuberated life in the staid office. Her chatty, carefree demeanor tended to relax any anxious patients in the waiting room. Adhering to the clinic's office procedure manual, Andi was careful to keep her forearm tats covered and her piercings free of flashy rings in nostrils, brows, and lips. Her punk haircut with shaved sides and a pop of maroon on the top could not be concealed as easily.

Finally, the day's last patient, along with Renita and Andi, left at a little after six o'clock. Lauren began making her rounds—turning off the computers, silencing Echo, and shutting the blinds. Just before she flicked off the lights, her cell phone rang.

It was Renita. "You remembered to fax Howard Beech's demographics to Mercy Sanitorium, right, Mother?"

Perplexed, Lauren frowned. "No. You never told me you wanted me to."

"Yes, I did, damn't. Yesterday, right after he checked out."

It seemed to Lauren her older daughter's cursing was increasing concurrently with her growing impatience with her mother. Cell phone cradled between shoulder and ear,

Lauren backtracked to her desk and flipped over her notebook's page to the day before. "No, I made no note of that."

A heavy sigh. "That's because you forgot to."

The Velcro cinched tighter. Six months ago, when suddenly rising from her office chair, she had suffered abrupt dizziness, which resulted in the chair rolling from beneath her when she went to sit back down—and in her striking her head on the filing cabinet behind. Since then, Renita and her sister Sylvie, fearing a mini-stroke, had been eagle-eyeing her for lapses of any kind.

This continued scrutiny by Lauren's daughters annoyed her, and their seemingly offhanded quips regarding her memory worried her. Sure, occasionally she forgot an intention or thought when passing from one room to another or misplaced her eyeglasses, as she used to do before cataract surgery abolished the need for them. Besides, did not everyone experience that kind of forgetfulness? So what if these episodes may have increased. No big whoop.

Still, since the dizzy spell she had begun keeping the notebook. She could imagine nothing worse than getting Alzheimer's.

With a flourish Rick Mosely unwrapped Lauren's birthday gift. "Sun Song—my favorite!" He looped an arm around her shoulders and gave an affectionate squeeze.

The high-end cologne had put a dent in her monthly budget, but then she adored the amenable man. He aptly managed her portfolio with its Pepsico pension fund and other investments. More importantly, he adored Renita, acquiescing to her highhanded ways. A health nut, he was the fifth partner for Lauren's adamantly single daughter in the last twenty-five years and the longest-lasting at eight.

On the other hand, Lauren's younger daughter, the portly Sylvie, had taken to marriage and motherhood early on, giving birth to twin boys followed immediately by another son. Thanks to her corporate-lawyer husband, Burnett Cohen, she had never needed to work outside the home. As of last fall, all three children were away at college. With the bedrooms vacant, forty-three-year-old Sylvie was suffering the empty-nest syndrome. Which explained why she had importuned Lauren to come live with them.

After the birthday candles were blown out and the store-bought cake passed around to the five of them, the desultory conversation was mixed with intent cell phone perusal.

Lauren thought how lucky she was to have grown up before technology had taken over the world. She recalled how, when she was a kid, her parents and their friends played games that involved the children, like Black Magic and Under the Blanket. And she remembered with nostalgia how her mother had made from scratch Lauren's favorite, Mississippi Mud Cake, as in turn Lauren had made for her own two daughters.

She had loved being a mother, having the children stepping on her feet. Later on, in the midst of her daughters' late teenage years, she had off and on allowed her home to serve as a landing place, lasting anywhere from a few days to a few months, for their friends, who for one reason or another were temporarily homeless.

Life these days seemed weirdly plastic, disassociated from genuine personal contact. Even that tactile act of touching and hugging. Or was she just growing old and senile?

Burney, who, as opposed to Rick, was prone to be on the heavy side, swallowed another mouthful of cake, then asked. "Well, Lauren, did you give any more thought about moving into that community in Tanglewood?" His hairline was a duet of cul-de-sacs.

Lauren blinked at him. She set aside her tasteless cake. Were her tastebuds dying off or were store-bought pastries leached of richness by lack of human touch? "Which community in Tanglewood was that?"

Renita hummphed. "Several weeks ago, I told you about that old-aged home in Tanglewood, Mother."

Sylvie glanced up from perusing her cell phone and squinted over her bifocals. "The community is inhabited by the crème de la crème, is that right, Sis?"

"Yes, but Tanglewood is less than some of the other old-people places I checked out."

Old-people places? One could never accuse Renita of diplomacy.

"Retirement home," Burney amended. If ever there was a role meant for the smooth-talking attorney he was, it was that of the crafty diplomat.

Was tonight's gathering some sort of tribalism that sowed in Lauren the TV series *Survivor*'s seeds of distrust? "I don't recall committing to investigating a move there, Renita." And she could not envision being confined to living with people of her age only—"old people", as Renita styled it. This birthday party was turning out to be about as pleasant as a gynecological exam.

Answering The Call

Renita sighed and rose to refill her brandy snifter from the buffet's crystal decanter. "Well, not to worry about your forgetfulness, Mother."

Something in Lauren's chest tightened. Now, she could imagine something worse than Alzheimer's: the oppressive feeling of being lovingly gaslighted.

CHAPTER 2

There has to be an easier way.

As usual, the phrase tumbled from Lauren's lips in tempo with her shower's pelting drops, word by word. There. Has. To. Be. An. Easier. Way.

She had not heard an insistent inner voice since her childhood. Maybe she had been more open to it as a child, when her father would begin his drinking.

He came from oil money that went back through the family's gene pool almost to 1901 when nearby Spindletop spewed its geyser. She had never lacked for anything. Her mother had ensured she attended the best schools, from modeling to music, in an effort to make her more appealing. At one point, her mother badgered her about plastic surgery. "Long, straight noses are out these days, precious. Pixie noses are in." She had managed to outflank her mother on that idea.

Somewhere toward Lauren's high school years, the money drained out, siphoned by her mother's compulsive spending and her father's obsessive drinking. His binges often precipitated one of his tyrannical rampages. At those times, Lauren's intuition might whisper *Run!* or *Hide!* Only a single word, never a complete sentence . . . like, *There has to be an easier way.*

She finished showering. Early mornings were always the worst for her. May's dawning light had yet to breach her condo's high bath window. She craved sunlight. Sunlight to dispel night's lingering despondency.

Often, she would wake at three or four o'clock, unable to return to sleep. In those nocturnal hours, she occasionally would ponder the merits of living to an advanced age. What was the point of living another 'Groundhog Day" life until one's last exhalation? One day after another the same.

As she drove to work in the pre-dawn dark, she considered taking up another hobby. Her family was occupied with its own affairs and friends, and her grandchildren were away at college. Most likely, any hobby she undertook she would eventually add to her discarded ones—macrame, butterfly watching, cycling, painting, and on and on.

She continued to dabble in music, writing sentimental lyrics that in these days and times sounded corny. And then there was stargazing. The most wasteful time of all hobbies most would declare—and among the more difficult pastime pursuits, given that the "Stars at night are big and bright, deep in the Heart of Texas" was not true of Houston's light pollution.

All these were good pastime hobbies in which she engaged. But was that all that life was about . . . merely passing time?

What was wrong with her? What had happened to the Lauren who had been salutatorian of Lamar High School?

Who had been exhilarated about what the future offered? Who in one *grande folie* that summer following graduation had forfeited acceptance to The Julliard School of Music to backpack through Spain?

She had fallen in love with another backpacker while hitchhiking on the pilgrimage route to Santiago de Compostela and married, that's what. A college student who, like her, was impassioned by music.

She sighed with the flood of might-have-been memories and was turning her attention to getting the clinic up and running that morning, when Andi entered at 8:28.

"OMG, what a night, Ms. L!" With painstaking short steps from the office's parquet entry, the girl targeted her front desk chair.

Lauren looked up from the printer, adjacent to Andi's desk. The fax confirmation for Howard Beech's demographics was printing out. Lauren was a day late in sending the fax if Renita's claim that Lauren had forgotten to follow up was correct. "Is that as in 'hot dang!' or 'hell's bells!'?"

"As in for real—a for real Cinco de Mayo party last night." She stashed her chartreuse and purple tote bag beneath the desk counter and, slumping into her chair, flung a forearm to her forehead, crushing her short, spiked coif. Green today. "But way too many margaritas. I don't know how those Mexicans do it."

Lauren snagged the fax confirmation and, skirting Andi's chair, said, "I would suggest the hair of the dog, but I doubt the concoction will work its wonders that quickly before our first patient."

"A what dog?"

"Never mind." At eighteen, the girl was too young to

understand that colloquial expression. Or Lauren was too old to relate to the contemporary jargon. Furthermore, at eighteen the girl was too young to drink, at least, legally. "Instead, Andi, I would suggest a couple of Aleve from the medicine cabinet before work gets started."

The girl managed a sickly grin. "Aye, aye, Ms. L. For real, you boomers got it down."

A wry smile tempered Lauren's reproving expression. She could not remember ever being that young and heedless. The younger generation's slang and, especially, their cacophonous rap music were incomprehensible to her.

She had only to hear the operatic "Un Bel Di, Vedremo" and invariably she would be swept back to that day at twenty-nine, when she sat in her beat-to-shit Pinto, its windows rolled up, and fell apart.

She had been driving back from her husband funeral, with seven-year-old weeping Renita and whiny four-year-old Sylvie, sitting in the back.

Marty had been a wonderful father but not much of a provider. A rock musician—a romantic and a dreamer and a drug addict—he had saddled her with a mountain of debts, not counting hospital bills, and two jobs to hold down. Along with a string of infidelities for her to deal with. One might say that over the years he had indeed been killing her softly with his songs. When he died, they had been separated for almost two years.

Suddenly, her Pinto's rear tire had blown out, and she swerved off the pavement, just missing a bicyclist. Shaken, she gripped the steering wheel and pressed her forehead against it. She had exactly $37 to her name. Not enough to purchase a new tire. And the spare tire had more patches than her daughters' tattered jeans. Worse, her credit cards were maxed out.

At that moment, the car's cassette player was scratchily pouring out the Puccini aria. She had yelled her rage and screamed her agony in accompaniment to Madame Butterfly's mounting, tragic finale. In stunned silence Renita and Sylvie had watched and listened to their stalwart, practical mother's tearful nuclear meltdown.

She had been angry with God. Over the years that anger had mellowed, if that was the best descriptive word, to a sourness inside. She had come to understand that awful day that her wild, mindless rage would bury her early. Over time, she could only grieve herself deep to the bone.

Afterward, in the years to pass, she arrived at the epiphany that each experience enhanced her, that each failure was a triumph. She was learning to be kind to herself. Learning that it was not always easy to be alive. She could relentlessly choose to be happy doing daily tedious tasks—or even doing something as far-fetched as traveling around the world searching for happiness.

CHAPTER 3

There has to be an easier way.

Showering, Lauren ignored, as usual, the morning's repetition of mindless words. One blessing to aging—she no longer had to shave her underarms nor legs. Another blessing—her stomach, pooched by pregnancies, prevented her from peeping directly down to see the scarcity of pubic hair. And its graying.

Not that anyone but her gynecologist would be noting that condition these days.

It had been an astonishing five years since she had been in an intimate relationship, and that had lasted a mere six months. She had met the guy in a grocery store checkout line. After he overheard the clerk, glancing at her driver's license, wish her a happy birthday, he had chatted her up. Turned out he and Lauren shared the same birthday, down to the year. A charmer, he had settled into pretty much the proverbial couch potato.

Since then, she had occasionally contemplated going online to one of the dating websites for older people but could not summon the energy nor enthusiasm. She simply did not get around much anymore.

Years before, in her late-fifties, she had signed up on a website for seniors. Apparently fresh meat, she received nearly a hundred responses overnight. And apparently, she culled the wrong five to respond to. The dates had been fiascoes of monumental proportions. Few resembled their photos. One expected her to pay. Another tried groping her beneath the table.

The subject of dating must have been in the air that morning. "A freakin' hottie!" Andi eased her body gingerly into her office chair and nudged her tote bag beneath the counter. "Would you believe, like, a total hunk, Ms. L? After last night's gyrations, I could use a chiropractor this morning."

Andi chalked up a different lay practically every week. But who was Lauren to judge, when her own private parts were atrophying? Like her life itself? "Where did you meet this one?"

"At last week's Cinco de Mayo fiesta at Fritz Park." She shook out her hand, as if her beringed fingertips were burnt. Her bubblegum-pink lips pouted. "When Vincente Talamantes didn't call me, I called him—and glad I am I did. He is one scorching Mexicano."

A feeble rejoinder was the best she could summon. "Ahh, yes—that cliched Mexican temperament for passion." Christ almighty, that sounded like some bon mot from the Edwardian age.

Perhaps, she should attempt online dating again. Back in her office, she searched several dating sites on her computer. She scanned down the list. Toward the bottom, Silver Singles displayed complimentary reviews. Should she?

Could she?

"Good God, Mother—you can't be serious! Dating sites?!"

Her head jerked around. Renita was peeking over Lauren's shoulder at her computer screen. "I didn't hear you come in, babe."

Renita's expression puckered as if she had tasted a lemon. Like a mini gavel, her long finger rapped the desk. "All men want from a woman your age is a nurse or a purse."

It was everything she could do to keep her molars from grinding to powder. "Or, maybe, just a fuck."

Renita's eyebrows shot past her shingled bangs. Then she scoffed. "This search is for Andi, right? That girl could benefit from some psychotherapy."

"Because?" Andi had rebelled against her Pentecostal parents, who had kicked her out of the house the year before, leaving her to camp out in a dump of an apartment. Feeling the teenager was merely seeking to establish her own identity, which was in actuality a first name of Miriam and not Andi, Lauren had convinced Renita to hire the teenager, despite tats, piercings, and spiked neon hair.

"Because the girl's clearly fucking just to be fucking."

"Isn't that judgment a tad bit harsh?"

Renita crossed her arms and glared down at her. "Not a judgment at all. My professional evaluation. Surveys show females are less likely to reach orgasm in casual sex and one-night stands."

God, give me the patience of Buddha. "I've managed your Behavioral Health Solutions long enough, babe, to know psychobabble."

"Then you should realize your behavior is abnormal for a

woman of your age, considering having sex."

Something was building in Lauren. Had been building for some time now. A cage's bars she had to break through. Bars of her own making. By acquiescing. By appeasing. By ignoring. "Ahh, for the good old days of 'zipperless fuck.'"

"What?"

"You wouldn't understand. Erica Jong celebrated the female fantasy forty years ago, where 'zippers fell away like rose petals and underwear blew off in one breath like dandelion fluff.'"

Aghast, the rigid set of Renita's mouth wobbled. "Mother!"

"You're shocked?" Renita had done the same over the years, bedded down with whatever male was available for the weekend. If Lauren did not know better, she would swear her daughter was going schizoid on her. But then was it not a given that the best therapists studied psychology to unravel what they deemed impaired themselves?

"Appalled is more like it. And disgusted."

Her daughter's accompanying roll of her eyes was the same reaction she had rendered at thirteen when Lauren had finally decided at thirty-five-years-old it was high time she thwarted societal mores. She had pierced her ears and worn gypsy hooped earrings. The same thunderstruck reaction Lauren's own mother had delivered when Lauren had asked as a teenager to pierce her ears. "Only trashy females pierce their ears, Lauren."

With a click of her finger, she deleted the search tab and glanced over her shoulder. "Well, Renita, it is getting to be increasingly apparent whom I have become—a staid old lady. And I am not liking it one whit— or more to the point—I don't give a fuck about your opinion."

CHAPTER 4

There has to be an easier way.

"What on God's green earth does that mean exactly?" Surprised to hear herself for the first time responding aloud to those words automatically muttered each morning, Lauren stood rooted beneath the showerhead and blinked against the pelting water.

Talking to oneself was not abnormal. But did they not say that when one began answering oneself, that was the sign of a mental disorder?

Her mouth slanted in a warped smile. Without a booming social life, to whom else would she talk? She recognized her days were devolving into grand monotony. Was there an easier way than forging through each day's routine of working and sleeping? Of repetitious weekends gardening or Sundays, dutifully singing in the church choir? Ultimately, she was stagnating.

At work that morning, Andi's attention was once again focused on Vincente Talamantes. Lauren said, "I take it this is getting serious?"

"Duh, I hope not. What with the guy jobless? He's an exchange student at Rice University, for Pete's sake. But that Mexican can do more with his über cock than, I mean like, a conductor can do with his baton."

Lauren bit back her laughter over the chit's outrageous imagery. Nevertheless, her mention of a baton reminded Lauren that the Houston Symphony Orchestra was presenting tomorrow night the legendary violinist Itzhak Perlman. Music was to Lauren what drugs had been to her husband Marty.

She considered inviting her lifelong friend from high school, Jayne. But lately Jayne's dementia had accelerated so rapidly, Lauren was not sure if come tomorrow Jayne would remember the time, much less the invitation.

So many friends of Lauren's age were incapacitated. Physically, like her second cousin Marsha, crippled by severe rheumatoid arthritis in feet and hands. Emotionally, like her neighbor Bill, a Vietnam vet suffering agoraphobia from severe PTSD. Or mentally, like Jayne. Too many other friends had already been claimed by death.

Her mouth scrunched. It had been a hard-learned lesson that life was about learning to let go. Still, she had to wonder what was up with her moodiness lately. Did aging come with an abrupt overnight plunge in hormones?

She thought about a wedding of a friend's granddaughter she had attended last week. Looking like a chaperon from England's Victorian period at the reception, Lauren had sat on the sidelines, watching while the youthful guests romped on the dance floor to music that did not resonate with her as music.

She recalled when she had been that young and full of enthusiasm and zest and anticipation. And she recalled the high school jock who had gotten away. And recalled her dreams of a grand singing/dancing career. Ahhh, the what ifs of life.

At that night's wedding reception, she had not remembered feeling so old, feeling more than nearly three-quarters of a century old. Drier than the biblical dust to dust.

She had to wonder why she was still here. Still on her terrestrial journey. To be of service to others? She was weary of always being on call for family members and friends. If a stroke keeled her over where she sat at that evening's reception, she would have been fine with "The End."

CHAPTER 5

There has to be an easier way.

That morning, as she towel-dried her upper arm's saggy underflesh, Lauren reflected, getting older was the hardest thing she ever had to do. In both youth and old age, suffering occurred. But youth normally possessed the exuberance to go past the bruising, to trudge through the suffering; while it seemed that, at least with herself, the accumulation of years had drained her of the energy, of the enthusiasm, to forge ahead after accumulating tsunamic setbacks.

These days, she was merely existing. Treading water while faced with the inevitability of sinking.

And soon she would turn seventy. All the years she had wasted. No, she could not let herself think that way. She had learned from all her mistakes, right? Wisdom came with age. Or should.

She tossed aside the damp towel and grabbed her panties. No sexy thongs for her. The outrageously thin strip not only chaffed her but was extremely unsanitary in her opinion. Not that her opinion mattered to the younger generations. Still, better to go without the invasive strip, even if it meant forsaking panties altogether.

Recalling the week she had abandoned her panties, a slight grin lightened her morning miasma. That magical, wondrous week in a thatched-roof bungalow outside Puerto Vallarta with a midlife fling, whose name she could not even summon. Reveling with him on the sand and in the sea, naked as Venus and Eros.

She sighed. Midlife . . . as opposed to Beginning of life and now End of life.

She finished dressing and headed to work, the last place she wanted to be that morning. But then that was the sum total of her problem. She did not know where she wanted to be. She felt like she no longer belonged, fit in, anywhere.

She could muster no enthusiasm for travel. Not Paris or London or Budapest or Cairo. Nor did she possess the funds for travel. Not if she wanted to ensure any semblance of future independence, the funds of which Rick was safeguarding.

If she thought she was feeling low in spirits, Andi's limp posture as she slumped into her office chair like a bag of mulch decreed she could win a limbo contest. How low could one go? Damned low was the answer to Lauren's inquiry if Andi was feeling all right.

"Vincente's exchange term is up. He's returning to his family in Querétaro, Mexico." She folded her arms on her desk and sunk her head into them.

This relationship had been hot and heavy for some time now. "Well . . . would you want to join him?"

"He's not interested in me. Not in our kid I'm carrying either."

"Fuck!" Lauren breathed.

Andi raised her head. A wan smile contradicted her perky pink lipstick. "It's the fucking that got me in trouble, thank you very much, Ms. L."

She withheld remonstrating that it was the lack of protection that got the girl with child. "Has he told you explicitly he doesn't want the baby?"

"Explicitly?"

She stifled a sigh. "In plain words, has he said, 'Andi, I do not want this child of ours?'"

Andi's head tick-tocked. "Well, no. He doesn't know. But he once told me, in plain words, he wanted a law degree before he started a family." She grimaced. "Besides, he's already flaked on me. Leaving on that jet plane—don't know when he'll be back again."

The girl knew John Denver lyrics? There was hope for the younger generation. "Do you want to keep your baby?"

Her shoulders hunched. "I don't know. It's too gross to think about right now. I can't stomach bratty kids." Her palm dropped to her barrel-like midsection, no more rounded at this point than before. "And I can't stomach having a larger stomach than I'm already cursed with."

Nevertheless, the girl jimmied open the lower of her desk drawers. It contained her stash of Cheetos, Orange Slices, Sun Chips, Snickers, and Cheez Its. Her palliatives when stressed.

Lauren dropped a consoling hand on the girl's shoulder.

At that moment, Renita sallied forth from her office and glared, as if her mother and front desk secretary were plotting a conspiracy. "Lauren, Kathy Bergstrom is due in fifteen minutes. Have her medical notes and billing records been updated?"

Lauren swallowed another sigh. "Yes. I updated you in an email yesterday, Reni—Dr. Hillard."

Her daughter humphed. "It's not in my email, Lauren."

For a psychotherapist, Renita was coming up short in the patience department. But then treating emotionally bereft and complaining patients for twenty years could leach patience and compassion out of any doctor. "Have you checked your 'deleted' folder?"

Renita's fist jammed on her high hips, a legacy of her father's physique, along with Lauren's long legs. "Of course. First thing."

Well, that was interesting. Renita was now keeping track of Lauren's activities. Why? To prove incompetency? In that case, Lauren would willingly resign. However, what if her daughter suspected dementia? Fear goaded Lauren to respond defensively. "Then I suggest you check your junk mail, Dr. Hillard."

Renita's temperament had never been an amiable one. Stout even in childhood, she had suffered from poor self-image. Reflecting on Renita's childhood tantrums, Lauren had to give serious consideration to how often she herself had come up short as a single parent.

Renita had suffered the loss of her father more than Sylvie. Renita had been a daddy's girl. Her severe depression would too often turn into rage. Once, during that stressful period after her father's death, she had inflicted cuts on her wrists and undersides of her forearms. That was when Lauren sought psychotherapy through a local nonprofit social welfare organization. And, most likely, that was later the gem for Renita's career choice.

But Sylvie had suffered, too. Nightmares of being buried alive had plagued Lauren's younger daughter for years.

With Marty's death and the ensuing financial struggles, multiple jobs at one time, sometimes working seven days a week for months on end, Lauren had to acknowledge that all too often she had been emotionally, mentally, and physically unavailable for her daughters.

Many sleepless nights she had feared she did not have the wherewithal to make the next month's rent, let alone continue a single day more. From where would the bus money come that she needed to go to work? And what about the lesser funds for hosiery required at work? Returning milk bottles for deposit money did not cut the cake.

Those harried days, she feared that if she let herself break down, if she started screaming, she would be unable to stop. Paramedics would haul her off to the loony bin . . . and who then would care for Renita and Sylvie? Not Marty's parents. He had been estranged from them since he was seventeen, when he struck out on his own. And her parents?

When her mother, at fifty-two, had begun showing signs of early-onset of Alzheimer's— though that specific diagnosis was not widely used at that time—Lauren's father, now a raging alcoholic, had been helpless in caring for his wife.

Initially, Lauren's mother had begun acting fearful about the least little sounds outside the house. She claimed someone was trying to break in. Her paranoia became more aggressive. She yelled that she was being held prisoner in her own home and struck out when Lauren or her father tried to calm her.

So, Lauren had to assume that duty of looking after her mother, as well . . . eventually committing her mother to a care facility, while continuing to care for her doddering father along with her daughters. Both her mother and father had died within the next three years. And Lauren could only feel guilty at the relief rolling off her shoulders with their early deaths, even though death had relieved them of their sufferings.

That was the scariest part . . . that, as Renita had been hinting these past months, careful to camouflage her wording, Lauren was transitioning to the beginning stage of Alzheimer's, as had her own mother. And if anyone would know for certain, it would be Lauren's daughter, the professional, the psychotherapist.

Oh, dear God, no! Don't let it be so.

Lauren went back to her office. She opened up her **sent** emails, also praying she would find there the email to her daughter regarding the patient Kathy Bergstrom.

CHAPTER 6

There has to be an easier way.

An easier way than the spirit being slowly suffocated in some mental health institution.

The last thing Lauren wanted was for her daughters to be burdened by caring for her in their homes. And, since she had not found the Kathy Bergstrom email in her **sent** folder last week, it would appear Lauren's mental lapses were increasing. But she could have sworn she sent the email.

She was frightened. Was she in denial? Giving this serious consideration, her morning shower altered from brisk scrubbing to distracted lathering.

From both professional experience, working alongside her daughter, and personal experience, genuinely solicitous attention to Behavior Health Solution's patients, Lauren should be able to diagnose the precursors to Alzheimer's. If she was indeed exhibiting symptoms, Renita could prescribe medications to help manage the symptoms.

Lauren felt backed into a corner. In silent reverie, she asked herself what could she do? What did she want to do?

Answering The Call

There has to be an easier way.

Never had those words drifted across her tongue twice in one day. So, what was the import behind this daily dribble?

That there was that other option? That drastic one? It was said the window of cognizance to end the macabre existence of life attenuated by Alzheimer's was small. Her gambit would be then a sort of now or never one. She had access to Renita's office cabinet of sample medications. Enough samples could produce the desired fatal result.

Mexico.

Lauren's apathetic scrubbing froze. As if the shower's water was suddenly pelting hailstones, she recoiled a step. "What?"

No response. But from where had that single, very audible word found its way across her lips?

Surely, a subconscious remnant from her conversations with Andi about her Mexican lothario, Vincente Talamantes.

Lauren finished bathing and toweled off. Nevertheless, that solitary word *Mexico*. . . and its exotic image . . . hounded her as she drove to work, opened the office, and worked throughout the day.

The addled Andi had her act far more together that day than Lauren. She dropped two calls with insurance companies, sent an email to a wrong address, and miscoded a patient's bill.

Her mind was truly squirrely, coming up with an outlandish idea that Mexico was the remedy for her crippling dilemma. Yet the idea had taken root. There she would either find a way to renew her life or end it, by the means easily acquired in that country. Doubtlessly, Mexico beckoned her, summoned her.

Toward closing time, her daughter summoned Lauren to her office with an imperious wave of her hand. Going to stand behind her desk, Renita ruffled through a sheaf of papers with impatient fingers. "Mother—Lauren—I never received yesterday's paid vouchers." Her tone was saturated with frustration.

Lauren sagged into the nearby green leather-upholstered chair. Her right hand rubbed at her pulsing temple. "What can I say? As I always do at the end of the day, I put the binder clip of vouchers in your inbox."

Renita dropped into her desk chair and, leaning forward, clasped her hands, their forefingers pointing at Lauren like an executionary squad's rifles. "I didn't want to bring this up, this soon, but I have ordered an evaluation of your mental faculties."

"What?"

"You understand, it's for your own good. For your safety, your security."

Lauren's backbone straightened like a yardstick. "What are you implying?"

Her daughter delivered what Lauren interpreted as a placating smile. "Only that Sylvie and I—and the rest of our family—have your best interests at heart. We are concerned about you, Mother, and we want to take care of you. You deserve this, after all you have done for us. No more working, no more watching every penny."

Silence while Lauren grappled with the intent behind her daughter's solicitous words. "What . . . what did the evaluation show? And on what exactly was this evaluation based?"

"Well, naturally, on my own professional observations—and on your correspondence with me and our patients, which I also submitted. You know, the psycho app's various tests. Cognitive Behavioral and—."

Anger roiled behind her eyes. "With two decades of service on behalf of your Behavioral Health Solutions, I am quite familiar with the tests. Which manifested what?"

Renita's fingertips drummed. "I am still awaiting the results."

Unsteadily, Lauren rose to her feet. After years of life's lessons, of learning to practice caution, moderation, and restraint, she could not believe what tumbled out of her mouth next. "While you're waiting, I'll be packing."

Renita's brows almost collided at the bridge of her very straight nose. "Packing?"

"Yes. You can send the results to me in Mexico."

"Mexico?" Disbelief widened the iron gray eyes. "You're moving to Mexico?"

"I'm finished with Behavioral Health Solutions. I want to be no part of this particular behavioral health solution, Renita."

She arrowed for the door. Her shaking, sweating palm had to make a second attempt to turn the knob. In that moment, she caved. She simply could not desert either of her children. Not fully, anyway. But for a change, she was going to put herself first.

She looked back over her shoulder. "I am giving you two months' notice to groom Andi, or whomever you choose, for my position. But tomorrow and the rest of next week, I'm taking off—the first week off in two years."

That next morning, she sat motionless in her tatty pajamas before her laptop. Tear after tear leaked over her lids. She was stricken to the core of her heart by her daughter's militant announcement yesterday afternoon. Love, compassion, caring? Lauren had detected no evidence of those traits in Renita.

To have one's own child turn on you . . . but if Renita was right, that Lauren was suffering the onset of a vascular dementia . . . there was still that option Lauren had stored on her mind's backburner. At least for now. Deal with the immediate present, she reminded herself and swiped at another tear.

She was as dumbfounded as Renita by her abrupt decision to quit her job of twenty-two years—and to move to another country. To Mexico. Sure, she had a rudimentary knowledge of Spanish from her summer sojourn in Spain. But that was, what, how many years ago? Sweet Jesus! Almost fifty years ago. Five decades!

She knew no one in Mexico. Where would she go? A google of metropolitan Mexico City indicated a population of twenty-two million people. No, she wanted to escape from the crush of anonymous humanity. Houston metro's population of seven million was already oppressive.

With a quiet desperation, she sensed the need to go inside herself and to find out what really was important as she navigated this final stage of her life. A life where it appeared the best of all her years had passed her by.

She blew her nose on a tissue, ran a hand through the rat's nest of her hair, then forced her fingers to her keyboard. Time was wasting, time to begin her online search.

Mexico's port cities, like Merida, Cancun, Cabo San Lucas, or Puerta Vallarta were far too hot and humid for year-round living, at least, for her.

Further research showed *National Geographic* proclaiming the Colonial Highland towns in central Mexico—like San Miguel de Allende, Ajijic, or Guanajuato—sported perfect

Answering The Call

year-round climates.

Yet these colonial towns were populated with American, Canadian, and other expats, making them too pricey for her meager Social Security-plus budget. And she did not want to tap into her reserve funds unless it was a last resort. Besides, if she was going to move to another country, why choose a Little New York?

She recalled Andi mentioning her lover Vincente returning to his family in Querétaro. She googled it. A 600-year-old baroque city declared a World Heritage Site, Querétaro was in the Colonial Highlands, as well. At 6,200 feet elevation, along with the perks of a perfect climate and an aggressive economy, Querétaro, the capital of the state of Querétaro, also had an international airport.

Check.

Next, she clicked on her online credit card's travel points. Few, but enough to get her there.

Check.

Her passport was up to date.

Check.

Then, most importantly, she searched her bank's locations outside the States. Bingo—one on almost every corner in Querétaro.

Check.

As for buying a home in Querétaro, using her savings, that was not an immediate consideration, given the legal ramifications involved—and the obvious point that she might not be able to bring off this absurdity.

She did a random search of rentals—houses, apartments and casitas—using Facebook's Marketplace. Rentals in Querétaro were one-third that of the United States, as was the cost of living.

If she was careful—if she avoided affluent neighborhoods occupied primarily by expats, like Querétaro's trendy suburbs of Juriquilla, Millennia III, or Jurica—why, yes, she might just be able to afford retirement in Mexico living off her Social Security solely.

Besides, Facebook posts on a Querétaro group page notated that the gentrification of upscale neighborhoods such as those forfeited old world rustic charm and atmosphere for convenience.

Scanning the rental photos that appealed to her champagne taste and beer income, her eye was caught by a charming two-story casita. Her innate skepticism whispered it could be a dump. Better to wait until she could actually tour rental homes on site. Instead, she made an online reservation at an affordable Airbnb with a string of decent reviews.

Check.

Before logic and practicality could dissuade her, she booked a one-way flight for two months out. Now, all she had to do was give her two-months' notice to vacate her condo, sell off her furniture and Audi, cram clothes, laptop, and what other belongings she could into three suitcases . . . and over that time ween herself from friends and family.

As if that last thought had conjured a family member, her cell phone rang. She glanced down at her laptop's time—8:05 p.m.—and then over at her cell phone. Sylvie was calling. A silent groan vibrated up from Lauren's ribcage. Naturally, word of her walk-out would be passed around quicker than a collection plate.

Before answering, she grabbed another tissue and blew her nose again. "Hey, babe." She called both her daughters by the endearment. Well, not Renita, not when at work.

Answering The Call

Before Sylvie could respond, Lauren schooled her voice to a neutral note. "By now, I am sure you've heard from your sister that I am retiring in two months. Calling it quits at seventy, which I will be by that time."

Sylvie knew how difficult the determined Renita could be, so there was no need to offer explanations about this afternoon's showdown or put Sylvie on the defensive. "Anyway, if you're calling to offer congratulations, babe, I'd much prefer an offer of a flute of Prosecco."

"Momma, that's wonderful, you deserve to take it easy after all these years. But, uhh, decamping to another country, to Mexico, well . . . do you think that might not be a little drastic?"

Drastic times called for drastic measures, and Lauren felt very, very drastic at that moment. She took a deep breath. "I have been giving this a great deal of thought for some time." And in a sense that was the truth. Every morning, something inside her—her intuition, her subconscious, her soul, whatever—had been asking, "Is this what you're settling for from life?"

"Well, Momma . . . all of us have, too. Been giving you a lot of thought. You know, about your future. Like how we will care for you." She had the grace to sound abashed. "You cared for us all these years. Now we want to make sure we can care for you."

"Which means, what?" She suffered the silence then managed to jest, "Like who gets saddled with me?"

A sigh. "No, Momma. The long-term financial ins-and-outs. The legal matters. Medical affairs. That kind of stuff all children have to consider about their parents at some point."

"Oh. Of course." She digested this information . . . and

Sylvie's uncustomary taut tone. "Fortunately, I am in excellent health."

Excellent health, aside from Renita's recent claims of mental incompetency. Lauren took no prescription medications, another plus in facilitating her move to Mexico. "Furthermore, I am solvent, owing no debts other than my Audi. So, no worries, okay, babe?"

"But what if something happens to you in Mexico? Say, you break an ankle on a loose cobblestone or—"

Now it was she who sighed. "Mexico has a great healthcare system. Its doctors are highly qualified—and I might add their medical fees are far below that of the United States."

"But what if . . . what if you should . . . you know . . . ."

"Bite the dust there? I have already secured a cheap Med-Flight plan to get my carcass back home. Anything else worrying you, babe?"

A pause. "All right, Momma." Sylvie's voice returned to its usual affectionate timbre. "Just trying to cover all bases. And luckily should any complications arise once you're settled in Mexico, Burney's law firm has a legal affiliate an hour's flight from Querétaro, in Mexico City—Kramer, Garcia, and Figueroa. Ask for Jürgen Kramer, should you need anything. He's Burney's liaison with the firm."

"Good to know. Kramer, Garcia, and Figueroa. I'll keep that in mind." Not that her mind possessed the faculty of memory retention, if Renita was right.

Memory retention or not, Lauren wanted to make the most of what was left of her life. She wanted to live up to the expectations she had set for herself in high school. She wanted to push herself to a place out of her comfort zone.

Whether the results were accomplishment or embarrass-

Answering The Call

sing failure, she would definitely not be sitting on the couch, vegetating as she watched reality TV. No, she would be participating in life.

CHAPTER 7

Strange how, while showering Monday morning, the usual phrase, There has to be an easier way, did not trip across Lauren's lips. Not since last week had the phrase nudged her.

Excitement about this quest bubbled in her like New Year's Eve champagne. How far she had come from the last New Year's Eve, five months ago, when she had danced by herself to *Rocking Pneumonia Boogie Woogie Blues*, all the while weeping.

Despite her exhilaration, something niggled at her like the hounds of hell. What? Was she overlooking some vital piece to her plan? Was this, indeed, the easier way?

Then, from her mind's bleeding ink came the written words, "For all the sad words of tongue or pen, the saddest are these: It might have been." From her core, she understood she would regret for the remainder of her life not exploring this road less traveled, regardless if it resulted in a dead end.

Sure, she was nervous about such a monumental transition, answering the call to adventure. Quitting a lifelong job, which equaled unemployment; moving to a different location; conflict with a beloved family member—these ranked within the five top causes of blood pressure-bursting stress.

Of those five principal stress inducers, only divorce, which she had ultimately survived, and death remained. And as to death . . . at her age she was on the fast track to death anyway.

These super stresses could certainly attribute to her memory lapses. But, sweet Jesus, she did not want to be in denial if her condition was worse, as Renita claimed, than mere occasional memory lapses.

Lauren's family did not deserve to have to wrangle with the emotional, financial, and physical demands of caring for a parent with Alzheimer's. She herself had barely survived as a caregiver to an Alzheimer's parent.

For some time she had intuitively known she had to shake up her comfort zone—to take a risk and widen her boundaries—or let them define her, and confine her, even more narrowly with each passing year.

And now it was imperative she had to take this risk so Renita could not have her defined as crazy or confined in an institution. If she was indeed demented, then let it end there in Mexico.

She fixed a latte and returned to her laptop to do more research on her new residence. She was going to give it a year in Querétaro. To enjoy the luxury of not having to work. She might just devote some time to explore the mariachi and Mexican folkloric music that had always appealed to her. And if this year did not work out? That consideration was futile.

She would have to go back to work. And what company would want her, at her age? Other than as a Walmart greeter. Her options were limited. Maybe she had been foolish to quit her job in a fit of fear and anger.

Her cell phone rang. Andi was calling. Had Renita put her up to making this call? "Good morning, Andi." She kept her voice at a cautious pitch. "What's up?"

"Plenty." The girl's voice was a whisper.

"Plenty? What does that entail exactly?"

"Nothing's getting done here. And Dr. Hillard is salty."

"What?"

"Salty—angry, bitter, hyper hot. Please tell me you'll be back tomorrow, Ms. L."

"I am moving to Mexico, Andi. Querétaro, in fact. In two months."

A quick intake of breath. "Querétaro?"

"*Sí*," she said with an effected lightness. "As in the hometown of the father of your baby. Have you changed your mind about seeing him?"

"Umm," her voice sank a decibel. "I got the Bloody Mary, Ms. L."

"What? Oh? You're not pregnant?"

From the background came, "Is that my mother you're talking to, Andi? Here give me that ph—"

Next a scrapy, swishing noise, and then a more audible, "Mother, you're acting irrationally. You're not thinking clearly."

"You're right, Renita. Thinking clearly, no? I am not. But I am feeling clearly, for the first time in a long, long time."

"Now listen to me. You're making rash decisions—to quit abruptly like this and move away. To Mexico, of all places."

Answering The Call

Lauren was determined to maintain her cool. "What better place? It has sublime weather, great healthcare, and a low cost of living. One-and-a-half million American expats all can't be wrong."

Renita hummphed. "You're exhibiting the behavior of an imbalanced mind. Now, the family is gathering at my house tonight. Let's all discuss this in a mature fashion."

Lauren felt the kind of shivery chill she would get when biting into ice chips. "Is this an intervention, Renita?"

"Oh, Mother, don't be so dramatic. We just want to address all angles to this insane decision of yours. Obviously, you are unable to understand how dangerously problematic what you are doing is."

Long ago, Lauren had learned her daughter was a skillful adversary when it came to analytical reasoning. To continue this conversation with her was a losing proposition. "I love you, Renita." Not: I love you, babe. "Goodbye."

Cradling the phone, she gulped back the salty tears. Her chest spasmed in soundless sobs. Alienating herself from the ones she loved had not been part of this adventure agenda.

CHAPTER 8

The next day, Lauren first called upon her second cousin, Marsha. She lived in a tiny, subsidized apartment that smelled of decay. Sad, because in her youth Marsha had possessed a lively gypsy spirit that disliked being confined any place for long.

She sat in a cracked leather lounger. Her knotted hands, mere claws now, rested lightly on its arms. Her gnarled, stockinged feet were unable to tolerate anything other than her customary Birkenstocks. Three years younger than Lauren, Marsha's face was much more deeply lined. Stress and pain had taken their toll but left unblemished the droll curve to her lips.

"You're looking chipper," Lauren said.

"Chipper? Fuck, it's definitely hard to feel chipper, much less useful, when we get old."

"Roger that." She shared with Marsha her off-the-chart plan.

Marsha squinted at her. "You are sure you have thought this through, Lauren? All the possible ramifications?"

Answering The Call

"Like Jimmy Durante's *September Song*, Marsha, I don't have time to play the waiting game."

"Then, by all means fling caution to the winds, take the leap of faith that is the Tarot's Fool."

She winced. "My decision does seem to be one of pure folly, doesn't it?"

Her cousin's lips tucked into a wise smile. "Yes, it would seem that. But the Tarot's Fool is a fool because only a simple soul has the innocent faith to undertake such an adventure as you are planning, with all its risks and misery—and the lure of unimaginable rewards, as well."

She leaned over and gave Marsha's bony shoulders a gentle hug. "Bless you, dear one. And I love you."

Next, Lauren stopped by to see her longtime friend Jayne, who live in her widowed brother's garage apartment. A book in hand, she answered the door. Her blue eyes, fading like her memory, lit with the pleasure of recognition. She waved Lauren into the living room/dining room/kitchen. Stacks of dusty magazines and books, a collection of myriad pitchers, and various sized picture frames of family members occupied every available space.

Jayne lumbered over to the small dining table and, slumping her overweight body into one of the mismatched chairs, plopped down her book, a Stephen King novel. "The best thing about reading," she said with a wry smile, "when I forget something, I can always thumb back through to find it. If I can remember that I forgot something."

Most of the time Jayne was aware that her memory was slipping away, but she dealt with it as she had with her and Lauren's high school misadventures—with humor. These days she remembered more of the past than she did the present.

"You're looking . . . well, Jayne." She would never lie to her friend; never say she was looking great when she was not. And she would not share that she, too, might be losing her own mind.

Jayne ran a hand through her thinning hair, now completely gray. "These damned medications. I've lost a lot of hair but found a lot of fat."

Lauren chuckled.

Jayne leaned forward, and Lauren detected the faint odor of urine. Her friend must have forgotten to change her adult diaper. Jayne lowered her voice in a conspiratorial manner. "My brother keeps me prisoner here. I can't even go for a walk around the block. Blake thinks I'll escape."

Lauren almost chuckled again. Then she realized Jayne was serious. She was retreating into one of those increasingly delusional moments. Lauren, also, leaned forward and managed a conspiratorial smile. "I'm escaping, too," she said gently. "I am moving to Mexico. Querétaro, Mexico."

Jayne's eyes widened. "You are? When?"

Lauren thought she might have seen comprehension return to those eyes, hooded now by the thief of time. "In three days." With last night's phone call from Renita, Lauren realized that her family was hell bent on keeping her from leaving. Instantly, she had decided to set forward her departure to this week instead of waiting two months.

Jayne's gaze drifted, as if her thoughts were drifting again. "Lauren, remember that weekend we pooled our money to catch that bus to Brownsville—we were juniors in high school—so we could party across the border in Matamoros?"

"I do. It was the senior field trip, and I had the hots for

Answering The Call

the captain of the baseball team, Steve—I can't even remember the jock's last name. We passed ourselves off as seniors to the homeroom mothers and got away with it."

She chuckled. "Yeah. Stevie-boy got sick and threw up all over you."

"He never called again." Looking back, maybe he had been too embarrassed. Maybe, she should have risked reaching out to him.

"Hey, wouldn't it be fun to go together to Mexico again? Like old times." Jayne clapped a hand heavily mapped with blue veins over Lauren's. "Let's do it! Let's escape together!"

She squeezed Jayne's hand and blinked back tears. "Sure," she said, breaking her sworn promise to herself never to lie to her best friend. "Let me get settled first, and then we can finalize plans."

Jayne smiled sadly. "Finality follows much quicker than we think, doesn't it?"

What wisdom from even the demented. She could only nod and take her leave.

Lastly, upon returning to her condo, Lauren walked across the green strip of parkway to her neighbor's duplex. Bill, sitting on a backless bench out in front, whittled, a pastime of his. His markedly jug ears perked at her approach.

She dropped down on the bench beside his gaunt frame. "Is that a cannon taking shape?"

He ceased whittling, and his seamed lips tugged in a dry smile. "Nope. That's the Finger of God, shooting old goats like me the finger." He paused in a wheeze. "And I'm whittling on a piece of deadwood about as dead as I am."

"Nonsense." She tapped the whittled piece of wood.

"It's only changed forms. This form has taken on a sheen its former existence never had."

His rheumy eyes shot her an appreciative glance. "Gonna miss ya, gal."

She started. "How did you know I am leaving?"

"How could the whole hood not know? Saw a van hauling off your furniture this morning."

"Oh . . . yes." She settled her head back against the brick wall. "I sold my furniture and household goods—lock, stock, and barrel—to a firm that offered the best price. I'm left with three suitcases, and a blow-up mattress. Tomorrow, CarMax is handing over a check for my Audi and its keys. I came over to tell you good-bye. "

"Where ya headed?"

"South of the Border, Down Mexico Way."

"You're shittin' me."

"No. Already made my flight reservations and booked an Airbnb in Querétaro."

"You're mighty valiant, gal."

She realized she was lonely, even supported by incredibly empathetic friends. She never thought loneliness could ever feel so lonely. She glanced sideways at him. "No, I am mighty desperate. I am not even sure I am doing the right thing."

"Old Henry knew what he was talking 'bout."

Where did this come from? "Say what?"

"Henry Ford. That if you always do what you've always done, you'll always get what you've always got."

Damn, if Bill was not right. She did not want to wrap up the last part of her life as she had been living it the last twenty-two years, working for Renita.

Truly, what did she have to lose? Her savings for

unexpected expenditures? What was money for but to use? Her family? They had their own lives. They loved her, but she was not that necessary to them. Her life? She had already lived a long life. Why not go out with a bang?

As for her mind, she may have already lost that. Her freedom she did not intend to lose.

"Bill, when you think back, do you ever wish you had accomplished more?"

"I've marinated on that a lot, gal—and fuck, no. I wished I had loved more."

CHAPTER 9

Late that night, Renita sat behind her desk. She was alone in the office. Andi and Renita's sister Sylvie, who had reluctantly agreed to help out by filling in Lauren's position temporarily, had long since departed. Renita was left alone to read and reread the printout of the latest psychological exam she had ordered.

Borderline Personality Disorder causes instability in mood and behavior. A fear of being abandoned and attempts to avoid real or perceived abandonment are main characteristic of this condition. Features of borderline personality disorder include:

1. Extreme moods, such as anger, depression, or anxiety
2. Sudden or impulsive shifts in values or career plans
3. Transference, when feelings or thoughts about oneself are redirected to another
4. Poor self-image
5. Self-harm or suicidal thoughts

Answering The Call

In many people, Borderline Personality Disorder triggers the onset of delusions and even early dementia.

Renita buried her forehead in her palm. Even given her expertise, she did not know what to do. All the signs were there.

She thought about her mother's abandonment issues, this ill-advised move to Mexico. For all intents and purposes, her mother herself had been abandoned at an early age by her alcoholic father. And now she was suddenly quitting her job of twenty-two years, not to mention being angry at Renita for trying to intercede.

And what with her mother's own mother beset by Alzheimer's, it was quite likely the mental disease had been passed along in the genes.

At the apparent hopelessness of the condition, Renita did not know whether to weep or rage. Rage won. Her fingers wadded the printout. She hurled it into her trash basket with all the force of a track athlete performing a shot put.

※

Waiting for her flight, Lauren sat in the seat nearest AeroMexico's gate counter. Just in case something went awry at the last moment. Her exhilaration about this . . . what would she call it . . . life's final adventure? . . . was tempered by anxiety.

Ahead of her lay so much she was ignorant about, so much she would not know how to handle. Her Spanish had been reduced to the grade school variety. And she knew no one to call upon when she would, inevitably, run into the wrinkles associated with living in a foreign country. From grocery shopping to banking to locating a dentist. From city bus travel to Uber, to which she never had need to resort.

Her fingers flickered through her packet of documents. Passport. Covid Vacs. Completed Mexican attestation form. Address and phone number of the Airbnb in Querétaro. Five hundred American dollars' worth of pesos which she had preordered from her bank at a hefty charge.

She would need the currency in pesos to pay the airport taxi and any other unanticipated fees and charges occurring before she would be able to locate a bank branch location nearest her Airbnb. Naturally, she could always use her credit card; but that meant conversion fees.

Besides, in the research she had done through Facebook's Querétaro expats groups, she had learned that unless one lived in Querétaro's historic district of El Centro or one of the affluent neighborhoods, a majority of the stores were mom-and-pop operations that accepted only *efectivo*—cash.

She was having second thoughts at this last minute. So much could go wrong. Just the initial concern of trundling her carry-on and purse plus the two large, checked bags from the conveyor belt through to Querétaro customs smothered her excitement and accelerated her breathing, as if she were laboring up one of Querétaro's many steep hills.

She thought of her forfeited future paychecks with no assurance of forthcoming monies. Just the meager Social Security now. Unless, she opted to fall back on her managed funds. She thought of her health. Medicare did not cover health crises outside the United States. And worse, what if she was to die in Mexico, alone, as Sylvie had pointed out?

Lauren glanced up at the flight monitor. Seven minutes

Answering The Call

until boarding began. She worried her bottom lip. She did not have go through with this outlandish, bizarre idea . . . facing the greatest of fears, the terror of the unknown.

She could rent a subsidized, antiquated apartment back in Houston, where she had friends. In Querétaro she had nothing. Sure, she would lose her deposit at the Airbnb. Sure, she would lose her non-refundable airfare. Sure, she would lose face with friends and family. Sure, she would be snickered at as a doddering fool. But, hell, she had lost a lot in her life already.

And maybe she needed to face head on what her family suspected . . . that she was becoming unglued. Maybe she needed to begin undergoing therapy. And begin getting medicated. A first for her, as her body hereto had needed no medication for aging's ailments.

A relieved sigh, coming with her change of mind, her decision to back out of this folly, eddied from her. She smiled ruefully. What she most likely needed was one of those '70s mood rings to signal her family what to next expect from her recently unpredictable behavior.

She stood, grabbed the handles of her carry-ons, and set off. She got no farther than the first set of escalators, when her cell phone rang. While balancing her carry-ons upright on the descending moving steps, she fumbled in her small shoulder bag. She saw her cell phone's caller: Renita.

"Oh, babe," Lauren breathed, "I'm so glad it's you. I realize my actions lately must seem like chop suey to you all, and rightly so. I have decided that I was—"

"I just learned from Andi that you are flying to Mexico today. Our family is in an uproar over this. It's all your fault. If you really loved me, you wouldn't do this."

"Renita, this had nothing to do with you—or my love for

you. It's about me. What I wanted for this last portion of my life."

"You're being petty, Mother. And selfish."

While maneuvering her luggage off the escalator at the bottom, she tried to keep the conversation on track. "I simply want to retire. Can't you understand that? Twenty-two years is long enough at any job. Even you will admit it's time Behavioral Health Solutions is infused with new blood. Andi and Sylvie can manage the office until you can find someone to replace me."

"You're lucky you work for me, what with all your mistakes these days." The churlish quality in Renita's voice modulated. "I only keep you on my payroll because you need to be taken care of. Can't you understand that?"

Her daughter had a way of covertly undermining her. A professional way. She made Lauren question herself. She knew she should pause, pause before saying something she would regret later. "Sometimes, Renita, you can hack off my self-esteem, beginning at my arthritic knees."

"Mother, you're too sensitive."

She was losing self-control. Not a good sign. She tugged her luggage from the path of other hustling gate-bound passengers. Despite her effort to plug her throat, the words tumbled out. "I have dealt with your criticism so many times lately, and I am fed up!"

Lauren heard a long, shuddering breath over the airwaves. "Look, I am doing what is best for you. Either you abandon this insanity, or I'll submit the documented information regarding your recent behavior I have been compiling to a couple of colleagues. I am certain they will certify you as incompetent to be on your own."

A 10,000-volt current shot up Lauren's spine.

CHAPTER 10

Raw loneliness assailed Lauren. The deflation of her image of Mexico as an arcadia only accentuated that loneliness.

As the arms of two mountain ranges cuddled Querétaro, smog hazed the city. In El Centro, the historical district where Lauren's Airbnb was located and where so many expats congregated, the next-door neighbor's four dogs barked all day long. Pyrotechnics in honor of whatever day's particular saint went off like cannon booms twenty-four/seven. And the next door tamale factory's noxious fumes permeated her Airbnb.

Zoning was non-existent. She reminded herself this was what made Mexico exotic, vibrant, and vivid—discovering a brothel next to one of the city's many cathedrals. But then what more perfect place for a brothel? Or a cantina next to a hospital. Querétaro could not be deemed boring, at least.

Because the city was located in the high desert, dust particles continuously floated and coated everything. This, despite *National Geographic*'s yearly proclamation this Central

Highlands area had the best climate in the world, which meant virtually every home and store did not have heating nor air conditioning.

With late May the hottest time of the year, she found the nights so uncomfortably warm that she experienced only a few hours of restless sleep, making her disposition even edgier.

She had spent the last five days in harried hunting for a place to rent outside the city's carefully spruced El Centro historic district.

Every single apartment and casita in outlying areas that were within her budget were miniscule, with a bedroom barely large enough to navigate around its bed.

The littering in various neighborhoods appalled her. Trash abounded. Graffiti stenciled walls everywhere. Fine sand coated everything. Pathetically thin, mangy dogs roamed free, growling and snapping and struggling for survival.

She was beginning to suspect she had made a calamitous mistake in this abrupt idea to move to a foreign country. She was a fish out of water, gasping its dying breath.

Then, she stumbled across that same posted ad on a Facebook Querétaro group for the two-bedroom, one bath casita. It was still available. The photo featured a two-story home with a salmon-colored courtyard in front, its wrought-iron gates open wide in welcoming.

The casita was in Corregidora, a town adjacent to Querétaro and far enough from El Centro's congestion and smog. Its monthly rental was an astounding $325 U.S. dollars. The price was right! What could she say, except that she had fallen in love with the casita, like the idiotic lyrics she wrote glorifying True Love.

Answering The Call

As her years and experiences had accumulated, she had belatedly realized that particular romantic figure of speech was a delusion. Hopefully, the casita would be no delusion. Immediately, she arranged a tour.

The casita was more than she could have ever hoped or dreamed for. The last house on the hill with a heavenly view of the surrounding mountains by day and a glorious city light show of Querétaro below at night, it was located on a private cobblestone drive—no traffic, noise, litter, or graffiti, and with grilled door-and-window reinforcements not even Houdini could have penetrated.

A bus stop, hospital, *farmacía*, and small stores, *tienditas*, were located below the hill, a block away. According to Google maps, a Walmart Express was a forty-minute walk's distance. She would need a hand cart for groceries.

Immediately, she had followed up with the casita's owner in Mexico City about signing off on a *póliza jurídica* or renter's policy. The owner had set up a meeting with the legal firm representing the transaction. Its designated attorney, or *licenciado*, would be responsible in resolving any issues between the lessor and lessee and would collect and disburse all monies.

For the first time in a long while, Lauren was feeling like a participant in life. She was feeling the knots of time's urgency seep from her muscles. She was enthused about the future . . . until later that week, when she learned a banking group with no affiliation to Mexican banks had bought out her banking services stateside.

She would have to live off her credit cards until she could close her account with her present bank in the States and open one at a bank with financial ties in Mexico. She hit on a couple of online financial institutions but closing an account with one bank and opening an account with another would require an expensive round trip back to the States.

That left her with the gargantuan issue of *efectivo* or cash. Renting in Mexico, at least renting prudently, required the prospective renter qualify and also make a hefty outlay of pesos for the renter's policy itself. This particular owner also required first and last months' rent in cash. No credit card charges accepted.

She would have to dip into her dwindling hoard of pesos to cover this *póliza jurídica*. More importantly, she would have to convince the *licenciado* with most persuasive eloquence to importune the casita's owner to let her instead make the required first-and-last months' rental portion on her credit card.

If the *licenciado* spoke no English, she was likely facing the obliteration of her plans and dreams—and her independence, if Renita had her say.

※

Through the floor to ceiling glass petition, Jürgen Kramer watched with narrowed eyes as David Escobar made his way through Kramer, Garcia, and Figueroa's outer office.

Striding among the desks, the renegade finger-saluted with easy confidence the attorneys, clerks, and secretaries. They greeted and made way for him like sycophants. As if he deserved preferential treatment. And he, in turn, treated Jürgen's employees with amusement, much as he would a trained parrot or favored pooch.

Answering The Call

Escobar annoyed Jürgen. The man took it for granted that he was an equal to a white man. Social mores automatically, and always would, revere blue eyes and fair hair above ordinary dirt colors.

With aggravation, Jürgen awaited at his doorway the man's arrival, repeatedly delayed as he exchanged shoulder slaps, winks, and gibes with the firm's employees.

Impatiently, Jürgen tugged at each sleeve of his expensive suit. At last, the man approached, tilting his sunglasses atop his head. It irked Jürgen that Escobar's eyes were not a common brown but the green of sea surf. And that the man stood a full half-foot taller. "You have some explaining to do, Escobar."

The *licenciado*'s attention wandered to something on the carpet directly behind Jürgen. "I'd watch that fountain pen. Its black ink might dilute your blue blood."

Jürgen half-rotated to find his prized Montblanc on the floor, alarmingly near one heel of his costly Testoni shoes. Swooping to retrieve it, he returned to his desk. The man fell in behind him. Jürgen settled into his desk chair. "What can you possibly claim in your defense, Escobar? Your information was abominably erroneous."

"You wound my pride," he reproached. Nudging aside the teak bowl of peanuts Jürgen kept on hand, the man hunkered a hip on the polished desk and reached for a peanut.

"That would be difficult to do, given your excessive ego." Though why an excessive ego, Jürgen could not fathom. The man's hatchet features and mane, gray-streaked throughout like a skunk's, bore witness to the street cur he was; and his Guns and Roses t-shirt, jeans, and tennis shoes were as scruffy as his jaw. "The whistle blower has been discharged from prison employment and is nowhere to be found."

Supposedly, a prison guard was leaking information to the press about Mexico's quasi-militarized security force, the GN—that it was taking bribes, engaging in extortion, and suggestively "asking" for gifts. The government's Internal Affairs Director was a friend of Jürgen's and knew that Escobar, who freelanced for various law firms, was often in and out of prisons on client matters. Had, in fact, done prison time himself.

Escobar was to do the sleuthing. And, once found, Jürgen's process server, muscleman Joaquin Macho Lopez, was to do the exterminating.

"Oh, never you worry about that." Escobar cracked the peanut shell with the crush of one palm and carelessly tossed the crunched hulls on the desk. "The guard will show up sooner or later at another prison and under a different name. My own informants will alert me."

The man was lying through his perfect teeth. With scant patience, Jürgen grunted and brushed away the crushed peanut hulls that littered his desk. He would not allow this piss pot of an attorney to rile him. Nevertheless, the Internal Affairs Director was putting the pressure on Jürgen. "Don't fuck with me, Escobar. I know you're playing both sides."

Escobar popped another shelled peanut into his mouth. He glanced idly out the glass partition of Jürgen's opulent office. "Pull the strings then, Kramer. Draw up a pardon for me, fully removing my record of offense, and have your kissing-cousin, the Texas governor, sign it." He looked down then at Jürgen with eyes as hard as jade. "And then I'll personally produce the whistle blower for you."

Answering The Call

Jürgen grew cold with rage. The man was a contemptible peon who had nothing to lose. While he himself, so much more the accomplished man, stood to lose everything—his estates, his authority, his wealth—were his personal undertakings ever revealed.

But never had he failed to bend circumstances to his will. He had been around a long time, and a lot of people owed him favors. From the slacker street cop-on-the-take, whom he made sure got a tab, to the fairy mayor of Querétaro, whose oft-plumbed asshole he once saved in a court case by keeping the record of an incriminating photo sealed.

Over the years that he had practiced law in Texas, before returning to his home state of Querétaro in Mexico, he had thrown his support to fat fucks like Bobby Andrews, campaigning for state senator, and to the reelection of the weasel George Brunner for governor.

The paparazzi had photoed Brunner diddling his mistress at a Motel Six, and Jürgen had kept it off newspaper headlines. As he had gotten off the Texas governor on a corruption charge, after the oily bastard had been caught with his left hand in the pot.

Businesslike, he replied to Escobar, "So done. It's on my agenda."

"I'm sure it is. Soon as you produce the exoneration, I'll produce the whistleblower."

"And I'm sure you will." The man would find a way to dodge doing that. He picked up the Montblanc. "Meanwhile, a *póliza jurídica* back on your Querétaro turf needs to be contracted." He glanced up, his smile thin. "It's yours—that is, if you're interested in something more than the prison fare provided by your moonlighting with that fractious bunch."

He began to scribble on a note pad the prospective renter's information, swearing with each scratching stroke he would one day write Escobar's death warrant, as well.

CHAPTER 11

Lauren was to meet with the *licenciado* at a restaurant within a short distance's walk from her El Centro Airbnb, which made sandals a requisite over heels, given that some of the narrow sidewalks were uneven and a few side streets cobbled.

As a tribute to the warmer climate, she had chosen white trousers with a turquoise-and-silver concho belt girding her flowing white peasant blouse—one of a mere half-dozen that now made up her wardrobe. A minimalist she had become.

Monday's midafternoon was balmy. Sunlight bathed Querétaro's baroque buildings with a gossamer glow. Here flourished gardens, plazas, flower stalls, and fountains. Magenta bougainvillea brimmed over terracotta walls.

Her usual clipped stride slowed into a leisurely, rhythmic stroll. Paradoxically, she felt invigorated. She found herself smiling, nodding at the people shopping or sightseeing around the 17th century Historico Centro.

Her shoulders began to ease from their Velcro constraint

. . . only to knot again when she passed a young couple, holding hands. She felt a pang that she would never again experience that romantic gesture or the taste of a lover's kiss.

The restaurant Pared Azul was tucked into a side street. More of an al fresco dining, the little restaurant fronted a half dozen sidewalk tables. As it was past lunch time, only one table was occupied, this by a pair of young college students, given their full-blown dark beards and bohemian attire.

Several more tables dotted the indoor dining area. Blue walls bordered this part of the restaurant, hence its name, she supposed. Here the mouth-watering aroma of sauteed chiles, sizzling fajitas, and freshly chopped cilantro seduced the olfactory senses.

She paused, her vision adjusting to the interior's cooler shadows. At a table in the rear, she made out a sole male diner. This had to be Licenciado David Escobar.

At her approach, he rose and came from behind the small table. His impressive stature was intimidating. Sunglasses shielded his eyes. "Mrs. Hillard?"

"Yes?" His ungroomed appearance dismayed her. Long, salt-and-pepper hair was banded at his nape. He wore ripped jeans that were not a fashion statement but the real deal, a faded black t-shirt, and grungy tennis shoes that looked as if they were on their last retread.

"You are Licenciado Escobar?" she asked, hoping her incredulity did not permeate what was intended to be the customary exchange when greeting a stranger, this one a supposed attorney. Was this some sort of a money hoax?

"David will do."

He pronounced his name with the Spanish inflection on

the last syllable. Good, he spoke, at least, passable English. Only a scintilla of an accent riffed through his voice like melodious piano keys.

With a brief, perfunctory smile that only slightly diminished the brackets at either side of his mouth, he pulled out for her the hard-back, mustard yellow chair opposite his chili red one.

"*Gracias*," she said, warily sliding into the seat.

He resumed his. "Would you care for something to drink?"

She considered a club soda, knowing its carbonated water would be drink worthy. Then she eyed his half-filled glass and bottle of Corona. Why not indulge? After all, it was 5:00 somewhere. Besides, would not the tequila kill bacteria? "Yes, a margarita—on the rocks—and rimmed with sugar, not salt, *por favor*."

Smirking at that last request, he signaled the white-aproned waiter and ordered. By then her eyes were adjusting to the room's lesser light, and she made out the attorney's tattoos laddering each muscled forearm.

He tapped a lemon yellow pocket folder next to his beer glass. "I have three copies of the *póliza jurídica*. I'll go over it with you and answer any questions. Afterwards you can sign one and all. I'll notarize the documents, you fork over the $8,000 pesos, and we'll each be on our merry way."

She unfolded her linen napkin and draped it across her lap. Well, she could play along with the game, if that was his intention. "You don't waste time, do you?"

He tucked his sunglasses atop his head. This smile he nailed her with was less perfunctory and longer lasting by only seconds. The lines fanning out from his eyes may have been from laughter, but she doubted it. She judged those lines were etched by a cynical disposition. "My country's reputation for its slower pace can sometimes drive me loco."

She canted her head and studied him, trying to determine his age. He looked to be in his late forties, considering the honed physique his tight t-shirt clearly revealed—or early to mid-fifties, given this harsh countenance. His nose had to have been broken more than once, and his macheted cheekbones and jawline could have competed with Mount Rushmore's presidents.

A rather fresh, inch-long scar gouged a path beneath his left cheekbone. His skin, the rich color of teak wood, could be attributed to his Hispanic heritage or could have been refined by years spent in this high desert's fierce sunlight, which she already could attest to as incendiary.

"Your country's reputation?" She returned his curt smile with one of her own. "Now why do I get the impression that you are a man without a country?" And without affability.

"My lingo give me away?" He shoveled back an unruly swatch of dark brown hair tweeded with gray that had tumbled across his forehead. "I'm half-and-half, if that is what you're trying to figure out. Half American, half Mexican. But back to business. Now regarding the renter's policy . . . ." He flipped open the pocket folder and took out a pen.

The waiter returned with her margarita, and the *licenciado* looked from the Tajín-rimmed glass to her. "You wanted sugar-coated, did you not?"

"This is fine." Actually, the stemmed blown glass, its blue rim coated with burnt orange Tajín and garnished with a slice of lime cocktail was eye catching. "Better than fine."

Answering The Call

"Good to know you are pleased easily." He smiled. "It makes my job easier then."

She thought how ironic that his mellifluent baritone contradicted his brusque manner. However, she was not about to allow him to steamroll her. She had allowed her parents and her children to do so. No longer. "I prefer *The Darkside of the Moon*."

He blinked. "*Perdóname?*" She raised a brow and nodded at his t-shirt, stenciled with Pink Floyd's *Live and Let Die*. He glanced down at his chest then back at her. The eyes, surprisingly a pale green, she noted, glinted with faint amusement. "You like psychedelic metal?" She allowed only a slight smile. "I prefer the counterculture music of Bob Dylan over being hustled out the door." She had not completed seven decades without learning to hold her own. Yet she didn't want to scotch renting the house. Those eyes with their naturally curling lashes flared, then narrowed, as if taking renewed cognizance of her. After a beat, his wide mouth crimped in a deprecatory smile. He closed the folder and knuckled it aside. Leaning forward, he braced his laced fingers on the table. Their knuckles were scarred but with well-formed nailbeds. "This," he nodded at the folder, "is strictly a sideline. To keep my cupboards stocked. My other line of work is pro bono but can have dire repercussions if not addressed in, shall I say, a timely fashion?" "Oh, please spare me what your pro bono work encompasses." Hacking off human heads as a hitman for a drug cartel was probably how his left cheek got its pumpkin carve-out—just a part of his machete hazard duty. "My apologies if I seem to be hustling you out the . . . ," he paused.

"Well, you're certainly not hustling me. I'll give you that." She was too honest with herself to be affronted. "A sicario you might be but a gigolo, no. You had to have read my financial information I submitted to qualify for the renter's policy and have known that my portfolio is not up to gigantic gigolo par."

At that, he laughed, his eyes crinkling and the creases at either side of his mouth easing. genuine smile that transformed him—or, maybe, her perception of him. She was blown away. He could be devastatingly attractive. And far too young, alas.

The man was a silver fox, by any standards. She sighed and lifted her glass. "Here's to being loco. I certainly am for thinking I could make this move work." She felt his eyes on her as she took a sip of the margarita. It was sublime.

"Okay, why don't you tell me exactly what your problem is."

The abrupt but effortless way he shifted his consideration to focus solely on her was flustering. Stalling, she reached for a tortilla chip and dunked it in the salsa bowl, then muttered, "I have little cash on hand. Most of it went to pay for your renter's policy. But I don't have enough to pay for the first and last month's rent. Only a credit card I can use."

It was his turn to sigh. "Another case of you American retirees leaping without looking, huh? Well, in this case, a credit card won't fly with the casa's owner. You can't withdraw cash from your bank's ATM here?"

Instantly, the salsa drained her sinuses and she grabbed for her napkin, only to find she was dabbing tears not snot. She felt like such a fool. She could only shake her head.

"Talk to me, Mrs. Hillard."

She took a hefty swallow of her margarita, then proceeded to explain in intermittent hiccoughs her American bank's recent buyout, leaving her with no bank affiliations in Mexico.

"If expediency is the key word—"

"It is. I want to rent this house before someone else latches onto it."

"Then I recommend you immediately fly back home to the states and transfer your funds to a bank there with affiliations here in Mexico."

She gulped. "I can't."

Exasperation accented his scowl. "Come on, your credit card—you can't even charge your airfare on it?"

She took another sip of the margarita and felt its glow eddying throughout her. Her spine relaxed against the chair's spindle back. "You think of me as a retiree. My family thinks of me as . . . well, loco." With her forefinger, she twirled circles at her temple. "Hell, they may be right. Especially, since I gave them authority as co-signers on both my financial and legal affairs."

While he made no comment, his expression intimated he was inclined to agree with her family.

So what? She did not like this younger man much. He might be the real deal, as far as attorneys went, but she did not care what his opinion of her was. She slumped farther in her chair. Her finger rimmed her glass. Absently, she licked the sugar from her fingertip. She glanced up and saw his attention was on her mouth.

The look in his eyes . . . her stomach did a loop-the-loop.

When she found her voice, it came out as a whisking of dry leaves. "Renita, my older daughter—a doctor of psychotherapy and my former employer—talks of confining me." The admission was embarrassing. But the margarita made it easier. "So, an airfare charge on my credit card, which my family monitors, would alert them I was back stateside." Her imagination ran rapid filling in the gaps on how her family would scramble to bring her back to captivity.

The way he studied each of her features, his narrowed gaze moving from her eyes to her lips, next to her throat, and then observing even her veined hands before returning back to her eyes . . . it was as if he was evaluating not only her age but also her character. Under his intense regard, she fidgeted with her glass, rolling its stem between her thumb and fingers.

"*Lo siento*, Mrs. Hillard," he murmured at last, "but my client would think *I* was loco were I to accept your credit card in lieu of cash."

Despite being sorry, he apparently had determined her mentality came up one Corona short of a sixpack.

She delved into her purse and dropped $150 pesos onto the table, enough to more than cover the margarita and tip. She stood, waited to make sure the room did not spin, then smiled down at the *licenciado's* startled expression. "Not *hasta luego* but *adiós*, Licenciado Escobar, because I truly trust I shall never have the dire necessity of resorting to your legal services again."

He draped one elbow over the chair ear. His grin mocked her. "So, just what do you intend to do, Mrs. Hillard?"

She pivoted from the table but glanced back. A taunting smile twisted her lips. "My general philosophy when faced with an unpleasant situation– or person, as the case may be—is to ask myself, 'What would Donna Summer do?'"

He was so much younger, she doubted he even knew who Donna Summer was, not that it mattered. She

Answering The Call

sauntered off toward the sunlit exit.

From behind her came his deep, taunting laughter. "She'd say, 'So, come on, baby. Let's dance tonight.'"

From over her shoulder she flipped him the finger.

CHAPTER 12

Joaquin Macho Lopez inched forward in El Buen Pastor's sinuous line. It snaked out beneath the soup kitchen's galvanized rollup door onto a side street fronting Carretera 57. The superhighway was part of the Pan American Highway that ran from Chile, the southern tip of South America, through Central America, bound for the United States and Canada.

Monthly, thousands of Latin Americans illegally tramped Mexico's Federal Highway to seek asylum in the United States from crushing poverty or political repression. At Querétaro, they would leave off their footslogging for a soup kitchen or a migrant shelter.

Today, El Buen Pastor, a former bodega or warehouse, was shoehorned with itinerants. An old man doubled up in a coughing seizure. A whining toddler yanked on his mother's grimy rebozo. A baby wailed because its mother's bared breast was shriveled of milk.

By habit, Macho sniffed through his left nostril. Snorting crack had collapsed the septum of his right one. Only the defunct nostril and one hunched shoulder impaired his massive physique.

Well, add to that a testicle recently punctured during his brief internment at the local Juzgados Penales. As always, Kramer bailed him out of prison and cleared his record so that he could continue to function as the law firm's licensed process server and enforcer.

Macho had a score to settle with the assailant who had inflicted the testicle wound. The scrotum support Macho was forced to wear was rackingly uncomfortable.

He studied the refugees directly ahead of him in queue; casually, he peered over his shoulder at those behind. He was searching for the healthiest from among the road weary. His keen eyesight, of which he was inordinately proud, could laser in on a hand lesion or decayed gums or the whites of the eyes, or lack thereof, with an accuracy that equaled the best of snipers.

Beneath his filthy denim jacket, he wore holstered to his hunched shoulder his FN5. It could penetrate a bullet-proof vest. Not that he needed a handgun when subduing a quarry. Most of the refugees were starved skinny and weakened by their thousand-mile treks. Besides, his quarries needed to be taken alive.

His hunched shoulder was a result of a childhood fall from a rancho's avocado tree in an orchard he had been raiding. The ball of his upper arm bone had popped out of socket, resulting in a dislocated shoulder. With his family, too poor to get him medical attention, the upshot of the damage to his shoulder blade was that the healing of its growth plate had been impaired. With the onset of puberty, shooting up in height and frame as he had, an obvious deformity had developed.

As he grew in stature, he also had muscled up. He had not tolerated any taunts from other kids—especially, their nickname for him of Camelback. Consequently, they suffered broken bones and worse. Nor would he tolerate the recent slur of Macho Nacho by the same pendejo who had delivered Macho's testicle wound.

He accepted his plate doled with two offal-filled tortillas and a small bowl of carne machaca stew and headed to a table, where sat a scrawny young woman alongside a gaunt older one, whom he deemed to be her mother. When he took a chair opposite the two, both females barely nodded and returned avidly to consuming their meal.

The stew's dried beef tasted like cardboard. He turned his attention to the younger of the two females. The whites of her coffee-brown eyes were bright. Her hair, caught back in a braid the length of her back, was still lustrous. Good.

"My name is Hector." He sniffed. "And yours?"

She hesitated, guardedly scrutinizing him from beneath her raven-winged brows. "Carlotta."

If she were not so beat down, so utterly exhausted she would have detected that his slouched posture in the chair was too indolent to be authentic; that his overall bearing was menacing. Especially, when he noted in a female's eyes rejection due to his deformity. But today he was not seeking sex.

Eventually, he cajoled her into chatting; learned that she was fleeing the government repression in San Salvador. Whether from Guatemala, Honduras, Columbia, they were all the same. Without hope, with dreams.

He learned that she was traveling only with her mother. The older woman with the sallow, sagging flesh would be easy enough to dispatch.

Answering The Call

    Her daughter Carlotta would bring a substantial profit in the organ trade. Usually a quarry he culled resulted in their awakening in a motel bathtub or alley clinic, luckily minus only a harvested kidney, for which there was always a shortage and which earned the most money on the black market.

    Unluckily for the rather pretty Carlotta, though gaunt, she appeared vitally healthy. All her organs would be harvested. He felt a momentary pang for her. But organs were like commodities to be bought and sold, and hers would subsidize his cocaine habit for some time to come.

CHAPTER 13

Tuesday at 8:00 a.m. sharp, the ping of Lauren's cell phone paused her in dressing for the renewal of her house hunting excursion. Perusing Querétaro's online rentals, she had located three suitable living quarters—two were apartments—that did not require a renter's policy and would accept a credit card charge for first and last months' deposit.

Of course, this was likely a negative indication of either the house's condition or location or both. And, of course, the credit card charge could be tracked back to Querétaro, which she was most reluctant to do. But she was down to her last resort. Soon her Airbnb deposit would run out.

In bra and panties, she crossed to the nightstand and stared down at her cell phone's incoming text. It was from Renita. Like approaching a spider's web, Lauren's fingertip dipped cautiously to retrieve the cell phone text message.

Under the Mental Healthcare Act, I have the authority to move you into a care home. If you do not return immediately, I will be filing with the U.S. Department of

Answering The Call

State's Bureau of Consular Affairs for assistance with international retrieval of an incompetent family member.

Her breathing corked in her throat. She had been verifying her checking account online. Her bank had posted her most recent Social Security check. And her credit card was still processing merchant transactions, the last one posted within the past week. So, Rick, in charge of her financial affairs, had not intervened yet and presented no crisis on her various accounts.

But legally? What damage could Sylvie's husband, Burnett Cohen, the attorney, inflict? This was at the top of Lauren's worry roster.

How much time did she have before Renita's threat could be implemented? Mere days? Surely more, given Mexico's backlog of civic affairs. Weeks, maybe a month or even more, if luck was on Lauren's side. Meanwhile, it was imperative she open a new bank account in the States before her present one was frozen. Renita's partner Rick could easily do that.

Under certain restrictions, Lauren could open an account here in Mexico, but an online transfer of funds from her U.S. account would also alert Renita as to her mother's exact whereabouts.

Renita. Her growing contentiousness struck Lauren deeply. Renita had always resented her for leaving her father when he was down and out. She felt her mother was responsible for his decline and ultimate death.

Lauren may not have been the best of wives or mothers, but she had done her best. To go on with life, she had to let go of guilt.

Yet, she had to ask herself . . . was it possible Renita was right? Not only about Lauren's past culpability but this also? Did she have the beginning stages of dementia and was in denial? And, if so, did she want to put her family through the suffering of dealing with the ensuing emotional, legal, and financial issues?

She glanced at her two larger pieces of luggage wedged in the Airbnb's small closet, its door forced ajar by their size. Should she return to Houston, her family, and whatever ramifications awaited her?

Why not? She was soul-lonely here. She missed her family, dysfunctional though they were, including herself; and she missed her friends, dwindling though they were with the passing of the years.

But . . . she had been lonely in Houston. Had awakened nights with a piercing loneliness, a longing, that family and friends had not assuaged. Nor could, for that matter, if anyone were to be totally honest. Loneliness, like happiness, was a choice. And this was her last chance at choice. Her last dance.

Her cell phone's messaging pinged again. She groaned. No way around it, she would have to reply to Renita this time. She glanced down at the cell phone's screen. The message was from David Escobar. Damn! He would be wanting his cash fee for preparing the useless renter's policy. The nerve of the man.

At that moment, she did not know to which sender she dreaded responding the most—her daughter or the *licenciado*.

*

Midmorning Wednesday David forked over the 57 pesos at yet another toll booth and accelerated his road-worn, ten-year-old Pathfinder once again onto the superhighway. The compact SUV groaned with the effort, and so did he. At least, inwardly.

Nine or so hours of driving would elapse between Querétaro and Laredo, Texas. Nine or so hours with the *gringa* as his passenger. So close he could smell her faint floral scent. So close that whenever the highway's edge sheared off in a precipice he detected an abrupt hiccough in her breathing and sighted the veins in her hands knotted prominently.

Lauren Hillard's rental policy stated she was on the cusp of her seventieth birthday, a week away. In her lavender tie-dyed t-shirt and form-fitting jeans, she did not look her age. She had an hourglass figure with a lush tush and ample breasts that begged to be fondled.

But, hell, he was loco for inviting her along on this hasty, last minute trip to Laredo, Texas. And people often went loco when flipping over to another decade, as she was.

He kept his cell phone's Spotify playlist at a soothing low pitch. Not because he was stressed, although his border crossing at Nuevo Laredo would be tense, but because the music precluded conversation. Hopefully.

The starchy *gringa* seemed content to say as little as possible, exchanging only the minimal pleasantries . . . the most important being she was grateful for this opportunity to sneak into the United States via the back door of Nuevo Laredo.

No mention of the fact that, despite her days' earlier acclamation to the contrary, she would, after all, be using his legal services to rent the house she so eagerly desired—once she switched her funds to a new U.S. bank account with ties to banks in Mexico.

In the morning's predawn, he had swung by her Airbnb to pick her up. He figured, since this ghastly prison discovery necessitated the trip to Laredo, Lauren Hillard could fly in under the radar with him, take care of her bank business before closing time, and head back south to Querétaro, all within twenty-four hours . . . and before her family had an inkling of her activity.

Why did he bother to bail her out of her predicament? In his line of work, it went against his creed. Show no emotion, feel no pain. Sunglasses came in handy for that technique.

On the other hand, he could read the *gringa*'s every emotion. Her own sunglasses, plowing back her shoulder-length mane, gray-streaked as a brindle cat, left her eyes—and their emotions—unmasked. She did not like him. Which bothered him not in the least. Her few attempts at civility provided him entertainment to alleviate the trip's boredom.

She herself was a paradox. Hardheaded yet openly vulnerable, if he read her right. And he usually did read people as accurately as any expert in human behavior. He conceded that she was intelligent, well educated . . . and good looking.

A classy woman, given the way she had strolled inside the Pared Azul with an easy, confident grace that whispered of wealth somewhere in her background. But it was the wry humor she had displayed upon taking her abrupt leave of him at the restaurant that made him curious enough to give it a go. Haul her with him to Laredo.

Donna Summer? What the hell?! He grinned to himself once again.

Just ahead, an oncoming 18-wheeler crossed the median

before swerving back into its lane. A jaw-tight, sibilant gasp whisked from her.

"Relax. Your Houston traffic delivers far more hazards."

She glanced askance at him. "You know I am from Houston?"

"Without question. Your driver's license."

But he knew oh so much more. Practically everything about her. Beginning with her recent retirement from Behavior Health Solutions and dating all the way back to her youth's marriage to the feckless, deceased husband, Marty. David always did his homework.

"You are not concerned about us being stopped by one of the cartels? I've heard they block the road and steal your vehicle and cash . . . and then, uhh, sometimes gun down the victims."

He lifted his shoulders. "It's quite possible."

He caught the pointed gaze her eyes, fanned by age lines, cast at his tats. They scored his right forearm where his wrist lapped the steering wheel. "You're knowledgeable about . . . uhh, incidents like this?"

He delighted in improvising. "We sicarios prefer the dagger in our line of work."

He was pleased to see her lids flare with apprehension. Her lovely eyes expanded as large as clumps of silver sage. "Then you really are a sicario?"

Something untoward in him sought to allay that apprehension. "Here along this stretch of highway, we're more likely to encounter a shakedown by the cartel. They pull you over, determine what you should pay as a 'toll,' then give you a receipt or a code to pass along later should you be hauled over farther up the road again by other cartel members of the family."

In a nanosecond, his attention switched from the *gringa* to the big horn ram bounding across the highway directly in front. The *gringa's* hands shot toward the dashboard to brace against the jarring. The Pathfinder skidded tail-end. When the brakes' screeching finally stopped, he could feel the Nissan's rear teetering backward in a true cliffhanger.

"What were you saying about the hazards of Houston traffic being greater?" she gasped. She went to dry scrub her face, and the Pathfinder teetered atop its precarious rock perch.

"Don't move!" he warned her.

Her eyes on his were wide with terror. She swallowed, then nodded, just barely.

"Look, we're going to exit at the same time. Understand?"

Again, the barest of nods.

He glanced over the side at the hundred-odd-foot drop-off and said, "Cautiously, slowly. Remember, coordinate our movements—to keep the car balanced. Got it?"

Once more, a terse nod from her.

At the same moment he reached for the door handle, she reached for hers. His did not give. Her alarmed gaze leaped from her locked door handle to join with his. He yanked this time. *Nada*—except he felt the Pathfinder's frame bobble, fluctuating its precious grip on the cliff's edge.

She shot him a horrified look.

"Not to worry. Okay, we exit via the windows." He pressed the window's down switch. Again, nothing. The electrical system was dead.

"I don't suppose you have one of those vehicle escape tools?" Her voice was a cynical croak. "You know, to break a window."

"Sure thing—and a winch, as well, to haul the SUV up off the cliff." His cell phone on the console had gone flying, who knew to where. "Is your purse—your cell phone—within reach?"

She glanced down at the floor. Then, cautiously, she craned to look behind her. "It may be in back or beneath the seat."

"Now is not the place nor time to scramble around searching for either yours or mine. Listen, I want you to follow along with me. Do exactly as I do. We're going to break our windows—with as few jerking movements as possible."

From the back of his seat, he detached the head rest with a modicum of motion. "Here we go—and, hey, lower your sunglasses over your eyes. And turn your head away."

Like *The Matrix*'s bullet-dodging scenes, she moved in slow motion to detach her head rest. He kept a sidewise eye on her to make sure she synchronized his moves from thereon. Aiming the headrest's metal prongs at the center of his door window, he crashed against it. She followed suit.

Thudding smashes resulted but no give from either his window or hers—except for the Pathfinder's infinitesimal tottering. No use in going easy now. Not when their mere attempt to break the windows resulted in the rumble of pebbles beneath the Pathfinder's tires. It was now or never. "Again, harder," he ordered.

He rammed the prongs this time. Splintering shards flew. And the Pathfinder lurched violently.

He froze, waiting for the fatal downward slide. The car's traction skidded, then stabilized for the moment. He speared a glance in her direction. She had shattered her window, as well. Sunlight glinted off glass that speckled her tie-dyed t-shirt. Pinpoints of blood freckled the lower portion of her face.

"Careful here now," he warned. "Knock away any projecting shards from your window frame. Then we scramble though." At least, he hoped that they could do so before his Pathfinder's wobbly balance veered too far toward the declining edge.

With the heel of his fist, he chipped away shards. With each thrust, the car seesawed minutely but perilously. At last, the window frame afforded a safe space to wedge through. He glanced back at her. "Ready?" he asked.

She broke off from her glass cracking and managed a rusty, breathless, "Yes."

He had to give her credit. Her lacerated hands were dribbling blood where the glass had sliced. Yet she had not panicked and gone wacko on him. "Okay, lady, let's roll. One, two, three—and here we go!"

As he wriggled through, the car tilted and slid. *Oh, ¡Jesucristo!*

He heaved himself fully out and bounced to a rolling halt atop a spiny shrub. He clung tightly to it until his dangling feet found purchase below the ledge on which he was stranded. *Merida*, but the prickly cluster stung!

Above him, the highway was out of sight. Next to him, the Pathfinder was teetering recklessly. Around him, a buzzard winged, as if observing its next meal.

A yard higher up, a pungent pine offered anchorage. With braced hands, he began to leverage his weight—only to jar to a halt. Out of sight, below the narrow ledge supporting him, rocks pinned his right ankle.

He yanked his right foot again. Loosened rubble showered the rock face beneath in echoing thuds. Still, his

Answering The Call

ankle remained clamped by the vise of rocks. He tried swiveling downward from his waist in an attempt to grasp and loosen his ankle. The ledge blocked his fingers desperate groping any farther underneath than his knee. He started sweating and not from the blistering sunlight. Dust and dirt clotted his nostrils.

Then, pebbles pelted the exposed right side of his face, pressed against the griddle-hot rock. Next, a shadow umbrellaed him. "Mr. Escobar, are you all right?!"

"*Si*, I am fine as wine in the summertime."

Crouching over him, the *gringa* did not look amused. Tiny scarlet pearls trickled down both sides of her face. She seemed impervious to her scanty perch next to him with its hundreds of feet drop-off. "Wine would be divine. Shall I see what I can find?"

"GodDAMNit, my right ankle is jammed, lady."

She chuckled, and there and then he thought he would burst a blood vessel.

She knelt on all fours, then flattened her body alongside his. Her jean's lush cargo was aligned close to his face, her own lined up with his thigh. "Hold tight. I'm going to lean over and dislodge your foot."

She slithered her weight forward. Once again, rubble rolled off the edge like playing marbles.

For him, heights were dizzyingly sickening. And for her, maybe, as well, because her movements stalled, and he heard her sharp inhalation. "Well?" he demanded.

"Uhhh, give me a moment."

He gritted his teeth. Moments were precious. Any moment, the ledge supporting both his weight and now hers could give way.

Her rump caterpillared forward a little more. At last, he

felt her hand compressing his calf. Next, with her outstretched body splayed at opposite ends alongside his and her head hanging over the ledge, her palm inched down his jeans leg toward his trapped ankle. He felt her tug, then waggle his ankle.

He flexed it ever so slightly. It was freed! *¡Gracias a Dios and all the wicked saints!*

Beside him, she pushed erect onto her knees and dusted off her bloodied palms. "I suggest I back off this ledge first. Give you room to move."

By the time they scrambled up to the highway, a dilapidated stepside pickup was headed their way. He hailed it over. The Chevy pickup rolled past, slowed, then stopped.

He trotted up to the driver's open window. The sombreroed old man slit-eyed his battered appearance. "The cartel bust you, *hijo*?"

"No, a *pinche* ram."

The man cackled.

He jerked his jaw over his shoulder. "Sent my car—and me and the woman back there—over the side of the mountain. Could you give us a lift as far north as you're headed?"

It was the leathered old man's turn to jerk his jaw over his shoulder—at his pickup bed. Its slatted wood sides held a cargo of chickens in wired cages. "Nuevo Laredo."

"*Perfecto.* You wouldn't by any chance have a cell phone?" He had to get his Pathfinder towed. And he hated like hell abandoning both his cell phone and his Sig Sauer P365, hidden in its heavy duty magnetic gun case within the auto's metal framework.

The wizened man flashed a jack-o-lantern grin at the glovebox. "Something better. A Stinger."

Answering The Call

Dubiously, David glanced back at the truck's poultry cargo. The Stinger was a device that mimicked a wireless carrier cell tower. It could force all nearby mobile phones and other cellular data devices to connect to it and thereby keep tabs—tabs on local cartels or Federales in the area.

"What kind of cargo you running beneath these chicken coops?"

"Just chicken shit."

"*Bien.*" He wasn't about to argue.

The *gringa* loped up beside him, and he told her, "Looks like we'll be spending the night in Laredo."

Against the sunlight, she squinted up at him. Over her pale gray eyes, her perfectly delineated brows knitted. "But I can't. You know this. A credit card charge for my hotel room will surely be picked up by my family."

"No, not at a hotel," he said patiently. Both their bodies had to be wracked with after-shock. "At my house. My other house." She stiffened, and he had to smile at her old-fashioned prudishness. "Don't worry your pretty self. My half-sister lives there now. She will make a good duenna. She's much older than I, about your age."

If the woman was stiff-necked before, with his last sentence her body looked like rigor mortis had set in.

CHAPTER 14

Lauren sat at the kitchen table which was draped with a faded citrusy-flowered plastic cloth. On one side of her sat the brash *licenciado*, though she now seriously doubted the authenticity of his attorney's credentials, and on the other his half-sister Irma.

A bare bulb above cast a dull yellow light on the late-night repast of tortillas, radishes, chiles, warmed-over and rancid frijoles, and some kind of meat with a gamey smell.

Lauren and David Escobar had arrived in Laredo too late to make it to the bank. She had expected crossing the border without IDs, left behind in his SUV, would at best take hours and at worst result in a fiasco resulting in their being denied entry into the United States.

The man had brushed aside her concern. He had used the cell phone of the old farmer who rescued them to put through a call. She did not understand very much of the Spanish exchange; but, after the farmer dropped them off on a side street near Nuevo Laredo's border crossing, her bodyguard had ordered her to wait.

Answering The Call

Uneasily, she had done so. Dusk was settling like a coating of desert dust on the impoverished Mexican city, sister-city to Laredo, Texas. She watched him approach an androgynous figure wrapped in a shawl, who sat on the opposite, trash-littered corner. Their conversation was brief. He appeared to peel off a few bills into a basket next to the seated figure, who passed up to him a woven dinner mat from the stack at hand.

When he rejoined Lauren, a sly grin deepened the grooves at the ends of his wickedly beautiful mouth. "What is going on?" she asked.

"Money talks." As they walked toward the International Bridge, he was speedily unraveling a portion of the wicker table mat. As if by magic, several twenty-dollar U.S. bills unfurled.

Ten minutes later, the bills were exchanged with one of the agents on duty at the bridge—a burly male who grinned conspiratorially—and then she and her sicario-cum-escort had been waved past.

Now, Irma, his half-sister, was talking, in English. She was skeletal thin with deep marionette lines and forehead wrinkles exposed by faded gray hair pulled severely back into a knot at her nape. "Your law degree . . . is that not enough, David? Earning money from the *ricos* while helping the *pobres* at the same time? You're no Robin Hood. What you are doing, this sideline, it is too risky."

Lauren, reaching for her chipped glass of tepid water, almost knocked it over. A possible confirmation—that his sideline was somehow wrapped up with the drug cartel, as she had fearfully suspected all along?

Irma's walnut brown eyes strayed from her brother to dart Lauren a chary glance then track back to him. "But this other thing," she swept a work-roughened hand as if swatting off a fly, "giving what little free time you have to that Human Rights Commission, it does not put food in your belly, ¿|sí?!"

Now Lauren's head pinballed between the two siblings. David Escobar's pro bono work was for Mexico's Human Rights Commission? Or, at least, that was a front?

He sighed and took a swallow from his scarred glass. "Speaking of belly, Irma, a three-month old baby's body was discovered this week—an abdominal incision had been made, and drugs were suspected to have been hidden inside."

The bean-laden tortilla wedge stuck in Lauren's mouth. Forcing the piece down in a gulp, she pushed away her plate. She could eat no more.

Irma's tortilla-filled uplifted hand paused. She crossed herself with her other. "So?"

With insouciance, he poured water from his glass onto his ratty, cotton green napkin. He shifted his chair to face Lauren's. Surprising her, he cupped her chin and began dabbing the napkin against her left cheek. She flinched, and he said, "When you washed your hands, you forgot the dirt and blood on your face."

His intimate attention unnerved her. Especially given this new perspective of him, as a possible Good-Guy-in-the-White-Hat. Or a clever double-crosser?

He slanted his head to look her over. "You've a few glass nicks here and there."

She made the mistake of looking into his eyes and was lost in their sea-green depths. Heat roiled through her. She felt like she was on a carnival tilt-a-whirl.

His hand paused in its gentle swiping, and his eyes met

hers in an appraising manner. He had to observe in hers her strong reaction to him. She had had a momentary yearning to lean against him. Abruptly he released her chin.

Laying aside the napkin, he turned his attention back to his half-sister.

"So, that's why I am here, Irma. The baby was found in one of San Miguel Prison's dumpsters—along with the surnames on the bracelet from the indigent hospital the infant was still wearing."

"Pepe?" Irma's voice rusked.

"Your son is all right. But the baby . . . it was your grandson."

Irma's triangular piece of tortilla she used as a scoop dropped from her fingers. Her hands knotted. She bit her lower lip, as if to stop her chin's quivering. Her eyes glistened. "How . . . how could this happen?"

"I don't know the particulars. I only heard about it from the Human Rights Commission. It advised me it'll pay for funeral expenses. Meanwhile it's doing an independent investigation."

"Pepe?" Irma breathed.

"I'll keep tabs on Pepe. . . but there is only so much I can do for my nephew through the Commission's auspices. I had already recommended that inmates' food be improved and called for a review on how punishments are managed." The corners of his mouth dipped. "Both recommendations remain pending."

"Recommendations? That's all you can do about a newborn taken from a hospital and gutted?!" Lauren's outburst surprised even herself, as well as the other two at the table.

For a brief moment, David's eyes measured her perturbed features. Then, calmly, "Do you have a better suggestion?"

"Well . . . well," she blustered, "for one thing I'd include better monitoring of the children in hospitals, especially indigent ones." After all, she did know something about coordinating with those patients Renita referred to psychiatric hospitals and the hospital staff.

He nodded, as if considering her response. After a beat, he replied, "Then, I would suggest you, as a would-be humanitarian, do exactly that—keep tabs on the impoverished children. Who was it who said—Gandhi, wasn't it—'Be the change you want to see in the world?'"

"But . . . but this isn't my world."

He raked a brow and smiled thinly. "Yet you're partaking of our world, are you not?"

First the grisly disclosure regarding the baby and now this, his insensitive retort. She simply could no longer remain at the table.

Pleading exhaustion, she repaired to the cubicle-like bathroom with its sink and shower's rusty plumbing and yellowed water that barely dribbled. At the sink, she finished her ablutions with a quick scrubbing of splintered cake soap. It would have to do.

She glanced in the tarnished mirror and was surprised at her image. She looked all of her seventy years . . . bags, sags, and winkles. Funny, with the tiny abrasions pitting her cheeks, she looked like a senior citizen with acne. Except it was not so funny. *Jesus Christ!*

A hopelessness flurried around her like cremated ashes. What was the point of all this, this life-force exertion at one's final years? She had felt like she merely existed, where she was not really a part of living life anymore.

Answering The Call

But this? This was a cosmic alternate part of life's spectrum.

The two-bedroom house was small, cramped, and cluttered. Irma had relegated David to a lumpy-looking couch and generously given Lauren the second bedroom's cot. Its pillow was flatter than a pancake, its timeworn sheets rough, and its tattered cover threadbare. Utterly tired as she was, depleted of all energy, she expected to sleep deeply. But, no. Aging had intensified nature's demand on her bladder.

The second time she arose for a rendezvous with the bathroom, she stuttered with eyes as gritty as shucked oysters through the partially closed door and stopped, as stunned as if tasered.

David stood naked before the toilet, one palm braced against the stucco-chinked wall, his thick, piss-hard penis in his other hand. His head whipped toward her, his expression startled.

In that bombshell instant, she felt simultaneously his lambent eyes ravishing her and her body zinging with a sweet, flaming sensitivity. She gave him a brilliant toothpaste ad smile. "You're missing the toilet." Then she turned abruptly, closing the door in her wake.

*

If Renita's assertions were correct about Lauren's mental instability, she believed her libido would have atrophied over time, along with her memory.

Last night's bathroom encounter with David Escobar proved that wrong—at least, the libido part. After she had whirled away from the startled man, forgotten yearnings had kept her awake. Yearnings that aroused her to levels of sensuality she had thought long perished, like winter's crunch on autumn's leaves.

Early that morning, the tow truck had delivered his Pathfinder. It appeared only slightly the worse for wear. However, she felt she appeared in poorer shape than the vehicle. She had not prepared for an overnight trip. Without a change of clothing or showering or makeup this morning, she was certain she looked haggard. Her aging appearance bothered her more than she would have thought.

On the other hand, though wearing the same scruffy jeans, David had donned a fresh black t-shirt that must have been stored away at his house there in Laredo. How appropriate that his pop culture t-shirt featured *The Grateful Dead* with a skull and roses.

On the drive back to Querétaro, neither of them mentioned the bathroom incident. The elephant in the room. Yet, they sat so close she could feel his energy's palpable heat.

After stopping off at first one bank to close her old account, and then another to set up a new one with ties to Mexico, they then drove through a *taquería* for breakfast burritos, which they had finished off within minutes.

She had anticipated the trip ahead to be as personally uncommunicative as the one the day before. She was still stinging from his goading the previous night, which essentially amounted to, "Do something then or shut-the-fuck-up."

He surprised her, speaking up at last. His gaze trained on the highway, he said, "To move to a developing country—

Answering The Call

like Mexico—takes what you Americans call grit."

She glanced sidewise at him, awaiting what was coming next. Another derisive comment?

"I'll give you that," he continued. "Grit. But you caught me flatfooted with the courage you displayed yesterday—there on the cliff."

Oh, so he was attempting amiability? "No, I am not courageous." She strove for honesty, more for her own integral reflection than a response to mere superficial conversation. With this move to Mexico, she was finished with subterfuge. At this stage of life, she was who she was, for better or worse. "I am simply not afraid of dying, Mr. Escobar."

"David, please," he reminded her. "After what we've been though the last twenty-four hours, I would think society's formality would approve us being on a first-name basis."

Was he alluding also to their early morning bathroom encounter? If so, she intended to ignore the reference.

Hands folded primly in her lap, she stared ahead at the road's dry and dusty vista. "It's the living this final leg of my journey that scares me. Will I be confined to a hospital bed, merely a blob of needles and tubes? Will I recognize family and friends? Will constant pain become unbearable?"

When being old affected the quality of life in an incredibly detrimental way, that was when she no longer wanted to live.

He glanced over at her quickly. "Are you terminally ill?"

Listlessly, she lifted one shoulder. "More like terminally defunct."

He considered this, then nodded. His silver-stranded hair partially escaped the sunglasses perched atop his head to slant across his jaw. "Things you don't think about when you are young."

"Oh, being old has its benefits, I suppose. Advantages like more time, a deeper and broader perspective, less striving to be the best and most successful." She thought sadly how it also focused on the urgency to repair important relationships, one of which, at least in her case, appeared to be irreparable. Would Renita's adversarial attitude ever relent?

"I have never thought of you as old."

Surprised, she glanced sidelong at him and tried to ascertain if this was an off-handed remark or mere flattery. He did not seem the type to resort to flattery. His dealings would be direct and blunt. His craggy profile looked perfectly serious, and her heart tripped a beat. She almost blurted, *How do you think of me?*

Oh, God help her, all she wanted was to retire from life with dignity, not some pathetic aging woman grasping at straws.

"But then, at fifty-three," he joshed, "I don't think of myself as old until I rise from bed in the morning with complaining and creaking joints."

Granted, he might be deemed borderline handsome. Or homely, depending on his smile or scowl. Next, the image of him earlier that morning assailed her—at the feral look that had leaped briefly to his face. The hard want . . . reflected in his eyes, his very stance . . . had been assertively male. Her lips had tingled, her eyes had felt languorously weighted. Her body had felt afire. Electric shock therapy could not have dazed her more.

She sought the safety of platonic conversation. "This was kind of you to let me tag along with you to Laredo."

Answering The Call

"If I were kind, I would have done your *póliza jurídica* pro bono."

She raised a brow. "But you invited me to ride along with you. Why even that kindness?"

"I figured rightly that once you got your finances straightened out at the bank, you would spring for the gas and food today."

Since he rarely allowed a genuine smile, this sidewise grin he pitched her stole her breath. Remember, her brain warned, he is seventeen years younger. Don't make an idiot of yourself. "You're a puzzling person, Mr.—uhh, David."

"Aren't we all? You know, dichotomies. I find people a remarkable study in contradictions." He flicked her a look that intimated, 'such as yourself,' before he returned his attentiveness to the stretch of highway ahead.

There was little traffic on it. A mirage of heat shimmered in hazy waves from its pavement. They were crossing the infinite expanse of the Chihuahuan Desert. And she was crossing an infinite expanse of fragile ego to reach out, to connect with him on more personal terms. Self-protection warranted her to stay impersonal. She could not help herself.

"You are educated. An attorney, and yet, judging by your actions at the border yesterday, you seem familiar with the . . . the underworld. Is that an appropriate term?"

He regarded her cursorily. Something profoundly painful shadowed his eyes. "That's a broad term. Underworld."

She half shifted toward him. "Look, I don't mean to invade your privacy. It's just that, after yesterday—the car accident and everything afterwards—I feel like I am caught up in one of those mind-bending kaleidoscopes. Trying to make sense of all this while everything about me seems to be spinning out of focus."

"I don't want to scare you off—but, yes, you might say I have connections with the underworld. Admittedly, it aids me in my work, my primary work—the Human Rights Commission."

"And these connections, are they with the under— ?"

"Ignorance is bliss."

Acknowledging his blockade of that question, she let a moment pass. "All right, I admit that I am ignorant, let's say, about this Human Rights Commission you are involved with. Who are you, really? I know you're an attorney, an activist, and, I suspect, a man who walks on the dangerous side of the sidewalk. How did you become that?"

He shrugged. "That what? There's the attorney and activist part who have made me what I am. And then there is the coyote and killer." The last was uttered with laconic amusement, as if he delighted in bedeviling her.

Although a chill wormed through her veins, she would not take the bait. She sought to keep her voice neutral. "All of that. We've hours ahead of us, and I make a good listener."

"Yes, you do make a good listener. A discerning listener, I've noticed. Most of 'all of that' is like anyone else's storyline. Mundane. There is not that much to tell."

"To tell . . . or will tell?"

"It's all about wrongs, I guess you'd say. I started out life on the proverbial wrong side of the Rio Grande border, here in Querétaro. Then, as a youngster, on the wrong side of the railroad tracks in Laredo, Texas. . . well, you either joined one of the gangs or ended up on the wrong side of the turf. Dead. To continue with my euphemism, I ended up on the wrong side of the prison bars in Laredo."

Answering The Call

Surprise widened her eyes, tempered by a wariness that followed. "So, how did you get caught on the, uh—wrong—track?"

"Good pun." He swiped her with a mirthless smile. "As a teenager, I was a coyote, smuggling desperate people on the wrong side of the Rio Grande to safety farther north of Laredo. It helped put food on the table, threads on the body, cardboard roof over the head, those sorts of luxuries. I got nailed ferrying the asylum seekers. Even an aftermarket off-road package can't outrun a government drone. Not that the cartel ever furnished me one of those packages."

"How long were you in prison?"

"Long enough—almost two years. While there, I observed that some wrongs needed to be righted. Made up my mind and became an activist. I knew, if I wanted to be effective, I needed a college degree. Not likely for a penniless Mexican-American kid—well, Yaqui Indian, too, but that tracks my genes back a ways."

She eyed him up and down. "Taking into account your extraordinary height, you couldn't get a basketball scholarship?"

"Nope. Never played. Basketballs were another luxury. And, besides, my prison record didn't help on the stateside of the Rio Grande. So, I got my jurisprudence masters at the Panamerican University of Nuevo Laredo."

"No family? You know, like a wife?"

"There's my widowed half-sister you met, of course, Irma. And her son, my nephew Pepe. The one in the notoriously lawless and overcrowded San Miguel prison. As for my wife . . . she's dead, murdered."

At his monotone, her eyes widened. Her breath backed

up in her throat. "You've explained the attorney-activist part of your life, and the coyote part." She mitigated her uneasiness into a poorly attempted jest. "But, the killer part, uhh, you didn't by any chance kill your . . . ?"

His sigh was more a huff. "I am a tired, used-up man. You don't have to be afraid of me."

She was more afraid of herself, of her strong reaction to this man with his unsavory background. The end of this return trip to Querétaro could not come quickly enough.

CHAPTER 15

Five days later, Lauren was able to move into her unfurnished casita, which meant sleeping on her blow-up mattress until the two beds she ordered, along with a refrigerator, were delivered. In Mexico, she was told, deliveries could stretch into days or weeks or even, occasionally, months of waiting.

Meanwhile, she made excursions around her new neighborhood, shopping for rustic Mexican furniture pieces at bargain prices to complete the furnishing of her casita—a pine dining table, a frayed upholstered couch, and two *equipale* pigskin chairs. With no TV, radio, or newspaper to raise one's blood pressure, peace and calm were tentatively reigning.

Still, a disquiet simmered below the tranquility of her days. With each passing year she had continued to think she would find fulfillment of a sort. Well, she was sixty-freakin'-nine-years old. If not by now, when? Certainly, no one could accuse her of being a slouch in her life. She had given her all.

She was not depressed or sad. Not even burnt out. She simply felt isolated from life. Was it due to Querétaro's language and cultural barrier?

Though curious about her, the people in her Corregidor neighborhood largely kept to themselves. Her neighbors on either side did not fully comprehend her Spanglish but tried to assist with well-meant smiles. How could she adequately express her abject loneliness to strangers much less in a strange language? The language barrier isolated her.

However, music united the world round. One evening she had Ubered into El Centro, where the expat's night life was rife. Hank's, a restaurant bar on Plaza Constitución, provided musical entertainment.

Alone, she ordered dinner and a margarita, then sat back to enjoy a cover of Creedence Clearwater Revival. The four-piece band was excellent, but her age clearly positioned her outside the coterie gathered to dine and listen, and she did not want to be crass and intrude without an invitation to join.

Another evening, she sat alone in her new casita and got slowly and quietly inebriated on her blender's margaritas. The next day, well past the lunch hour, she made a determined effort to connect with others there in Querétaro. She went online. Surely, the capital of the state of Querétaro would have Meetup groups as had the United States.

Browsing online, she missed the familiar things of life, like efficient appliances and Whataburger and inside jokes. Even given her rudimentary knowledge of Spanish, she would still be an outcast for not picking up on the innuendos of inside jokes inherent only to the Mexican culture.

Answering The Call

Occasionally, her thoughts strayed to David Escobar. Often, she felt drawn to the too-much younger man. Was tempted to connect with him again, if only for companionship with someone who spoke fluent English.

Then, she would remind herself he was young enough to be her son. And immediately, she would refocus her mind on something less mortifying.

Neither could she let herself dwell for long on the ever lurking fright of dementia and Renita's next move.

A few weeks later she tried reaching out through Facebook again. She met up with a cadre of recently retired expats in her community of Corregidor. Like her, they were new to life in Mexico. Croissants and cappuccinos at a local coffee house with five members in the chat group assuaged her loneliness somewhat. Yet she sensed an anxiety in each. A desperate looking for a rope thrown.

Like them, she still felt at loose ends. As if she had been fired or demoted. At the heart of her disquiet, she supposed, was an older person's feelings of uselessness or worthlessness. Once again, she considered getting involved in volunteering, perhaps at one of Querétaro's pet shelters. An unimaginable number of vagabond dogs roamed the streets. Yet volunteering years before had not fulfilled a lacking she could not name.

Hands behind her head, she lay awake one night, as she did every night in that small, overly warm upstairs bedroom, and wondered if she had made a titanic mistake. She did not feel like she belonged anywhere. Absence from her family ached to the bone, but Renita's tyranny stabbed to the heart.

Maybe with time, Renita's fury might burn itself out. Maybe by the time Lauren returned to the States to renew her Mexican immigration permit, five months off, her family would relent and welcome her with open arms. If not, she would automatically renew her Mexican immigration permit for another six months.

Meanwhile . . . meanwhile . . . . should she, could she, take up David's challenge? How on God's green earth would she involve herself with protection of indigent children in a hospital? Her Spanish was not proficient enough for hospital administrative work.

The next morning, while lunching on her patio, she was still pondering the issue of how she could make a difference, given the overwhelming number of destitute children. Impossible, for a sole woman, much less a foreigner.

Saints preserve her, she had retired, had she not? The last thing she needed or wanted was to go back to work.

Her cell phone rang. She glanced down at the caller ID, and her brows knitted. She put down her slice of mango, nudged aside her cup of cherished *café de olla* and picked up the cell phone. "Andi, what a surprise. But good to hear from you."

"Maybe not so good," came the teeth-braced tight voice.

"Why? What's going on?"

"Your daughter, Dr. H, filed some kind of psychiatric hold against you. First thing this morning. They want to lock you up for 72 hours."

She sucked air between her teeth. "Renita? What do you mean? A psychiatric hold for what?"

"Can I tell you when I get there?"

"There—where? Here? My house?"

"Yeah. I gotta find Vincente."

"Vincente? Because why?"

"Because I want him to have the chance to meet

Vinny—his son."

"Oh, sweet Jesus, Andi." Then, "I thought your menstrual period had resumed."

"Only spotty, for a couple of days. Please, please, Ms. L, please can I come? I already bought the airline ticket. With the last of my credit card points. I'm at the George Bush International airport now."

To consent to this plea would be a fiasco. Just draw the line in the sand and say no. She sighed. "Okay, give me your flight itinerary."

Five hours later, she was pacing Querétaro airport's small waiting area for arrivals to exit the customs area. She almost did not recognize Andi. Rings dangled from every appendage—nose, brows, lips, and ears and graced all fingers and thumbs. Her spangled bangs and spiked hair were now sprayed a neon orange. She carried only her chartreuse and purple tote bag.

"Yo, Ms. L!"

Lauren bussed the young girl on the cheek. "You look as if you have smuggled the Times Square New Year's Eve ball beneath that t-shirt." Sporting a genie's lamp, the tent-sized t-shirt's logo penned, *Here I am ~ now where are your other two wishes.*

Andi made a face. "Only there's no sweetheart to kiss at New Year's midnight."

"Here, let me help you with your tote." Its weight almost tilted her off balance. "What do you have in here, a 15-pound bowling ball?"

She toothed a Cheshire grin. "Everything from my hair wand to my joystick. I didn't want to fork out for checked luggage."

"Your what—your joystick? Wait, never mind an

explanation. I'm too old to listen. I've ordered an Uber for us. The trip to my casita takes a good forty minutes—time enough for you to expand on your delivery of Renita's filing an order for a psychiatric hold this morning."

She guided Andi past the glass doors to the curb outside. "And, by the way, how have you explained your peremptorily exiting the office this morning to my daughter?"

Andi's rubber band mouth stretched into a tight smile. "Told Dr. H I had started bleeding, and that the doc recommended bedrest for a week. That news deflated Dr. H like a punctured tire. Luckily for her, Ms. S has been filling in since you left."

"Ms. S?"

"Your other daughter, Sylvie."

Lauren felt like that deflated tire. So, it would seem her family had circled their wagons, leaving her outside them. An almost unbearable depth of despair gutted her. She had always told her daughters that it was she and they against the world. Now it was they and the world against her.

Windows rolled down, the Uber she ordered pulled to the curb. Normally, air conditioning was not part of the package—which meant traffic noise and desert dust with which to contend.

Once she, Andi, and the suitcase were stashed inside, Lauren asked the apprehensive question. "What can you tell me about this order for a psychiatric hold?"

Andi slumped onto the backseat beside her, her hands netting her domed stomach. "I was waiting at the office printer for a fax to come through, verifying a patient's insurance. Instead, what came through next was a fax from your son-in-law's law firm. What's its name—?"

"Cohen, Muller, and Levy."

"Yeah. Something about a psychiatric hold—"

"A psychiatric injunction?"

"That's it. They're filing a temporary psych paper through their affiliate, headquartered in Mexico City—Kramer and something or the other."

Combined with Lauren's heartache was another feeling . . . fear. A monstrous fear that control of her life would be snatched from her. How could she hope to combat her son-in-law Rick, who managed her investments; her daughter, a psychotherapist; and Sylvie's husband, Burney, an attorney renowned for his debate tactics in the courtroom and who could manipulate Lauren's legal affairs all too easily?

"On what basis, Andi? On what basis are they filing this injunction?"

"That due to your mental incompetence, you are a danger to yourself—something like that. Oh, and quite possibly a danger to those around you. That you need to be under supervised care. That is as far as I got, when Dragon Lady walked up. Holy Shinola, she went nuclear. She snatched the fax from me and yelled at me to go make tomorrow's patient reminder calls, which I had already done this morning and told her so. I swear, Ms. L, she's getting more forgetful than you are."

"Thanks for that backhanded compliment, Andi."

But Lauren took no offense. Her mind was already foraging through her scraps of knowledge about legal matters. She knew a temporary psychiatric hold, good for only ten days, could be issued without notice. Any federal, state, or local court could do it.

Could Cohen, Muller, and Levy's legal maneuvers in Texas extend to their Mexico City affiliate, Kramer, Garcia, and Figueroa, and from Mexico City to Querétaro and her? She shuddered, her flesh prickling.

Andi glanced at her askance. "You can't be cold in this furnace heat?"

"Tell me about the little one." She nodded at Andi's mounding belly. "Vinny. When is your son due? How has your pregnancy been so far? You *are* seeing a gynecologist, right?"

Her fingers, sausage-like from pregnancy, embraced her burgeoning womb. "Vinny is due in a little more than four months. I'd put off making another appointment with the gynecologist—like, until I knew for sure what I wanted to do." She peered out the Uber's window at the passing Easter egg-colored houses.

Lauren was well aware that with Houston so close to the Mexican border the option to terminated unwanted pregnancies quite late was easily available. Was that what Andi had in mind as a backup plan?

Andi darted her a side glance. "When Vinny began squirming around a few days ago, I decided. That's why I am here. To find that hot tamale."

"Hot tamale?"

"Hey, Vincente's chili is as big as a poblano and hot as a habanero."

She rolled her eyes and hoped the Uber driver did not understand English.

"Look, Ms. L, I want to find Vincente. You don't want your daughter to find you. I figured we could work this together."

Shaking her head, she smiled wryly. "All right, Mata Hari."

"Matter what—Matterhorn?"

Answering The Call

"Never mind. I'm showing my age. It's nearing six o'clock. You've got to be hungry." She leaned forward and instructed the Uber driver to drop them off at a café near her home.

In the café's tiled-and-tree-shaded courtyard, Andi scoped the tiered fountain. "OMG WTF!"

"I take it that exclamation means you like the place?" The black-aproned waitress threaded among the patron-crowded tables to take their order. After the arrival of freshly squeezed *limonadas*, along with chips and salsa, she turned to the more serious matters they both faced.

"Look, Andi, I am grateful for what you've shared about my daughter's . . . recent behavior . . . regarding me." She tilted her head back, stared sightlessly into the overhead boughs where birds chattered the advent of evening. "But I feel . . . well, crummy. Spying on my own daughter's activities."

At the sight of the *antojitos,* Andi's round face lit like the moon. Immediately, she dug in. "I look at it this way," she crunched with a mouth full of chips, "your daughter, Dr. H, is spying on *you*."

She considered this. "Fair enough." She still felt uneasy. Renita was her first born. Her heart and soul. In Lauren's mind, one could not sanely, emotionally, conspire against one's own flesh-and-blood. Not if one truly loved. But then was she herself sane? Renita insisted not.

Pensively, she leaned forward to dip into the spicy salsa one of the few remaining freshly fried chips Andi had left. Lauren stalled for a thoughtful moment to take a sip of her *limonada.* Then, reluctantly, capitulated to Andi. "Okay, first, we have to find Vincente. Second, we have to see if he is willing to concede the baby is his. If so, do you want to marry him?"

Andi reached for her *limonada*. Took a long sip. "I don't know. I only know I have this scorching hot thing for him. I need to see him again. To be with him again. I know I am only a teenager, Ms. L. But you tell me. How do you deny these insistent, plaguing freakin' feelings? If you're for reals, how do you go on, without giving it everything you got? If not, that's not living. That's existing."

Well, Lauren could buy into that.

CHAPTER 16

"*Bueno?*" David snapped without looking at his cell phone's caller ID. He was watching the latest news feed of *El Orbe* tickertape across his laptop screen.

Ten undocumented Venezuelan migrants had sewn their lips together while demonstrating in Tapachula's prison. Migrants crossing Mexico's southern border at the city of Tapachula were generally arrested and forced to wait three to four months for a response to their applications with immigration authorities.

He calculated if his business account contained enough *dinero* for him to grab a flight out of Querétaro. If not, that meant a long, hard-on-the-ass drive to Tapachula.

"Hello? . . . Hello?"

He blinked, recovered his focus, and responded automatically in English, "Yes. Hello. David Escobar, attorney, speaking."

"Mr. Escobar . . . David . . . this is Lauren. Lauren Hillard. I rode with you to Laredo—you negotiated my renter's policy last month, remember?"

One end of his mouth wrenched in a smile. Here, she felt like she had to identify herself, when he had recognized that soft southern accent once she began speaking. "Yes, I remember you, Lauren. Quite clearly."

And he would wager she remembered him, quite clearly, from the night she interrupted his piss. She had been on his mind on and off since then. He doubted the American woman entertained the same kind of thoughts he did. And doubted seriously she even mused about a half-broke Mexican American.

"How can I help you, Lauren?"

"Well . . . since we last met, a couple of legal issues have arisen. Really, I am not even sure you can help. I don't know why I am bothering—this is all so crazy. I apolo—"

"Tell me about them. These issues."

A pause, and he could feel her uncertainty about reaching out to him accelerating. "Look, Lauren, I realize a cell phone is not conducive for certain disclosures. I'd come to your house to discuss this, but my son Antonio will be home from school soon. Can you grab an Uber and come to my place?"

"Oh." Confusion colored her voice. "I thought, I don't know why, I thought that you had no family. Umm, just a moment, please."

He could hear her muffling the phone then indistinctly conversing with someone. Finally, "David, when I mentioned a couple of legal issues, they also involve a friend, here visiting. Andi Lyons. We'd both be coming."

"I'll make a double batch of sangria. It's cheap and easy." He gave her no time to change her mind. He wrapped up the conversation, giving her his address and a "See you in an hour. *Hasta luego.*"

Answering The Call

He figured his hundred-year-old hovel should be a cultural shock to the *gringa*. Good. He was not one for pretenses. He went online, checked his meager business bank balance, made an el cheapo red-eye flight reservation to Tapachula for later that night, then headed to the kitchen.

In the refrigerator, he kept for him and Tony a pitcher of sangria, diluted with seltzer water and loaded with diced fresh fruit. It was healthier than beer or tequila shots, he figured. And the customary afternoon refreshment gave him a chance to chat with Tony; to keep tabs on his son's social life.

As a junior at the university and only twenty-one, the young man was open to the fast lane. And David had already been down that highway but only as a junior in high school. He had wanted to get his own life straight, to get his degree, granted a late start at thirty, before having children.

Pilar had wanted to start earlier. Her blandishments in bed would certainly have achieved that if she had had her way. But then her way had been cut far too short.

He was tossing a diced green apple into the blown-glass pitcher when he heard the vrooming of Tony's hammered Kawasaki. Moments later, the bespectacled young man shrugged his backpack off onto the ear of one of the rickety kitchen chairs. He was as muscle-roped as David but not as tall,

"Hey, Papi. Overdoing the fruit aren't you" He chipped a grin. "More wine would be fine."

"More fruit dilutes the brute." David had always made it a point to speak only English with his son. English was the umbilical cord to a better life. "I have some clients dropping by. Cut up the orange, will you." It was not a question.

Tony squeezed by him to wash his hands in the rust-stained sink. "There's a rave playing out at Corregidora's event venue a weekend away." He dried them and picked up the paring knife. "Can I go with some of—"

David squinted at him. "A what is playing?"

"You know, a rave—a musical festival.

He scowled. "You mean an Ecstasy festival."

"No, no. Not those loco drug-fests like you've heard of."

"I am thrilled to note your linguistics course is paying off—and, no you can't go. I have to fly out on business late tonight. More like the wee-hours of tomorrow morning. I'll take the Kawasaki to the airport. A day—day-and-a-half max—I should be out of pocket. Meanwhile, you can stay at your grandma's."

"Come on, Papi. I'm old enough now to stay home alone."

"And your Abuelita Marta is too old to stay home alone." Since Pilar's death thirteen years before, her mother had been caring for Tony whenever David's work took him away from home. Which was far too often with David juggling the two jobs. "We need to be checking on Abuelita Marta more frequently."

And that got him to thinking, how wrinkled and hunched his mother-in-law was at 72, only a couple of years older than Lauren Hillard. Yet the difference in their appearance was like comparing one of the Guanajuato mummified bodies with a stylish window mannequin.

Except that opposed to a varnished mannequin, Lauren Hillard possessed a patina that could not be overlooked. A life force that could not be ignored. A wisdom that could give Mensa a run for its money. The kind of woman in whose embraces you could lose yourself.

Answering The Call

Tony chucked the orange wedges into the pitcher. "But the rave goes on the entire weekend, and my friends—"

The rope bell chimed visitors, and David forestalled Tony with a negative wag of his forefinger over his shouldder. "That's a no-go."

He navigated through the small front room congested with a dumpy couch, two split-leather chairs, an off-kilter coffee table, and his small, littered desk. With only two bedrooms in the decrepit stucco, a separate office was not a consideration.

A relic of the post-revolution 1920's, the *cucaracha*-infested cinderblock house, in the same derelict barrio as his mother-in-law's, had been a domicile windfall to an out-of-work widower from Nuevo Laredo with a nine-year-old son and a weeks-old diploma in criminal justice.

Behind the concrete patio's high *zagúan*, its wrought iron gate as rusted as the kitchen sink, waited Lauren Hillard and a short teenage girl. He was surprised to note she was very pregnant—and his very male reaction to Lauren. It had not waned in the interval. Never a good thing to mix business with pleasure.

With a token smile of welcoming, he stepped aside. "Come on in, please." He nodded at the girl. Her spiked orange hair, body rings, and tats made Gen Z look humdrum. "I am David Escobar."

"This is Andi Lyons," Lauren said. "I mentioned her in our earlier phone conversation."

"Happied-up to meet you," the girl said with animated aplomb.

"And I am Tony," his son supplied from the laminated peeling front door. Thumbs in his jeans pockets, he was eyeing the girl through his rimless glasses. His expression was a mixture of bemusement and amusement.

Uh-oh, David thought. "Tony, would you finish up with the sangria?"

With a disappointed moue, his son retreated to the kitchen.

David shut the gate and stepped aside for the two women to enter. Following Lauren Hillard to the front door, his thoughts preoccupied with her, he almost forgot to duck. The doors' low lintels were a curse of the barrio's century-old houses, for which his exceptional height had paid with many noggin knocks.

Inside, he extended a hand toward the sitting area. The two females took the frayed upholstered couch. Dust fluttered. Oh, well. He settled his lengthy frame into one of the two broken-down pigskin chairs, reclaimed from an upscale restaurant dumpster.

He did not miss how Lauren Hillard's glance quickly took in the room's shoddy furnishings. Hands clasped between his knees, he leaned forward. "All right, ladies, tell me how I might be of help."

The teenaged Andi glanced uncertainly at her older female companion.

Today the woman's graying brown hair was caught up atop her head in a careless swirl that exposed the graceful sweep of her neck. She interlaced her fingers atop her jeaned thighs and, emulating him, leaned forward. Her white peasant blouse, its drawstring ties dangling, presented a low decolletage that revealed the slope of her breasts.

Her smoky-gray eyes met his, and he wondered if she was experiencing the same sensual stirring as he. Likely not. "Andi's issue is less convoluted than mine, so, I suppose we should start with hers first."

Answering The Call

The pregnant girl's toothful grin turned tense. "I'm trying to find a dude by the name of Vincente Talamantes." Her beringed fingers cupped her stomach like a protective shield. "The father of our baby."

"What do you want from him? Child support? A marriage certificate? His head on a platter?"

Her purple-tinted lips formed a quavering grin. "I don't know. For right now, like, I just want to see how he feels about me. To see how I feel about him, after all this time. Like, if it's still white lightning."

He nodded, absorbing this. He could identify with that same feeling for Lauren. Sizzling hot white lightning. "Vincente Talamantes is a rather common name. Do you have any other information? His parents' names? A street name? Where he worked?"

Tony returned and passed around a plastic tray of the sangria-filled chipped glasses, serving first the girl, who dimpled a grin up at him. *Not good*, David thought.

Lauren said, "Should you be drinking, Andi—given your pregnancy?"

"Whatever. I'm an adult." She then looked back to David, "No. None of that kind of info . . . uhh, except I do seem to remember now that Vincente mentioned returning here to finish up his degree—like some kind of law program, if that helps."

He glanced at Tony. "Do you recognize the name?"

His son set the tray on the coffee table, plopped into the other chair, and rubbed his cleft jaw that so reminded David of his own.

Shaving its cleft was a ritual bloodletting. He occasionally thought about the convenience of sporting the mountain-man beard in style these days, but that was hardly advantageous to winning legal cases. When appearing in court, he made it a point to wear a suit jacket, his tats hidden, and his long and heavy hair inconspicuously knotted tidily at his nape.

"Vincente Talamantes," Tony mused with a slow blink. "The name's not familiar. Do you know which campus? There are several."

Swallowing a sip of her sangria, the girl shook her head and in a grooming gesture raked her fingertips through her spiked hair. Per force, David had become a social analyst of body behavior. The gesture in itself was not indicative of being deceptive, merely a motion at being presentable. She flashed Tony a sheepish grin. "We never got around to that."

Lauren set aside her glass, "Listen, I don't want to take up a lot of your time. We just need some advice, legal advice. And, clearly, I want to pay." She drew a deep breath then expelled it in a rush. "But I guess I need to know up front what kind of fee I am looking at here for the two of us."

David was not going to let sympathy get in the way of business. He had a son's future to save. "My fee would depend on what your own issue entails, as well."

She licked her lips. "I told you my family thinks I am loco. Especially with my decision to move here." She paused. Her lips flattened, suppressing what he suspected was a traitorous trembling. She looked down at her sangria.

He could see was laboring under her pain of admission. He made no move to assist her. All the while he was imagining what it would feel like for his lips, his tongue, to explore that soft, lovely mouth.

She looked up, her unflinching gaze meeting his. "My

oldest daughter Renita is a Doctor of Psychology. I managed her office until recently." She extended her hand toward the pregnant girl. "Andi here works the front desk for Renita. It seems, based on Renita's professional opinion, my mental competence—or lack thereof—makes me a danger to myself and society."

Perforce, he had undertaken to learn her credit score, her traffic violations—there had been few over the years, and her health history. He knew even about her partial hysterectomy. He probably was more intimately familiar with her than her husband and lovers. He knew of only three but possibly there had been more he had missed in his detailed research.

"I recall your referencing something to that effect that day we met for lunch—your family's objection to your move." And he recalled quite vividly the landmine effect she had on him. Disorienting. Skewing his certainty of the validity of his internal compass.

Given his experience that demanded instantly reading people, he would relegate her to the caretaker type of person. But his finely attuned senses, generated mainly by his gut feelings, whispered this was a woman of far more depth and complexity.

Lauren proceeded to fill him in on the more recent details of her quandary, with the pregnant girl putting in, "I faxed the document for Dr. H—Dr. Hillard—early yesterday. It was going to a law firm in Mexico City."

"Burney Cohen's law firm—my son-in-law—issued the temporary restraint order," Lauren clarified. She bit her bottom lip, sighed, then said, "I need to know what ramifications I am facing here under Mexican law."

"Which law firm?"

"What? It's Cohen, Muller, and Levy."

"No, the legal firm in Mexico City your son-in-law is affiliated with."

"Oh. Give me a moment to think." She set down her neglected sangria and rubbed her temples, then looked up at him. "Yes, the firm he uses in Mexico City—it's Kramer something or the other."

"Kramer, Garcia, and Figueroa," the younger woman interjected.

"Yes," Lauren said, "that's it."

David mentally winced. "I'm familiar with the firm. Occasionally, I handle minor cases for it when it is overloaded. It tosses me the scraps. In fact, it was that firm that turned over to me your rental policy."

"What can you tell me about it, about Kramer, Garcia, and Figueroa?"

Can or will? He was not inclined to share much with anyone. Like for instance, Joaquin Macho Lopez, Kramer's quasimodo of a process server and henchman for the firm's illegal side. Macho had inflicted David with a nasty facial scar five months ago. If ever a human was half-made per the French term *quasimodo*, it was Macho Lopez. The man reminded David of the pitiless hitman Anton Chigurh in the film *No Country for Old Men*, set on the Texas border.

Following a meeting with a prison inmate one afternoon, David had opposed Macho's barbarous tactics on the prison exercise grounds and taunted him with the name Macho Nacho. The hulk had sideswiped David's cheek with a melted down toothbrush used for a shiv. However, it was tit-for-tat.

The bored inmates were ripe for hostile entertainment. They had gathered round, goading the two combatants with shouted cheers and catcalling. David knew how to fight dirty. He wrestled the shiv from Macho and drove it up into his testicle. You made sure what you gave was worse than what you got. That effectively stopped most bullies. But then Macho Nacho was not most bullies.

"I'll put it this way. Jürgen Kramer, the firm's founding attorney and senior partner, is a formidable opponent both in and out of the courtroom. He makes use of our corrupt legal system quite effectively."

The man was a Little Napoleon. For all his refinement, there was something brutish about him. Flashy and crass with a nasal accent, he sported a sense of taste to match. In the courtroom, his Armani suits were custom tailored; in private, his leisure suits were adorned with a colorful shirt slashed to the chest to reveal a heavy cabled gold chain. In or out of court, Kramer possessed a mind like a whetted blade.

Her narrowed gaze reflected her consternation. Her fingertips massaged the hollow at the juncture of her collarbones. Which stymied his breathing. "Is there not some kind of judicial resolution to which I can resort under Mexican law?"

Contemplating the question, he rolled his half-empty glass back and forth between his palms. "It's like this. A court ordered injunction might be their next move. You could be ruled not to possess the legal capacity to make decisions for yourself."

"But surely the order can't be enforced here in Mexico."

He smiled grimly. "With *mordida*—the bite, the bribe—anything can be done. Legalities do not necessarily apply in Mexico. *La mordida* accomplishes far more and far more quickly an objective than does the plodding process through legal channels."

Andi's shoulder's slumped, pronouncing the swell of her stomach. Her lips formed an inverted horseshoe. She slid a sideways glance at Lauren. "Like, so what now, Ms. L?"

Absently, Lauren fretted with one of her blouse's drawstring tassels. "I'm thinking. I'm thinking."

He took pity on her, a sentiment he rarely allowed himself to bestow upon the prisoners requiring his legal help. "For the moment, you have one saving grace. A psychiatric hold or even a restraining order, for that matter, cannot exceed ten days without additional and time-consuming court proceedings that with luck might entail years. You merely have to stay out of sight, avoid being served, during the next ten days or so, depending what day the court signs off on the order."

"We can't stay anywhere that I would have to use a credit card," Lauren was muttering, more to herself. "Where we could be traced. However, I do have enough cash on hand to cover a hotel for us for a couple of days—if the accommodations are dirt cheap."

Andi affected a shudder. "I don't cotton to *cucarachas*, Ms. L."

Lauren's lips twisted. "Neither do I, babe, but beggars can't be choosers."

She looked up at him, then nodded, as if reaching a decision, and a lock of hair tumbled down from her clip's messy anchorage. She lifted an arm to nudge the tendril back up, which drew his attention to her hiked breast. Jesus, Mary, and Joseph!

"I'm sure you're familiar with the hood," she said, delivering a devastating smile that decimated his professional intention always to remain objective. "Any suggestions for a place to lay low?"

Tony interjected, "You can stay here."

David shot his son a taser glare.

"Papi, you already said you'd be out of town tonight and maybe tomorrow. They could have your bedroom. When you get back, you and I could double up in mine for the next ten days."

"Umm," Lauren asked, "what about things like toothbrushes and such? We brought nothing with us."

"Papi has a collection of unused travel toothbrushes."

"I got my tote." The teenager gestured toward her huge purple and chartreuse bag. "It's loaded with tools, like everything from makeup to masturba—"

"Umm, Andi, we're talking essentials here," Lauren interrupted. She shook her head, and the silvery curl drifted loose again. "Look, I don't want to put you two out."

"I'm flying back in six days," Andi chimed in. "Next Wednesday, Ms. L. So, you wouldn't have to worry about me. For the next ten days or so you just need to make sure you keep off the radar."

With an exasperated sigh, Lauren dropped her chin to her chest, then peered up at David. Her eyes were pinpoints of pain, of a deep sadness.

He could not even imagine what it would be like for his child, for Tony, to turn against him in later years as had her daughter against her.

"We haven't even discussed your fee yet," she murmured.

Stalling, pondering, he stared up at the ceiling, and noted an extensive corner cobweb he had somehow missed in his last cleaning. Several varmints were snared by those tenuous filaments. As he was by her particular mesh of feminine wiles.

Granted, when was that last household scouring, half-a-year ago? He grunted. He was such a chump. "The house could use a good swabbing."

"Done deal." Her answering smile of relief smote him. He was not the good guy she surmised.

CHAPTER 17

That next morning Andi suffered a momentary twinge of guilt, leaving Ms. L swabbing the squat little house in the marginal neighborhood. But Andi could not pass up the opportunity when Tony offered to drive her around the various University of Querétaro campuses in search of her elusive Vincente Talamantes.

With Tony's father on a flight to somewhere in the far southern region of Mexico, his dusty, dented SUV was his son's for the day. One hand lapped casually on the steering wheel, Tony navigated the Pathfinder among the darting autos like it was an extension of his body.

She found the danger of the calculated near-misses both harrowing and exhilarating. "Like, you ever thought of becoming a test driver for Ferrari?"

He slid her a rueful grin. His face held a warm intelligence. He wore his hair in an outgrown buzzcut that played off rather decently the contours of his square shaped face. He was dressed in chinos and a camo t-shirt. "Only if I could afford a Ferrari on my own, because my father will publicly execute me if I don't get a college degree first." He stroked the shift knob. "But I do find driving a sensorial experience."

Her eyebrows shot up. *Sensorial?* She had a good idea of the word's definition. But who tossed off a word like that? She studied the young man next to her with serious respect. He had overlapped his spectacles with sunglasses, and he looked bad ass. "So, what do you do when you are not in class or studying, Rambo?"

"Rambo? That's my father. I'm what you *gringos* call a nerd. Carrying eighteen hours eats up a lot of my time. But I don't mind it that much. Let's stop by the main campus first. See if we can get a lead on your guy there."

She scowled. "That's the worm in the apple. He's not my guy."

He shook his attention off the road to glance at her belly. "But he is . . . uhh . . . your baby's father? That is why you want to find him, right?"

She sighed, smoothed her loose smock over the bump in her belly. "I want to find him to find out if I still want him."

He returned his focus to his fearless driving. "And if you still do . . . but he doesn't want you—or the baby. . . then what?"

"Then I hire one of your Mexican hit men."

His head whipped toward her, and she grinned. "Just messing with you. Are you for hire?"

"Not as a hit man."

"Is your father? A hit man?"

He chuckled. "Hardly. Papi contracts out his legal expertise, but his main focus is our penniless *pinche* Human Rights Commission. No pay but his way, as he reminds me often enough."

"And his way is, like, you're getting that college degree?"

"Yeah. But in the United States. He wants me to have a better life than one afforded here in the barrio."

"Your father may have a one-up on your druthers."

"Druthers?"

"Yeah, like, I'd druther get high than bottom out. Your neighborhood is bottomed out. A dump."

At this, laughter rolled out of him. "Tactful, you aren't, *gringa*." He wheeled abruptly into a diagonal parking spot before a tree-shaded cluster of contemporary-looking buildings. "We're here. Let me do the talking, *bien?*"

He surprised her by coming around to help her as she struggled with both her girth and tote bag to exit the Pathfinder. *Gone With the Wind* gallantry was still in force in this day and age?

Circumventing one imposing white building, he led her down a hallway, weaving in and out of both young and old students lugging backpacks and computer bags.

Occasionally she would give some thought to attending college. Then she would scoff at the idea. She had barely made it through high school. Unfailingly, her bored mind drifted, unable to concentrate, unless the subject involved math. It contained no confusing variables.

One teacher had mentioned ADHD, one of many abbreviations ascribed to her—like CD, for conduct disorder, and SD, for standard deviation, and G&T for gifted and talented. The last which proved her point—what did teacher's know?

At a doorway on the left, Tony steered her inside and approached a long counter topped with baskets of forms. Behind it, on a tall stool before a computer, perched a bored but pretty chick, her shiny brunette hair snared back in a ponytail. At their approach, she glanced up and pitched them the mandatory inquiring smile. Then her eyes glowed. "Tony!"

"Hola, *hermosa.*" Smiling, he leaned one forearm on the counter, addressing in Spanish the now lively young girl. To Andi, who knew only a few Spanish endearments acquired from Vincente, Tony's following words ran together unintelligibly.

Something he said set the girl to giggling. Her caramel skin flushed a becoming pink.

He lowered his voice. Whatever he was next saying caused her to peer over her shoulder at a couple of coworkers at desks in the back of the office. Next, she shook her head at Tony, her ponytail swishing like a horsetail at flies.

From somewhere he produced a one-hundred peso bill slid across the formica counter by his covering hand. Andi calculated five dollars would be a lot to the student worker.

The girl quickly palmed it then turned back to the computer. Her fingers danced across its keys. For a moment, her dark eyes scanned the screen. She reverted her consideration to Tony, completely ignoring Andi, and, frowning, spat out a spate of Spanish in a hushed voice.

Tony nodded. "Gracias, Carmen." He winked at her, then took Andi's elbow, steering her out of the office.

"Well?" she asked, as he propelled her down the hall. With the burden she now carried, her short stubby legs had to quicken their pace to keep up with his longer strides. "Is Carmen the love of your life?" Somehow she could not picture this techy as a lover boy.

His wide shoulders hunched. He jammed his hands in his pockets and kept walking. "Carmen loves life."

Okay, so the subject of Carmen was off limits. "What did you find out?"

"She couldn't—or wouldn't—provide an address or phone number. She did pass along the info that your Vincente Talamantes is attending the University's Juriquilla campus. Juriquilla is the *Beverly Hills 90210* of Querétaro. We're heading there next."

"No TV in your house—how would you know about *90210?*"

He tapped toward the cellphone in his back pocket. "Lots of re-runs here in Mexico."

"From that machine gun-fire exchange with the *chica*, I gather she does not hold Vincente in high esteem."

Opening the Pathfinder passenger door for her to climb aboard, he looked down at her with a pitying expression. "If this Vincente Talamantes is the same one you are looking for, it appears your Romeo is engaged to none other than the daughter of Querétaro's police chief."

As he closed the passenger-side door, she felt as if he was also closing the door on her hopes. But then what *was* she hoping for?

Initially, she had thought she merely wanted to find out if she still felt the same stomach-quivering sensation when with Vincente. Now, this disappointment she felt at learning he was engaged . . . was it that she had wanted, expected, Vincente to marry her? And the stomach quivering sensation she now felt, that of her baby moving within, well, it was an entirely different kind of thrill.

Or, as it was nearing four o'clock, was it that her stomach's present activity could be nothing more than mere growling with hunger? Oh, for Houston's authentic creole cuisine.

Juriquilla was bad to the bone rich. Mostly expats, Tony said. American, Canadian, and an assortment of other wealthy internationals. Aside from a mega-moneyed mall, a major portion of Juriquilla centered around an immense sparkling blue lake with whitewashed, multi-tiered houses clinging to a sky-high bluff. It looked like a travel photo of one of those Greek islands.

At the Juriquilla campus, Tony grasped her elbow to support her as she lumbered up a flight of stairs to the super-modern administration building. "We'll try the admin office first," he was saying, "although I don't have the pull here I do at the main campus."

"You mean you don't have a crunch here like Carmen."

"I mean you don't have much of a chance of finding your Romeo here," he said, opening one of the building's expanse of glass doors for her.

Entering, she retorted, "Wrong, Tony Escobar."

Because the six-foot dark god with the voluminous pompadour hairstyle striding toward her was none other than Vincente Talamantes. Beneath an unbuttoned white linen shirt, a red t-shirt looked pasted to his pumped-up pecs. *Oh cripes.* He was chatting up a cute girl with pixie black hair. The tiny thing gazed up at him as if he were the Second Coming.

Andi watched Vincente's expression closely, those molten-hot brown eyes and that ultra-lush mouth. She had not contemplated how she expected him to react. Or what she had been hoping from him. But it was not what followed.

He gave her the *abrazo*, an embrace, followed by a pecking on each cheek. He released her with a smile. "What a surprise, Andi." He eyed her up and down. "Motherhood becomes you. And this is my fiancée, Gabriella Marquez. Gabby, this is my American friend, Andi, and . . . uhh . . ." He inclined his head, indicating he was waiting for her to supply her surname.

"It's Andi Lyons, *cabrón*." Tony said.

Vincente's shoulders jerked wide in a boxer's stance, and he drew back his fist. Faster than a blink, Tony, a good two inches shorter, shifted into some kind of black belt position, one fist drawn to his opposite shoulder, the other fist shooting diagonally across his midsection.

Palms upraised, Andi thrust between the two adversaries. "Whoa, yo! Vincente, wait. Is there somewhere we can talk?"

At her pleading expression, he frowned, his expression one of confoundment. "Talk? What is there to talk about?"

Stunned, her palms dropped to her stomach. "Why, about . . . about our baby."

"*Our* baby?" he held up his palms and stepped back. "I have not the slightest idea what you are talking about."

She fisted now nonexistent hips. "I'm talking about how you fucked me inside out, that's what."

Vincente's fiancé—Gabriella, Gabby, Gangbanger, whatever—tilted her head, her gaze raking Andi from round face to round belly. "I think you are a foolish American girl."

Tony grabbed Andi's elbow and rotated her around, steering her toward the exit door. "Wait, wait," she said, her feet trying to put on the brakes. "I want to see what Vincente says."

"He's not going to say anything, Andi." He propelled her outside and down the steps toward the Pathfinder. "He's not going to marry you. And he's not going to claim the baby as his. And you would never win if you tried to fight him in court here in Mexico. He's a dud." He yanked open the Pathfinder passenger door for her, and she could almost see the smoke coming out of his ears. "And you are brainless to have even considered coming to Mexico." He slammed the door shut.

CHAPTER 18

David slung his backpack over one shoulder and strode toward the airport's sliding door exit. Tropical heat, so different from Querétaro's high-altitude climate, steamed his sunglasses.

Tapachula, Mexico was a city socially and economically the equivalent of United States border towns like Laredo—except Tapachula was not on the northern border with United States but on the southern border with battle-strafed Guatemala.

He hailed a taxi and caught a ride to Tapachula's Olympic Stadium. Undocumented migrants from Central and South America, crossing into Mexico, were generally arrested and sent to a migrant detention center here in Tapachula for an indeterminate period. Its Olympic Stadium was a crowded refugee camp where The National Migration Institute, the INM agency, did not provide humanitarian services such as food, bedding, or sanitary disposal.

The overwhelming migrant influxes had collapsed the

INM, leaving the migrants waiting for responses to applications that were unlikely ever to come. In defiance of authorities, thousands of these migrants opted to join the dangerous trek of migrant caravans to the United States.

Ironical, how so many Americans, Lauren Hillard among them, were headed south of the Mexican border and these migrants were headed north of its border, both chasing different American dreams.

The largest migrant flow into Mexico was individuals from as far away as Haiti and Cuba, seeking political asylum. He knew very well that he could have numbered himself among them with that same urgency to protect one's family. But he had been unable to protect Pilar on his own turf. Tony, he would protect.

And Lauren? Bitter experience was teaching him that when he let himself love someone he put that beloved in jeopardy. He would not do that to her.

The helmeted and combat-vested Guardia Nacional, toting assault rifles and abetted by snarling guard dogs, positioned themselves in front of the Olympic Stadium's twin ramped entrances. Gathered behind the ring of soldiers were local government officials, various press corps, and curious spectators. From the primeval forests, contiguous with the stadium, brightly plumaged birds cawed a warning.

He had arrived just in time. From within the stadium, ten individuals, led by a woman in Mexico's vivid *folklórico* red-white-and-green garb, proceeded down one of the two entrance ramps.

He presented his Human Rights Commission Agent pass to the guard on duty and met the spitfire and her protestors halfway up the ramp. "You've always made it a point to capture the press's notice, Angela."

But his focus was beyond her, on the grotesque sight of the ten people plodding behind. Their dry-bloodied, sewn-shut mouths were a bid for attention to their political cause. Three of the ten migrants were females. One of the male protestors had also sewn closed his eyelids. At the sight of these protestors, David thought that even an atheist would feel the need to pray.

Shiny coils of ropy black braids wreathed either of Angela's ears. Behind one was tucked a large white blossom, a margarita. The thirty-six-year old's carmine lips bestowed a cheeky grin. She had a supreme confidence about her beauty. "But not capture—nor hold—your notice, not long enough anyway."

Occasionally their paths crossed, as she worked the refugee agency COMAR. She was a brilliant tactician with a fierce dedication to feminist causes, as well . . . and an engaging partner in bed.

It occurred to him that she was seventeen years younger than he—the same number of years that Lauren was older.

So what was the allure Lauren possessed that continually tugged at his interest? The depth that came with maturity? Perhaps, as with fine port, scotch and the best wines, aging enriched her essence. Her subtle, beguiling sensuality contrasted sharply with Angela's blatant sexuality.

His male's sharply honed instinct told him Lauren was oblivious to her sensuality . . . that basic part of nature repressed when sometimes emotional, mental, or sheer physical survival demanded that potent energy be channeled more effectively.

"Lately, you've been ignoring my God-given charms," Angela teased.

"Your charms are undeniable," he said with a good-natured grin, "but God-given is questionable."

Uncannily, that same basic survival instinct of his slipped into overdrive. He detached his gaze from her avid one and canvassed his surroundings. Just beyond the stadium ring of spectators, his surveillance skidded to a stop.

Reposed against a towering palm tree was a familiar figure. Though the palm's fronds shadowed the face's identity and the man's arms were crossed in nonchalance, the hunched shoulder exuded menace.

For this very reason, and many other situations that had posed a possible threat all these years, David had always made sure his address and accounts were listed under pseudonyms and password managers were used—in order to protect Tony. Yet Macho Lopez had somehow managed to crack one of David's codes.

After wrapping up his meeting with the various self-mutilated protestors, David glanced once more in the direction where Macho had loitered. Like a bogeyman, the man appeared to have melted into the jungle foliage.

But, upon arrival in the stadium's parking lot, appended behind one windshield wiper of David's rental car was a bull fight advertisement. Poorly scribbled at the top was, "Tony Escobar does not need his eyeglasses. Nor his eyeballs. But his corneas the black market needs."

CHAPTER 19

"He doesn't want me—or our baby!"

At the shrilly screamed words, Lauren winced and tilted her cell phone away from her ear. "Andi, it's going to be all right. You knew this was a possibility. Have Tony bring you on back to the house. We'll figure out our next—"

A tear-choked, "Nooo." A hiccough. Then more soberly, "Listen, Ms. L, I am going to eat myself beyond silly right now. I've bullied Tony into hauling my bloated body to the nearest *taquería*."

The phone went dead. Lauren sighed. Food, Andi's solution to every crisis. But then the girl needed to be eating for two.

Which reminded Lauren it was late afternoon and she had not eaten since David scrounged leftovers for dinner yesterday, before he flew out on his business trip.

She scavenged through the family fridge and found among its meager stock an opened cellophane package containing two quesadillas. Standing at the counter she had polished to a Medici gleam, she did her own pigging out, while fretting what Renita's next possible move might be.

No closer to an answer, Lauren finally went back to her cleaning, for which that morning she had redonned her standby peasant blouse, jeans, and tennis shoes. As both Andi and she had brought no change of clothing, it was going to be a long ten days holed up in this wretched neighborhood.

Recollecting her dash with David to the U.S. border and now her stranded stay at his casa, it would seem when with him her wardrobe, already ruthlessly reduced before her move, presently consisted of little more than Eve's fig leaf.

His bedroom required her Merry Maid's cleaning services next. She had already located a set of wash-worn sheets in his closet, the size of one of those antiquated telephone booths. After she changed the bed she and Andi had slept on the night before, she put her hands on her hips and shook her head with a sigh. Andi was the first person with whom she had shared a bed in years. A sad commentary.

With a dust rag, she attacked the single window's crumpled venetian slats, then shifted her attention to swathing the dust from the laminated tops of the dresser drawers and nightstand. Next she set to sweeping the room, but beneath the double bed her broom hooked on something. Kneeling, she fished out the object. A guitar.

Sweet Jesus, it was a Strat Sunburst Fender. She reckoned the high quality acoustic guitar had to be worth close to the neighborhood of a grand. Gingerly, as if it were a Stradivarius Viola, she went to cradle it. Out of the sound hole fluttered something. A photo.

She scooped it up. It looked to have been snapped at a small venue, considering the closely crammed, tiny tables, each occupied by groupies of a long ago era, with more patrons standing behind.

A very young and very sexy David was on the stage, the guitar strap slung from his neck. He was leaning around a microphone stand toward a female fan below, his long hair freeze-framed in one swishing motion.

Gazing up at him, the young woman's hands were clasped beneath her chin, as if in ecstatic prayer. With her dark hair cascading below her shoulders, her profile was Madonna beautiful.

Lauren flipped over the photo. *Mi héroe, mi esposo, mi todo.* My hero, my husband, my all. It was signed, *Con amor ~ Pilar.* Whew! Love personified.

Dazed, she thrust the tell-tale photo back inside the guitar's cavity, eased the guitar beneath the bed, and returned to her cleaning. All the while her mind was centered on David. He was such an enigma. A master of impersonations? Whatever, he was shoving her lightyears beyond anything she had encountered.

According to Tony, his father was not due back until the next morning at the earliest. And, more importantly, where were Tony and Andi?

She finished her housecleaning with the single bathroom, which both males had obviously failed to notice the accumulation of soap scum in the shower stall. In addition, she beat to death with her broom a scorpion that had the misfortune to cross her path.

After nine o'clock came and went and filthy and exhausted from the sweeping, mopping, dusting, she popped into the cramped shower. Its heated water was fitful and issued in resentful spurts.

In the dark, she redonned her drawstring blouse, sans

bra. Like most houses, David's had neither air conditioning nor heating. The weather at that high altitude was generally mild, but she was finding the high desert's summer nights could be uncomfortably warm.

Not that she would sleep in the raw . . . and not because of any notion of modesty drummed into her from childhood. No, she was simply disheartened by the flabby muscles and crepey skin the years has stockpiled.

Far too often these days, she was reminded that her time on this terrestrial plane was drawing short. But then, was that not why she had set off on this sojourn initially? To answer this call to adventure in whatever time might remain?

It had to be well toward midnight when she was awakened by Tony's low admonishing voice and Andi's weepy, giggly response. When several minutes passed and Andi still did not show up in David's bedroom, Lauren could only surmise Andi had elected to dally in Tony's bed. Ahh, for the spontaneity and energy and passion of youth.

Punching her pillow for a comfortable spot for her head, Lauren at last succumbed to a fretful sleep, rolling to her stomach, then flopping onto her back. Periodically, she flipped her pillow, seeking its cooler underside.

Sometime much later she stirred, awakened this time by the mattress's sagging. Aggravated and groggily, she threw back the covers for a tardily changing-beds Andi.

"*Lo siento*" came a deep masculine voice, "but I'm fagged."

Lauren shot up onto her elbows. In the faint gray light seeping from the window's shuttered slats, she could make out David's shadowed torso—his broad shoulders and his muscled back tapering to his waist. He was shrugging off his t-shirt.

As her adjusting vision sharpened, she picked out the silvering in his dark hair—and his back's various nicks and scars and punctures. It looked like a knife-throwing or shooting range's human target practice.

He tossed what sounded to be a shoe into a corner. "Your young friend has co-opted my side of Tony's bed." He tugged off his other shoe. "And hold the chili, because I'm not doubling up this body's high-rise to sleep on the couch." Standing, he stood to drop his jeans, and next slumped his magnificent, toned length down alongside her.

Lying on her back, as rigid as her principles, she stared sightlessly up at the ceiling.

"By the way, I sleep commando."

"Well, I don't." She pounded her pillow again and rolled to her side, facing the wall.

He must have felt her tension, because he mumbled, "Like I said before, you don't have to be afraid of me." He turned onto his side, away from her, and within minutes began softly snoring.

She closed her eyes tightly, determined to summon sleep as quickly as possible. Her spine tingled from the heat of his body. Her sense of smell, which she thought had deteriorated, prickled with the faint scent of his citrusy aftershave and other purely male odors identifiable with him.

God help her, she was erotically stimulated. More than she had been in years. And at her age! This was not how it was supposed to be, damn it. Her aging body was supposed to slip compliantly into dormancy followed at some point by numbing death. Instead, it was acutely aware, highly sensitized. Was that her heart, whispering it was time again?

Time to fall in love? The last time?

Her fingers crumpled the bedsheet. Nonsense.

Yet she did not want these sensations to end. They might not come again. For those few moments she was feeling pulsatingly alive. She wanted to remember this time, lying beside this man, for the long, lonely winter nights ahead. If only she could reexperience how it felt to touch a man. No, to experience the sensation of touching him, David Escobar.

She released the bedsheet, her hand creeping out to reach toward him . . . and then withdrawing. Those feelings belonged to the young. In her head and heart, the dreams and yearnings had remained the same. But not her body. She was older but no wiser. Foolish old, lonely woman.

*

Eyes closed, David could feel his body curled around another's. His lids flickered. Morning's buttery light swept one wall. Long, smokey-gray hair splashed across his bicep. Lauren. His arm mantled her ribcage. He detected her breath, felt her chest's soft rising and falling. His nostrils flared at her skin's fresh scent of soap combined with her hair's herbal smell of shampoo.

Of their own volition, his fingers drowsily drifted lower to caress her belly, cocooned within her linen peasant blouse. What was it about the magic of night that intensified each sensation, that sharpened the sharing of stolen love?

And what was it about poverty that possessed the power to disillusion magic? Sure, if he wanted, he could earn a more substantial salary to equal that of Mexico's average household income. But that would never be able to compete with the high society status of Lauren's youth. Besides, he wanted Tony to understand the value of human dignity, regardless of class.

He heard her sharp rake of breath. She shifted, twisting toward him, her face turned up to his. In the dimness, her eyes were as smoky as her hair. "You can't be serious."

"What? This wanting of you?" That last utterance surprised him as much as it must have surprised her.

Her breath shredded in her throat. She pushed up, braced on one forearm half over him, her hair falling from her shoulder to sweep his temple. "I am old enough to be your mother."

"Older than I, yes. But not old." He, too, raised onto one elbow, his mouth a breath away from hers. "What has age got to do with loving?"

She spun toward the edge of the bed and sprang to her feet, her slender, shaking frame a chimerical silhouette. "Age is a turn-off in the merciless light of day."

Confounded, he could only mutter, "What? Expression lines?"

She yanked open the venetian blinds. Morning's sunlight scalded the room. "And I won't be used for your gratification under the cover of darkness. Have a better look."

He eyed her with blatant appreciation.

She sputtered, grabbed clothing from the chair, then pivoted toward the bedroom door, swung it open and shut. Next followed the bathroom door's muted swishing closed.

Stunned, by his own responses more than hers, he lay there, reflecting. He recalled how on the unscheduled flight back he had entertained reveries about this unique woman,

Lauren Hillard.

Reveries of her warmth and ageless feminine power had dispelled for that little while, at least, the haunting recollection of the suffering Tapachula migrants. These reveries had beckoned him when he had begun to lapse further back, into his lonely past. Had shoved away the specter of Macho, now shadowing him.

What was Macho up to? Did it have to do with the *cholo's* thirst for revenge? Or a possible more pernicious mission having to do with locating Lauren Hillard?

As far as an intimate relationship, she clearly wanted nothing to do with David. Because she felt he was too young for her? Or because he patently was not in her stratosphere culturally or financially? Or both?

One could not fight innate feelings and prejudices like those, and he certainly was not going to try. Nope, no hard feelings that way.

CHAPTER 20

That morning, Tony located a music channel on the wall-mounted television. Succumbing to his persuasive charm, Andi and Lauren helped stow the furniture against the walls, creating a dance space.

He held out his hands to Andi. "*Bien*, now show me the West Coast Swing."

She collapsed on the couch and, giggling, warded off his importuning with a negative shake of her hands. "No way, dude. My dance style is a cross between Simon Says and a stripper whose rent is due."

His head canted, his expression puzzled, then he grinned in understanding. He rotated to Lauren. "Then you will have to teach me."

She threw up her hands and chuckled. "I haven't danced in forever, Tony. I'm not sure I even remember how."

"Once you start, you will remember. You know, like riding a bicycle." He took her hand before she could object and pulled her into the cleared circle. *Boogie Shoes* by KC and the Sunshine Band was playing.

He was right, once she let her body feel the pulse of the music, she began to sway. Her musician's soul telegraphed the music's beat to her feet and arms. "Okay, Tony," she relented, placing her hand on his shoulder, not as muscled, nor as broad, as his father's. "First, you walk backward, two steps, beginning with your left foot, then a triple step in place and a forward, walk, walk."

She showed him, and then he mimicked it. "Good," she said. "Now, take my hand again. You simply push me away, slightly, then draw me back in."

He caught on rapidly, and he fell into rhythm with a natural ease. However, he lacked yet the smoothness that came with practice and made several missteps. When he pushed her away and lost his grip, she spun out, collided with one of the pigskin chairs, and tumbled backward over its arm, sinking butt first. He and Andi cracked up laughing, and their hilarity set Lauren off in helpless laughter, as well.

"Here," came a rum-rich voice she instantly recognized. "I got you."

She looked up, up. David's damp hair sprinkled her with droplets. He leaned over to scoop her from the chair. The music must have drowned out his showering. He had not shaven yet, because a dark stubble shadowed his jaw.

She knew he had slept in late, having arrived in the early hours of the morning. She had awakened . . . no, her body had awakened . . . to his touch, to his caressing her belly. A sweet heaviness had taken root lower in her abdomen. Until logic barged in to remind her she was truly losing her mind.

He let her feet swing free and inch by inch lowered her to the floor. As her body slid down his, seizures she had never experienced jolted her. She risked staring up into his eyes. Was the same smoldering desire that rocked her what she saw in the depths of his?

His smile came slowly but fully, transforming the severity stamped onto his face into a lightheartedness pervasive in the room. "Now pay attention, Tony," he said. "I am going to show you how the West Coast Swing is done properly. You take the woman's hand, palm down, and press your thumb atop, with your forefinger extended, like a pistol. It's all in the control I exert through my hand and arm."

She could feel the energy's current surging from his hand to hers. Jimmy Reed's bluesy *Baby, What You Want Me to Do* was playing now.

Following its slower, sultry tempo, David walked her out, then drew her back to him. His eyes remained locked on hers. Fluidly he led her through the dance patterns. When next she stepped back into his embrace, her entire body was supercharged. He wrapped up the dance, whipping her out and drawing her back to hold her firmly to him through the strain's last smoky notes.

"Bravo!" Andi was clapping enthusiastically.

Lauren blinked, trying to restore some sensibility to her shattered composure.

"*Híjoli*, Papi," Tony exclaimed, "I had no idea you could dance like that!"

Never taking his eyes from hers, David replied, "There is a lot you have to learn about your old man, *mijo*."

※

Later that day, on the miniscule back patio, Lauren was struggling to wash the voluminous bedsheets in the *lavadero's* washboard sink. Creeping red bougainvillea softened the harshness of the laundry room's concrete walls.

Breaking loose from an afternoon Zoom meeting, David located a plastic tub of detergent for Lauren and was dousing the lavadero's water-soaked bedsheets. Tony was in his bedroom, tending to an online college course, and the lethargic Andi was napping in his bed.

Using rubber gloves Lauren had uncovered, she vigorously began swabbing the sheets against the washboard's concrete ridges. She was not in the best of moods. Each day, each hour, proclaimed this adventure of hers was a mortifying blunder. From alienating her family to selling off all her belongings to isolating herself by moving to a foreign country. And now this, a fixation on a much younger man, who just might be scamming her.

"Why *did* you come back early?" Lauren asked.

With a twist of his wrist, David recapped the bright orange detergent tub. "It seems the two of us may share a Mutual Adversarial Society member."

She paused in scrubbing, her shoulders and upper arms already welcoming the momentary physical relief. "And that would be?" she asked, looking up over her shoulder. He was standing just behind her, his height eclipsing hers by a good foot.

"Macho Lopez, aka Macho Nacho, my term of endearment for him. He contracts out as a process server for Jürgen Kramer, my erstwhile employer—and your daughter Renita's legal contact here in Mexico. I spotted Macho tailing me on my trip to Tapachula."

"Shit!" Her gloved hands flung the top sheet against the laundry room's pockmarked wall. "Can Mexico get any shittier?!" With a mournful twist of her mouth, she watched the wet sheet slither down the concrete blocks.

Answering The Call

Even more forcefully, he slung the detergent tub into the piling sheet. "So, this shithole and more to the point—its poverty—doesn't suit Her Majesty?"

She blinked, her head shaking off his scornful sarcasm. "I've lived in poverty before. I and my daughters. What does poverty have to do with the here and now?"

"Because I am here and now." The play of reaction across his animated features said so much more than his words. At once fierce and, opposingly, questioning.

She sparked, "And was—is—your love for Pilar here and now?"

"Pilar?" He stared down at her with incomprehension.

"Yes, Pilar."

"What do you know about her?"

"Your guitar. While cleaning your bedroom, I found it beneath your bed. Her photo of you two fell out of it."

"Oh. Yes." His gaze strove backward in time. "My wife." He crossed to collect the detergent tub and shoved it back on the high, board shelf. "And thanks for cleaning my adorable abode."

She was not going to let him off that easily. "Your wife—and the love of your life?"

"Tony is my life." He strode back toward the patio door.

She sighed. He had neither defended nor disputed his feelings for Pilar. "And your music? What about it?"

From over his shoulder he shot her a wooden glance. "It died *The Day the Music Died*. With Pilar."

And so am I, Lauren thought. . . dying.

CHAPTER 21

That night Lauren found sleeping just inches from David unbearable. Not that she slept, more like dozed. And she suspected from his own restless turnings he had not slept well either.

In that double bed, it was difficult not to touch one another unintentionally. Her hand sliding off her pillow to fall on his wrist. His knee, in shifting positions, grazing her calf. Toward morning, his arm draping possessively over her waist had stirred her awake . . . and in slumbering disregard, she had fallen asleep again.

At some point, she awoke to find she was cuddled into the crescent of his lengthy body.

He must have awakened at the same time, because he withdrew his arm at once. Moments later he arose and began dressing. The window's slatted, muted light silhouetted his classically ideal physique. She knew then she was hopelessly infatuated with the man.

She had cabin fever. That had to be it, had to be why she could drum up no immunity to his potent male pheromones, testosterones, or whatever it was that powered his core.

Obviously, he had picked up on her tension that morning—most likely the tension of all four of them. That need to break out of the confines of the stymying stucco. He suggested he felt it safe enough for them to hit up a neighborhood *tienda* and restock the pantry to cover the next ten days' worth of food.

She cast a critical eye at her well-worn jeans and peasant blouse. "Buying a badly needed change of clothing would be a welcome diversion, too."

Grudgingly, he relented. "All right, we'll stop off at a department store. But make it pronto inside. And buy only what you can pay for with cash."

After a swift raid for food on the *tiendita*, so small she had to step aside in the narrow aisle for a butcher hauling a hog carcass on his back, they headed next to purchase a change of clothing.

She and Andi were riding in the back of the Pathfinder, behind David at the wheel and Tony in the passenger seat. Lauren noted several times how David's head would swivel ever so slightly toward both side mirrors and then the rearview mirror.

Tony half turned in his seat to face her and Andi, directly behind him. "While you are in the Coppel Department Store, also buy swimsuits." He glanced over at his father. "How about it, Papi? After they finish, can we run up to Pinal de Amole and Puente de Dios?"

"You've got a class this afternoon."

"Only an online one I can do tonight."

"Never will this body fit into a swimsuit," Andi grudged. "It'd take a bed canopy."

149

Lauren knew she never would expose her own body's grapefruit-dimpled cellulite in a bathing suit.

Tony waved a dismissive hand. "Well, we can wade in the pool beneath the cave's falls. And do lunch at Pinal de Amole. They've the best *pancholes* and *gorditas* anywhere to be found."

"You had me at 'lunch'," Andi said.

Lauren could see David's reflection. While his sunglasses gave away nothing in the rearview mirror, the easing of his stringent mouth indicated he deemed the afternoon outing . . . what? Only tolerable for him, given that he had reluctantly agreed to harbor her from a process server over the next week or so to come?

"It appears then you have today's agenda lined out, son," he said, his tone noncommittal.

After he parked in front of the upscale department store, Tony popped out to open the back door for Andi, and David swung open the back door for Lauren.

"Coming with us?" she asked, sliding out from the back seat to face him.

"Clothes shopping is the seventh level of hell for me."

With a withering look, she peered over her aviator sunglasses and eyed him up and down. "I would say your duds' lack of sartorial splendor would confirm that fact."

He gave her a slow grin. Her stomach did a free-fall; he had that kind of sensually devastating effect on her, on a woman long past her prime. Implausible. Unimaginable. Ridiculous.

"Count me in with them, Papi," Tony called over the car's roof. "I'm going in to get a pair of cutoffs."

David only nodded. Already, his head was swerving by degrees like a video camera recording its surroundings. He stepped back to allow her to pass and shut the door behind her. "Don't dally anywhere," he said.

She saluted smartly. "Aye, aye, captain."

He did an eye roll. Smiling, she sauntered off.

Inside, she, Andi, and Tony split in different directions. In the dressing room, she settled on a blue-flowered, flounced skirt that lapped her bare calves and elected to keep it on. She figured if she did go wading, she could hike its hem between her legs and anchor it with the elastic waistband. Her white peasant blouse would do for now but would need several hand washings over the days to come.

Cautious about spending too many of the pesos left in her purse and heeding David's warning to make haste, she lastly snatched from hooks a pair of *huaraches* and a bergère hat, its wide brim trailing blue ribbons.

Outside, however, her quickened pace faltered then stopped altogether. Several steps away, near the store's trash dumpster, two small boys who could not be more four or five-years-old were tussling over an ear of roasted corn, its husk shredding with their scuffling. Their shaggy black hair looked as grungy as sludge.

Startling the scruffy pair, she stooped between them and asked in Spanish where were their parents.

The kid who now held possession of the corncob eyed her suspiciously. The grimy little face of the other urchin puckered. "Our mama, she left us."

"When?" she asked. "How long ago?"

He shrugged. "I don't remember. A long, long time ago."

"Where do you two live?"

Another shrug. "Wherever we—"

"*Callate*, Felipe," the other hissed at his brother.

At the same time, both boys' heads tilted back to look

upward, a hand grasped her upper arm. She yelped.

David hauled her to her feet. "Didn't I warn you about returning directly to the car?"

She tugged loose. "You also told me keep tabs on the impoverished children."

He sighed. "You know very well that was a rhetorical remark. Besides, the last things those kids want is some zealous do-gooder who might separate them in order to find them shelter.

Andi and Tony, exiting the department store, caught up with her and David. She could tell he was still put out with her, because, as he opened the rear seat door for her, he snapped, *"Pues,* dressed like that you are sure to go unnoticed."

Looking up, she gave his dull white long-sleeve shirt, rolled at the sleeves and hanging loose over a dark t-shirt, the same endless perusal he had given her. "Think so? When it comes to best dressed men, you're no James Bond."

A low groan rumbled from the expanse of that wide chest, and he muttered, *"¡Dios mio, ayudame!"*

Dear God, she was the one needing help before she thoroughly disgraced herself by succumbing to David's magnetic machismo.

Sliding in next to her, Andi quipped, "No cap, fam, in this black muumuu I look basic."

David arched a derisive brow. "What did she just say?"

"Let me translate," Tony said. "No lie, friends, in this black muumuu I look boring." He grinned back at Andi. "Outrageous you may be, but boring, never."

Both Lauren's brows arched. So, where was this unlikely relationship going?

Answering The Call

The drive up through the Sierra Gorda biosphere reserve revealed breathtaking views of deep canyons planted with banana and sugar cane fields and steep mountains timbered by conifer and oak forests. Along the way, they passed old mesquite trees shading long-neglected, centuries-old ranchos.

Enthusiastically, Tony was explaining that the area protected species in danger of extinction, "Like the green parrot and the jaguar and puma."

"When do we eat?" asked Andi, patting her muumuu's black mound. "Vinny here is protesting."

Once again, David checked out his rearview mirror, then conceded, "Up ahead is the pueblo, Pinal de Amole. We can grab a bite there."

Hacienda ruins engulfed by leafy vines heralded the approach of a civilization of sorts. A civilization dating back to pre-Columbian times by the looks of the green-lichened dwellings.

Finally, houses painted red, ochre or yellow came into view. Here and there, people were leaning out their windows or lounging on their balconies or hanging washing from atop their roofs.

Just past a plaza, he pulled in front of an oblong stone building with a colonnaded porch. Along with the others, she mounted its railless plank steps. A few wood tables dotted the porch. Toward the back, what looked to be the scorched carcass of a goat, head and all, rotated on a spit. Its dripping fat sizzled on the coals below.

Lauren stopped short and gagged. "You all go ahead. I am not really that hungry. I'll just scout around the place."

Without waiting for an acknowledgment from them, she retreated back down the stairs. Her steps hastening, she headed around back of the building. Her stomach demanded to retch. However, as she rounded the corner, a heavenly scent caused her steps to falter. Squinting against the harsh sunlight, her eyes scanned beyond and found the aromatic source.

A small field of blueish indigo carpeted the rocky soil and stretched up the field's incline, toward the wall of purple mountains. How astonishing to find a lavender field amidst that high desert's mountain hideaway. A serene retreat.

Lavender's soul-soothing fragrance beckoned her. Closer, she could detect the humming of bees, the slight cooling of the air, and nature's restorative remedy, vegetation. Her stomach's knotting settled. The Velcro's tension across her shoulders eased.

Wandering the rows, fingers trailing the lavender leaves, she inhaled deeply time and again. The place was a haven of tranquility and calmness. Was not lavender the color associated with old women? The Lavender Ladies?

She bent to pluck a violet sprig and tucked it behind her ear. She had read that students in ancient Greece wore lavender just such when studying, so beneficial was its inhalation for memory.

She sighed. Had she at last bypassed that window when one is aware of dementia's onset? Here she was desperate to affirm her memory was sound, when all these sensations could now be delusions . . . the lush verdant colors suffusing her vision right now, the rich pealing of a chapel bell vibrating against her ear, the lavender sprig's velvety texture against her temple's frail, pulsing vein.

And if she was delusional, did it matter if this vibrant life she presently entertained was not reality? She was reminded of the visually stimulating film *What Dreams May Come*, where a plucked flower turned into a radiant oil paint in the palm. Its star, Robin Williams had been cursed with a form of dementia and had committed suicide.

Should she?

"You are in a pensive mood." She whirled. David was holding out to her a parchment paper bundle. It wrapped a steaming, savory confection. "You must be hungry."

"What is it?"

"Not *carne de cabra*—goat meat." He hiked a wry grin. Whatever danger he presented instantly shut off her warning alarm whenever he smiled like that, with one corner of his mouth. "*Pan de pulque. Pulque* bread."

She raised one brow.

"Not even enough *pulque* to make you pleasantly aroused," he qualified. Then, realizing the suggestiveness of his words, his mouth compressed. "We should be getting back on the road to the Bridge of God."

If this were her version of delusion, he would have taken her in his arms, would have slowly and thoroughly made love to her right there and then on the fecund earth. Or mere rutting it might have been. It would not matter.

But she had to be quite sane, because she patently knew, and kept reminding herself, that she was merely an aging woman desperate for a love relationship in this last part of her life.

CHAPTER 22

People tended to feel uncomfortable around David. They sensed his inability to suffer fools.

Right now, he felt the biggest fool. Stumbling over his words, his thoughts, his feelings when in the presence of Lauren Hillard. He could not figure out why he kept on wanting the gringa, thinking about her.

She had to have some kind of special magic because she continued to enthrall him. Her smile gave him such a delightfully wicked burn, a fast and hot and hard knife to the heart and manhood. The knowledge and wisdom behind that inscrutable smile rekindled his hopes and dreams that had taken a lifetime to destroy. She understood life, and he suspected she understood him, though they were worlds apart as defined by culture, class, religion, race . . . and finances.

Pues, in the latter, financial status, he could have contended with her. At least, until he had been six-or seven-years-old, given the astronomical wealth his Mexican father had created and the familial one his American mother had

Answering The Call

inherited. She had been a *gringa* socialite. But unlike Lauren, his mother had been a shallow woman.

Few outsiders were aware of the isolated approach to Puente de Dios, a natural bridge, located on the slope of a small mountain. A tiny, bamboo shack community at the edge of the sinuously climbing highway charged an entrance fee.

Parking the Pathfinder on the dirt lot, he paid a gap-toothed pig farmer the obligatory pesos for the four of them. They set off afoot, with Tony in the lead, trailed by Andi, then Lauren. He brought up the rear. And what a pleasure it was to watch her sensuous sway beneath the long, flowered skirt. So fully female.

They followed the Rio Escanela, about a mile's hike to the Bridge of God. Banked with dense vegetation on one side and a steep canyon wall on the other, the small river pooled in scattered limestone shallows along the way.

Lauren and Andi took off their sandals, hiked their skirts, and waded with delight through each successively chilling pool. He and Tony shucked their tennis shoes and rolled their jeans up past their calves. Macaws shrieked their welcome, and parrots gave wing to colorful flights.

From beneath the dip of her hat's wide brim, Lauren flung him a twinkling glance over her shoulder. "Oh, I had forgotten how much I used to love birdwatching. Thank you for this."

He loved the feeling it gave him to please her. "The best is yet to come."

The narrow river, swimming with gigantic trout, flowed through a series of miniscule caves. Climbing the limestone path ever upwards, they passed water rushing around boulders, its enormous whooshing deafening all other sound.

After shouldering between a slice of rocks and mounting a plank ladder, they traversed a natural stone bridge, then confronted a moss-covered rock resembling the head of a monkey and next an elephant head, both of which were said to act as guardians of the gate to an unbelievable fairy land.

The Rio Escanela, high atop the sparkling, spacious cavern, performed like a multitude of showerheads. Its chilly water filtered down through the grotto's limestone ceiling, shimmering like cascading liquid silver. From below the grotto's floor seeped a warm spring to light the cavern in a translucent azure blue. The comingling of the two extreme water temperatures manifested a magical mist.

Stunning him, Lauren laughed aloud, then shouted "Shangri-La!" With a flicking of one wrist, she sent her wide-brimmed hat sailing, threw wide her arms, and plunged into the pool in a stinging belly flop.

Tony and Andi looked on in shocked surprise. When Lauren surfaced, she stood mid-thigh deep and, with a whip of her neck, tossed back from her face her gloriously gray-streaked hair. Cascading water streamed it over her shoulders. Her wet skirt and blouse were plastered to her earth-mother's body. "God, I love this place!"

And, Christ's bloody cross, he loved this mind-bending image of her . . . resplendent and regal in all her bravura.

Later, he did a quick google search for further interpretation on his fuzzy recollection of the term Shangri-La.

The fictional place has become synonymous with any earthly paradise, particularly a mythical Himalayan utopia—an enduringly happy land, isolated from the world. In the novel, the people who live at Shangri-La are almost immortal, living hundreds of years beyond the normal lifespan and only very slowly aging in appearance.

※

Lauren watched—this time from the passenger front seat's side of the car, as David had chosen to ensconce her there—while he thumbed through his cell phone's screen. His lips hitched in a slight smile. His thick salt-and-pepper hair, almost dry from the mile hike back to the car, riffled his shoulders.

He started the engine and, looking in the rear-view mirror at Andi and Tony in the rear seats, said, "On the way back, we'll stop by your Abuelita Marta's and check on her."

Lauren's mouth crunched. With her damp hair straggling down her cheeks and neck like seaweed, she did not relish meeting anyone. Much less the mother of his beloved Pilar.

As it turned out, Lauren did not have to. By the time they arrived back in Querétaro, daylight was waning. After David parked the Pathfinder in front of a barrio's dwelling that looked like a smoke-smudged kiln, Tony towed Andi along with him to the rusty grilled gate and punched the doorbell beside it.

"You're not going in?" Lauren asked David.

His wrist, resting atop the steering wheel, wagged a finger. He shook his head.

His reticence disturbed her. That and what she considered his rudeness. What had happened to the lighthearted man who had romped with her and Tony and Andi in the grotto's lagoon-like pool, splashing one another and cavorting like children? Did this visit to his mother-in-law have anything to do with his absorption with his late wife? Sweet Jesus, Pilar had been dead thirteen years now.

Tiny and hunched, a white-haired woman shrouded in black hobbled to the gate with the aid of a cane to admit Tony and Andi. Lauren could not repress her irritation. "Is it something I've said or done that has us sitting outside here in the car?"

He shifted toward her, his arm overlapping the back of her seat. "No. It's something I have done—or, more to the point, didn't do."

Brow furrowing, she inclined her head. "I don't understand."

"At one point, my wife Pilar was earning extra money to supplement our college education fees and the soaring cost of caring for our three-year-old, Tony, by working in the evenings at one of the many *maquiladora*. These factories exploited workers this side of the Texas border."

He paused, rubbed absently beneath his rolled sleeve at his forearm's tattoo. The one inked with the word, *Madre*.

She said nothing, giving him time to collect himself.

"Returning from work late one evening, on the way to our house, Pilar was kidnapped." Another excruciating pause. "She was murdered . . . as happened that year to five hundred or so females on both sides of the border of Laredo's vicinity."

Surely he heard her sibilant inhalation, but he gave no notice.

"The rapes and murders . . . the slave trade and organ harvesting . . . the horrors have escalated monstrously since. The press tends to gloss over these border murders with the generic term 'femicide.' Because the reality is too awful for fashionable folks to read about. Her lovely body had been mutilated beyond recognition by a trafficker harvesting her organs."

Lauren choked back a gag. He paused, his voice raw, and she waited for him to collect himself.

"Her mother Marta never has forgiven me. For not protecting my loved one—her loved one. I had permitted Pilar to be exposed to danger."

"Had she not already been in danger, growing up there?"

"No, Pilar grew up here in Querétaro, one of Mexico's safest cities. One weekend, she and a couple of high school girlfriends traveled by bus to Laredo to party. That night my gig was at one of its dives, where we met." He gave a laconic shrug. "It was nuclear combustion at first sight. We were together for the next nine years, until . . . ."

She waited then filled in the heartbreaking silence. "And after that, after her . . . ," Lauren's tongue and lips found it impossible to form the morbid word "murder."

"After that, as soon as I graduated and landed my degree as a *Notario Público*, I moved Tony and me out of the danger zone. To Querétaro and Tony's grandmother, Marta. Her grandson was all the family she had left. But the sight of me . . . " he lifted one shoulder, " . . . well, it's easier on her old heart . . . and mine . . . the less often we see each other, the better."

Lauren's cell phone rang. She dug into her shoulder bag's tiny compartment, stuffed with her passport, pesos, receipts, and essential lip gloss, along with her driver's license. She was beginning to think Andi's huge tote was a good idea. The caller was Sylvie. Lauren affected a cheerful tone. "Hey babe!"

David hiked a brow at the endearment, and she mouthed, "I call all the people I love babe."

He rolled his eyes.

"Mama, I'm still at the clinic."

She spared a glance at the cell phone's time. 6:41 p.m. "Sylvie, it's way past quitting time. Is there a problem?"

"Mama, I was emptying the trash baskets . . . ."

"Yes?"

"And . . . and I found a partially wadded printout in it. I could see a portion of the letterhead—*Psychological Assessment Advocates*. I smoothed it open."

Oh, God! Then this was it, here at last. The confirmation she was indeed delusional. Cradling the phone with her shoulder, she leaned forward in the car seat, as if to curl into a protective fetal position. "Go ahead."

"Mama, the mental health report . . . it confirms and details the psychological findings of the test applicant. Frontotemporal dementia."

Her physical pain was so great that her scalding tears could have transmuted to pebbles. She could only gasp her fear like some acidic reflux cresting over and over.

From her experience at the clinic, she knew frontotemporal dementia referred to a group of disorders, where nerve cells in the frontal and temporal lobes of the brain start to shrink and the sufferer begins to exhibit bizarre behavior, somewhere between the ages of forty and sixty-five.

Her expelling sigh was as heavy as David's hand was light, stroking her curved spine as it was now doing.

"Sylvie, although I am past the age when usually . . . " she swallowed, tried again, " . . . I will be the first to admit I have behaved, well, radically. I confess, Sylvie, I, too, have been overly concerned about my mental state lately, what with this abrupt move to a foreign country. . . and, well, everything else." Like, her crazy-ass enthrallment with

Answering The Call

David. "So I suppose I should not be stunned." Yet she was.

"But, Mama," came Sylvie's strained, insistent voice, "the test subject designated on this evaluation was not you."

"What?" She set up straight and swiped at a wayward tear. David's large hand continued to cup her shoulder supportingly. "What do you mean?"

"The person who took this test was— was my sister, Renita."

Shocked, she dropped the cell phone in her lap and scrambled to retrieve it. She wanted to weep again, this time for her daughter Renita. She sniffled. "Then . . . " she wanted to be sure she understood the implication of what Sylvie relayed, " . . . then this accounts for your sister's vitriolic persecution."

"And, Mama, I fear it is not over. I don't understand it, but Renita's entire angry energy is fixated on you. I am afraid of what she is going to do next. Her patients are going neglected. I am embarrassed when I have to keep rescheduling them."

"Sylvie, please keep me apprised of whatever—" She broke off as David 's hand on her shoulder tightened. She glanced sidewise at him.

He mouthed, "Tell her you'll call her next."

Puzzled, she could only nod. "Look, Sylvie, let me get back with you first. Umm, some things have come up here. And I love you, babe."

She went to restore the cell phone to her purse. "I guess you overheard our family's dysfunctional details," she told him apologetically.

She gaped as he yanked her cell phone from her, powered it off, and removed the battery. He tossed it on the floorboard and handed her back her cell phone. "I'll get you a burner phone. No apps—but good enough for the basics."

She frowned. "Why . . . why all this high-tech precaution?"

"If it were just your daughter Renita's wrath, protecting you here in Mexico should be fairly easy enough. But she has linked up with a rather influential person here—one who does not take kindly to me—Jürgen Kramer, et al. This puts you not only in legal jeopardy but—" his mouth tightened, "—*also in life jeopardy.*"

CHAPTER 23

Tony scanned his bedroom to make sure it would be cohabitable for a longer period than the initial ten days a warrant may have officially designated.

He checked the Remington XP-100 handgun, then stowed it within easy reach beneath the bed. No point in alarming Andi with his arsenal. Since he was knee-high to his father, which was a greater than average height, his *papi* had made sure he was familiar with the myriad martial arts and a variety of weapons.

After his father pulled him aside to brief him on this escalated alert regarding the older *gringa*, it was decided it was safer if that night and future quarterings remained the same as the previous ones—he and Andi in one bedroom; his father and Lauren in the other.

Tony suspected his father's decision was based on more than mere caution. His *papi*'s eye had alighted on a female that both stirred his cock and his mind. But his heart?

With his father and Lauren in the kitchen preparing dinner—*chile rellenos*, Tony's favorite—he had Andi all to himself. The footbath prepared and towel overlapping one shoulder, he opened his bedroom door. "Andi, you can come in now."

Her swollen bare feet were propped on the couch's opposite arm. Grumping, she levered herself up. The roundtrip hike that day had clearly laid her low. "I'll come in for one margarita and maybe sex, but that's it, Tony."

He burst out laughing. This tangerine topknotted ball of fire was brash and brilliant—and sported a fun side. Something his father had not exhibited in years, until today in the grotto horsing around with Lauren and them like a kid. "I have something even better in store than suds and sex, Andi."

Attentively, suspiciously, she entered his tiny bedroom. "Why all the hush-hush?"

"Something special only for you."

She scanned the walls, covered with his San Antonio Spurs pennants, the still rumpled bedsheets, the cheaply made hutch that served as his chest of drawers, and shrugged. "Home sweet home."

He had anticipated her dry observation but her singular comment was more of a soft pleasurable purr. "This way, *cariña.*"

He led her over to the wood chair, where he had buttressed a bed pillow against its laddered back. At the base of the chair legs awaited a pan of steaming water filtered with the crushed leaves of eucalyptus and Epsom salts. He made a sweeping bow. "*Por favor, sientate, señorita.*"

One beringed brow rose. "You're serious? You want me to sit? Not spread my legs on the bed?"

He took her upper arm and tugged her into the chair. "Is a pig's ass pork?"

She laughed and punched him on his shoulder. "I knew I liked you, Tony Escobar."

And he her. He liked her total disregard for others' opinions of her unconventional looks. Once he had her seated, he knelt before her and grasped one puffy ankle. He lowered her foot into the water, then the other swollen ankle. He wanted to keep her occupied while his father masterminded the sketchy situation with Lauren.

Andi sighed again and slouched. "Oh, heaven help me, this is better than an Ecstasy pinger."

This was another thing he liked about her. Her ebullient banter. She was intelligent but not an intellectual. The philosophical and political discussions of the world's woes by his female classmates got too heavy, too wearisome, for him after a while. Andi was raucous and lively.

He set about lathering her one foot, concentrating where the ankle swelled, and next worked the supple muscles of her calf. Finally, he massaged each toe with dedicated attention. "So, this little piggy went to the market," he joked.

She giggled and moaned her pleasure. "Don't stop, Tony. Ever."

Childhood memories left over from his Abuelita Marta's playful, loving care assailed him. The way her thumb rubbed his palm when she held his hand. The stroking of his hair from his forehead. Touching was as vital to him as breathing. Elsewise, what was the purpose of one's human body? Sadly, technology was abolishing the need for human touch.

Throughout the years, Abuelita Marta had been his bridge between him and his father's father. Don Ricardo, as the media and Mexico at large deferred to him, kept tabs on peon and professionals; on foes and family, estranged or not. Like Tony's father, his grandfather Don Ricardo Escobar was unreadable and therefore unpredictable.

Tony's grandfather was a demagog, one of the world's leaders who appealed to popular passions and prejudices. He could deign on the turn of a coin to lend his mighty influence to a foe instead of family. The cell phone mogul, Mexico's equivalent to Verizon's CEO, had no scruples.

Tony tweaked the next toe. "And this little pig stayed home."

She laughed. "And the next little piggy cried wee, wee, wee all the way home."

And he felt a big pork, playing footsie as he was with her. Could he be attracted to her as a romantic interest? Impossible!

※

Numbers do not matter to me. I find you irresistible.

This, of course, David did not tell Lauren that night. Skeptical as she was about him, about herself, she first had to see—had to feel convincingly—about herself the way he felt about her. That her beauty was not skin-deep but a beauty-to-the-bone deep.

Having showered, she returned from the bathroom and donned his black t-shirt for sleepwear, an old Waylon Jennings of his that looked like it could be the label for a bottle of whiskey. With her long legs bared, she was decidedly sexy.

The excessively elongated false eyelashes, the microbladed eyebrows thickened to grotesque proportions, the

Botox-injected lips and cheeks plumped to bizarre exaggeration by this generations' females . . . what exactly was the appreciative beauty in artificiality? More stunning was natural beauty. At least, to him.

He recognized that it had taken experimental courage for her, or anyone for that matter, to make this international move. She radiated grace and charm and tenderness. The last of which he sorely appreciated right now.

This endless, mostly fruitless fight for even basic human rights dragged him out. Made him forlorn beyond the darkness of night. A forlornness that even the precious connection he shared with his son could not assuage. What could he say, except he loved the feeling Lauren gave him? A sweet madness. She possessed an empathetic and understanding heart.

He shrugged out of his long-sleeve white shirt and doffed The Eagles band t-shirt. Lauren had been right. He missed the magic of music.

With an embarrassed gesture at the sight of his bared chest, she turned from him and began folding back the bedspread and sheet on her side of the double bed. "I really don't feel right," she murmured, "bringing all this down on your and Tony's heads."

He toed off first one tennis shoe, then the other and peeled off his long socks. He kept his tone neutral, light. "We discussed this. This house needs a woman's touch." As I need your touch. "Your housekeeping in exchange for my house over the ten days or so."

She settled on the bed. Those fathomless gray eyes above perfectly hewn high cheekbones peered at him from over her shoulder. "But not your life—or Tony's—or Andi's—is worth this . . . this avoidance of the looming confrontation with your Mexican law firm's process server."

"Not my law firm—but one backed by Mexican authorities," he reminded her. "A Mexican mental asylum is no place any mortal would want to be."

She sent him a wry smile and slid those luscious legs beneath the covers. "Sometimes I think I belong in an asylum. And then when I look around I think maybe I already am."

He grinned back and dropped his jeans. Her face swerved away. Well, he was not going to change his style of sleeping nude for her. "The one who belongs behind bars is the attorney your daughter has teamed up with, Jürgen Kramer—who, as I mentioned, just happens to have it in for me, as well. So, we're together in this. I say we keep to the plan I outlined before dinner."

"*Si, señor.*" She yawned and rolled to her side, presenting him with the lovely length of her spine. "Safety in numbers," she mumbled, "and no digital or electronic contact with the outside world, right?"

"Right. Make ourselves scarce."

In the buff, he switched off the nightstand's lamp and climbed in on his side of the bed. He faced the enticing, shadowy contour of her body—her narrow shoulder, sloping to the indenture of her waist, then swelling lushly with her hip. She was brave, smart, and impulsive—which was what had landed her in his bed.

Incomprehensibly, he wanted to explore more than those physical components of this woman; he wanted to explore the uncharted recess of her psyche.

Then the baser thought of her alabaster skin contrasting with his mocha-colored body, pumping into hers, chased away any and all other higher thoughts. His cock thickened painfully. Shedding a groan, he hitched the covers over his erection.

※

Coffee cup in hand, Andi braced her bulk against the cracked and chipped, blue-and- white azulejo-tiled counter. "Instant human," she sighed ecstatically. "Just add coffee."

"I hope that's decaf," Lauren teased. "You'll have that little one doing jittery kicks." Observing her, Lauren thought there was something softer about the girl. Maternity? Or a lover's gentle stroke?

Lauren took another sip of her coffee. She needed a strong stimulant to combat her very stimulating reaction both to Michelangelo's nude David throughout the sleepless night and to his chiseled body in khaki t-shirt and tight jeans during this early morning's kitchen work detail. Her stomach fluttered frenziedly like the Monarch butterflies that migrated to Mexico's national reserve each year.

Oddly, that morning there had been something indiscernible but more intimate between her and David while she made the coffee and he cooked the *chorizo* and cheese than the night spent sleeping with the stark naked man.

From where she sat at the table, she turned her head slightly to observe him, cooking at the cast iron stove. He was watching her. Their eyes locked. That moment of voyeurism sexually intensified the complex relationship existing between them. Then Tony said something, and their gazes ricocheted.

"Come on, Papi. The rave will be fun."

"Rave?" she questioned.

"A music festival," Andi supplied between bites of her *gordita*. Pregnancy had only augmented her love of food. "With lots of electronic music and dancing."

Tony grinned and doused his *gordita* with the red salsa his father had fashioned in the blender. "We need something to lighten us all up."

David tunneled fingers through his disheveled, silvering dark hair. His features, accented by the sharp ridges of his cheekbones, indicated his lack of enthusiasm.

"Come on, Papi," Tony urged.

Finally, he nodded. "I grant this *casa* will be little better than a playpen over the coming days." He shot each of them a stern look of resolve, the last reserved for Lauren. "But keep in mind we do nothing that would draw attention to ourselves."

She shrugged. "My wide-brimmed hat and sunglasses camouflage me sufficiently."

Andi was licking her salsa-tipped fingers. "I would be hard to camouflage."

"My San Antonio Spurs cap for your hair, then," Tony said. "And many of the young people who will be attending, they sport as many tats as you." He glanced pointedly at her stomach. "A serape of mine should shield your fair skin from the sun and . . . how do you say . . . prying eyes?"

David's scrutiny landed on Lauren. His frowning dark brows matched his stubble. He had not bothered shaving that morning. "By the way, how did you and Andi get here, to our house? I never asked. I hope by bus, not by Uber. That would mean a charge to your credit card that could be traced here."

"No, we took a taxi," Lauren said, "and I paid cash."

"Where did the taxi pick you up? At your house?"

She grimaced, trying to recall the activities of the past few days. So much had happened in the interval since. Life changing events.

"We caught the taxi at that *pastelería* we walked to," Andi put in, "where we had late breakfast, remember? You didn't finish your bagel, Ms. L."

"Right." Andi had finished it for her.

He nodded, but he looked dissatisfied still. "*Bien*. But once there, we separate in pairs. Make it more difficult if anyone is trying to tail us." Those eyes, as dark as lodestone, magnetized hers. "And you stay with me."

Something within her longed for just that; something else warned of heartache that would await her.

CHAPTER 24

Her chartreuse and purple striped tote slung over one shoulder, Andi surveyed the scene. The music festival sported more tents than her deranged parents' entire Old Testament . . . parents who believed a beating a day kept the devil away. They embraced the biblical admonition, "Spare the rod and spoil the child."

Held on the grounds of an estate replete with a rodeo-like charro arena, the rave hosted several stages studding an immense pasture that whiffed of pot. Ahh, the sweet smell of satisfaction, at last.

The revelers, almost all who looked to be in the twenty-to-forty years' age range, wandered among the various food trucks and curio vendors, stationed a distance from what appeared to be a sprawling hacienda.

At one stage, a loud five-piece band was performing before an audience of several hundred, just sitting or sprawled on the ground. Another hundred or so were dancing up front in a sluggish fashion.

What the freakin' heck? This society needed a vibe

check.

"Let's grab a beer," Tony said.

His dad and Lauren, who would have been a more attentive mom or grandmother than what Andi had known, had strayed off on their own.

"Get me two, one for each hand."

He raised a brow.

"Going to dance."

Both brows cleared his forehead. He tucked his thumbs in his jeans. "I thought you didn't dance."

She shrugged off her tote bag. "Duh. So, I'm learning a new art form."

"Two beers can't be good for junior." He nodded at her expanding waist.

The dude was living rent free in her mind. She allowed he was kind, clever, interesting, self-aware . . . and a very good kisser, judging by that single kiss she had permitted him in return of her tentative "gracias for the footbath" one. But chemistry counted for nothing. It was the damnable math that counted for everything, the one plus one that equaled three.

She tossed him a moody eye roll. "All right. Okay. *Bien.* Only one beer." She watched him depart for the nearest vendor. "Hey, Tony," she yelled after him.

He turned around. The sun glinted fairy circles off his eyeglasses.

"You're a GOAT."

His ropy body squared off. "What?"

She grinned and shouted against the music, "Greatest of All Time."

She sluffed off her sandals, comfortable on her bare,

duck-wide feet, and headed to the rim of the catatonic dancers. The females were wearing short skirts and either tennis shoes or knee-high boots. Knee-high boots in this warm weather? Their male partners in fundamental jeans or cutoffs shuffled a few steps to the music, never varying from their box-like perimeter.

Arms crossed atop her stomach, she watched, studied, and assessed her chances of success in the ring with her ungainly body. Nope. No way. Not on this group's dance card anyway.

Tony came up behind her and passed her a cold bottle. She liked the fact he was taller than she, visually reducing her behemoth width. She took a long guzzle from the chilly bottle. Beneath the sun's blistering ultra-rays, the velvety liquid cooled her jitters.

The band switched to a cover of *Gangnam Style*. The dancers frittered away except for a few who, without a clue to this K-pop song, lapsed into apathetic, disjointed movements. They looked deathly bored.

She started to take another long gulp then changed her mind. She handed the bottle back to Tony. She now had another to think about beside herself. And her next move . . . well, she had to do this solo—or else what was her point?

She strolled out across the grass. Once she reached the center of despondent dancers, she let it rip. Arms outstretched, head swiveling right to left and back, she let loose with The Pony combined with hip hop and a mingling of funky improvised moves.

She was the only one barefoot. Did not care. Ahh, the freedom of being herself. Fulfillment, as usual, bubbled up from her when she gave a finger to life's grind.

She was vaguely aware of astonishment rippling among

Answering The Call

the onlooker's expressions. The remaining couples dancing cleared way for her. The number of spectators increased. Better to be an oddity than a nobody.

Then, glancing around, she noted a few shucking their tennis shoes and boots to join her. Shouted whoops and laughter and "Oppa Gangnam!" bobbled among them like Karaoke's lyric bubble. The area grew crowded. She was no longer alone.

Then Tony was in front of her. He was grinning. Reflected in his sunglasses she could she her bobbing, smiling self. Did not matter if the bottoms of her bare feet were a dirty green. She was pretty. Not passably pretty but uncommonly pretty. Fancy that.

CHAPTER 25

While Tony and Andi occupied themselves at the rave's main stage, David steered Lauren away, toward a tiki-bar stall. It specialized in craft beers and beverages in *jarritas* garnished with colorful cocktail umbrellas or the zingy Tajín with exotic fruit wedges.

She looked at him and raised a brow. "Potent?"

He grinned. "It'll curl your toenails."

She laughed. "Then for starters, I'll have three, please."

He ordered for them, then looked down at her, "You don't do anything halfway do you?"

He said it with such seriousness, that she had to pause. "Why, yes, I suppose you are right." She had given all she had to her marriage and children. And then, after the marriage had gone sour and the children had grown, she had resigned from Pepsico and given her all to working for Renita at a reduced salary to help her daughter get her therapy clinic up and going.

Finishing off their *jarritas*, Lauren and David gravitated back toward the stage areas. As usual, the weather was perfect, with low humidity and a cloudless, turquoise sky, discounting marijuana fumes that delineated the event grounds.

The place might have been a mini-Woodstock, with the amplified thudding repetition of the drums, the hopped-up bass guitar, and the '70's psychedelic frenzy taking place in front of the main stage.

At least, it was not rap music. She just did not "get" this popular craze. Like many people of her vintage, she felt that the current society seemed completely unhinged when it came to real music. Of course, the younger generation with tongue-in-cheek derisively labeled easy listening music from the '70s and '80s as "Yacht Rock."

At the main stage, she stopped short. Its frenzy consisted of a crowd encircling Andi. Like some Aztec goddess of fertility, she was dancing with wild abandon to the hyper-charged music. Her free-spirited gyrations infected the onlookers. Captivated, one by one, couple by couple, they were drawn into her lively enchanted circle.

Lauren recognized the dated song. It was rap—and she had to admit it was catchy. She turned to David, standing slightly behind her, and took his hand. She felt the tingling rippling from his to hers. It set her body humming. "Your son is right—it's time for light-hearted fun."

Dubiousness raised one of David's brows, but he permitted her to tug him into the rim of the musical melee. Plucking her blue-flowered skirt to her knees, she joined in with the boisterous moves—swooping an elbow back, wobbling her knees, hands shooting up in pistol style. Exhilarated, she glanced aside at David.

He sent her a "you can't be serious" stare.

She nodded, grinning. Following the others, she jumped

forward, feet spread in a crouch and aimed her finger guns at him in a James Bond stance.

He burst out laughing. "You win!" he shouted over the music. He swung in behind her and mimicked her moves. She could feel his body heat sensually molding hers from shoulder blades to derriere. She twerked her booty like Andi was doing and heard his husky, carbonating laughter.

They danced till she was out of breath and paused, hands crossed at her chest, at which point he took her elbow and pulled her along behind him. He shouldered his way through the press of people and struck out for the less populated pastures beyond.

Here and there beneath large parasols or on spread blankets a few couples were being lightly affectionate, and at each witnessing Lauren glanced away swiftly, as if in doing so she was putting away that longing characteristic of her younger years when passion excluded the rest of the world.

They roved farther afield. Nearing four o'clock, despite the relative cool afternoon, at that high elevation the sun was intense because of the thinning atmosphere. She was grateful now for her lightweight clothing, hat, and sandals.

By accord she and David roamed toward an isolated grassy spot, shaded by a spindly ficus. Here the music, a rendition of Journey's *Open Arms*, blared less. Legs tucked beneath her, she settled a half-yard away from where he dropped down.

From under her hat's wide brim, she sent him an oblique look. "I'd say you don't do anything halfway either. In fact, it's all or nothing with you, am I right?"

He reclined with legs stretched before him, ankles crossed, and his weight braced on his elbows. Through curling lashes, he watched the performance in the distance. "Why idle when you can live at full throttle?"

She was tempted to comment that the idle mode that often came with aging accommodated advantages like perspective. But then what did she know about anything? It seemed the older she got the less she knew.

He turned his head to stare at her, making her feel uncomfortable. "With your skirt spread around you, your sunhat's brim slanted to half-shade your face," he said, at last, "you remind me of one those Belle Epoque portraits of a shepherdess."

She did not know which startled her more, that he was familiar with Belle Epoque paintings or that he saw her as something elegant and enticing that characterized that period. "Don't go there," she breathed.

His lift of one shoulder was expressive of indifference but his tone was one of amusement. "I can't help it. I suppose it's the stereotypical Latino's passionate temperament in me."

Although she fought it, her libido, which she had believed atrophied, responded to the high wattage signals of his quintessential maleness. From their first meeting, it had been this way. This powerfully seductive mesmerism.

She countered in defense. "You want to talk about passion. Passion involves pain as well as pleasure, and in my experience the pleasure has not been worth the pain."

His smile was a wry twist. "You cannot compare apples against bananas in terms of value. When you love, obviously, you also risk getting hurt. But passion filters that pain."

She busied her hands in removing her hat and shaking free her hair. "Risking coming here to Mexico, risking defying my family, is about as much as my brain and body can afford to risk."

"You did not mention your heart."

Languidly, she fanned her face with her hat, but her pulse was doing double time. "My heart is a part of my body, right?"

"Word games." Exasperation underscored his rebuttal. "To cover your fear of your age? Or is it your prejudice?"

Her jaw dropped. "Prejudice?"

Glancing around absently, he rolled a shoulder. As if such a touchy subject were nothing to him. "Yeah. Like class prejudice. Racial prejudice. Age preju—"

In the blink of an eye, he flung his body over hers. Her hat went sailing. He buried his face in the mesh of her hair. His stubbled jaw rasping her neck's tender flesh, he warned, "Don't move until I say so."

"What?" her shredded throat got out. "Why?"

"We are being observed—a man with binoculars."

She should feel frightened about the possibility of discovery. Instead, she felt only the pleasure of his painful weight. It had been so long since she had lain thus, beneath the wonderfully crushing weight of a lover. "How do you know we are the one this man is watching?

"There's not that many men built like Quasimodo. That's got to be Macho."

"Macho Nacho? How did he find us?"

She felt his warm breath whisper near her lips, "Did you pay for your purchases yesterday with the pesos I gave you?"

Her mind darted back to earlier. "Yes, of course." Then, "Oh my God! I forgot to pay for Andi's. She may have used her credit card."

"¡Escúchame!" He grabbed up her straw hat. "Listen!" he

said with emphasis, tugging the hat's beribboned brim low over her face, "We've no time. We're going to wind our way back to where I parked. I'll text Tony and have him and Andi Uber back home. Understand?"

Her mind flashing through alarming scenarios, she could only nod.

He wrapped an arm around her waist and lifted her upright. His body blocking her quivering one from view by either the frenetic dancers in the stage area or the milling crowd, he splayed his hand alongside her jaw and lowered his face over hers.

From beneath her hat brim, she stared up into his determined features. Then her eyes closed. He was kissing her. Just a mere, lingering brush of his lips across hers. Nevertheless, for her, at least, it was spontaneous combustion. Only his arm around her waist, supporting her, kept her knees from giving way.

His lips deserted hers. He raised his head. His reassuring smile was swift. "We go."

Their circuitous path back to the hacienda estate's parking lot cut through calf-high grass, circumvented an outlying volleyball group, and skirted an amorous couple writhing in the shade afforded by an elephantine cactus.

As if not to be outdone by the couple's affectionate display, David strode at a sedate pace, casually lapping, his arm draping her shoulder. Occasionally, he nuzzled her neck or dropped a light kiss on her cheek. If only he knew how his theatrical gestures undid her, set her body vibrating at an unsustainable high pitch.

Once over a rise and out of sight, he started off in a trot, tugging her along by one arm. Moments later, when they were within partial sight of Querétaro's acclaimed pyramid, he released her to yank his cell phone from his rear jeans pocket. He began texting rapidly.

Only the snorting of a solitary bull plodding toward them with tail swishing alerted them of a new danger.

Still texting, he swerved off down into an arroyo to avoid the bull, only to catch his foot on a rock. She latched onto his muscled bicep, preventing a fall.

He shot her a grateful grin and huffed, "You're not just another pretty face."

Pretty face?

At last they reached the parking lot and the Pathfinder. Panting, she leaned against its fender and warily surveyed the area's haphazardly parked vehicles for any lurking threat. He opened the passenger door for her and nodded at her to get in. Despite the interior heat of the Pathfinder, she was shaking. Chill bumps prickled her flesh.

"They've found me." Her voice was rotgut raw.

He unleashed the SUV into reverse, spraying dust and sand. "We don't know that." The Pathfinder roared from the graveled parking lot. Forgoing the estate exit, he careened the vehicle out over the deserted pasture toward sandhills scattered with cactus clumps. "But just in case, we'll take the scenic tour back home."

Ploughing and bouncing over unimproved terrain, the SUV spewed a sandy wake. She knuckled onto the door latch. Glancing at his bladed profile, she sensed he was in his element. He thrived on pressure, stress, obstacles. She had to ask herself, was his interest in her generated by merely the challenge she presented?

At last, when her clenched teeth seemed jarred loose, the vehicle regained traction on pavement. Her pent-up breath expelled in a whoosh. "I'd wager that scenic route isn't rated on Trip Advisor."

He surprised her with a wink. "Maybe on Flight Advisor."

The next moment, his strong features were once again a harsh sculpture. Gone was his humor. "And as your legal advisor, I think it's time you and I strategize."

She nodded slightly. "Yes?"

"Here's what we can only surmise." As he drove, his fingers ticked off on the steering wheel his reasoning. "One, we are not certain Jürgen Kramer has picked up on your trail." His lips curled derisively. "Macho Nacho could merely be tailing me, not you."

This was surreal. Seventy-year-old grandmothers did not get caught up in . . . in what? In Love and War dramas? "And the second?"

"And two, if they did track you through Andi's credit card—and by way of that her information such as her cell phone and its current location, here at the festival—it is highly unlikely they were able to link her cell phone to my home's location. Yet."

With one hand, he extracted his cell phone from his rear jeans pocket. "I'll text Tony to ditch her cell phone in the nearest body of water on the way back—after wiping it clean of data."

"Unless they got your license plate back at the rave."

He finished texting. "Which leads us to my third point."

Arching a questioning brow, she turned to him. Something about the fierceness of his gaze rattled her.

"If they did, if they have made the connection between you and me, it's only a matter of hours before they can serve you with a court order issued by the local magistrate."

"The bottom line, please." The setting sun was casting

sporadic shadows within the confines of the hurtling car, and she could not decipher his expression.

"It will be easier for your elder daughter, given the various authorizations you previously provided her, to arrange to have you deported. Mexican immigration authorities, in cooperation with U.S. law enforcement agencies, have been aggressively making use of Mexican immigration laws to deport non-Mexican fugitives to the United States."

"So? We covered this possibility earlier."

"Well, an attorney acting on your behalf could mount a temporary defense. To stall, you understand. As your attorney, I could do that. But to counter that defense your daughter's attorney here could then opt for extradition. Mexico extradites fugitives for serious crimes like drug trafficking, murder, kidnapping, and such."

"But . . . but I don't fall under any of those categories."

He pulled up in front on his *casa*. He shifted in the seat to face her, his left arm draping the steering wheel's curve, his other cradling the seatback. "No, but these legal issues could tie up your case in court here for a lengthy time. Meanwhile, you could find yourself not in some quality care facility for Alzheimer's patients but behind bars in a five-star hell."

"Impossible!"

"With sufficient *mordida*, anything and everything is possible here in Mexico." His unrelenting gaze pinned her to the seat like a collector pinned a butterfly to a board. "A woman has to be brave, smart, and very impulsive to get herself into as much danger as you have. I am just prompting you continue to be impulsive."

She grabbed for the door handle. "I've got to get out of here."

Answering The Call

His hand grasped her wrist. He leaned in, his face inches from hers. "Where would you go? You cannot use your credit card. You have no access to cash. No friends here to offer refuge."

Her free hand rubbed her temple. "Maybe I am losing my mind. Maybe I do have dementia." She could barely breathe. Her world was falling apart like a jigsaw puzzle. "Maybe I should just surrender and go back."

"You are not losing your mind, I can assure you. There is another option that may work."

Her hand dropped away. She turned her face to him. What she had learned about him was that he was daring, cool, alert, aggressive. So, she had no option but to trust him. "What?"

He released her wrist and shut off the engine. "An option that I suspect would be abhorrent to you. We'll table that discussion for now. Panic mode is not the time for critical thinking."

She could not think of anything more abhorrent than being confined against her will. A living nightmare, her heart screamed.

CHAPTER 26

That evening, while Tony and Andi were helping Lauren prepare supper, David disappeared in the Pathfinder. Given the shortage of ingredients stocked in the pantry, she was resorting to her no-fail version of King Ranch Chicken Casserole.

A short while later, as she was splashing mayonnaise with apple cider vinegar to substitute for the lack of sour cream, he returned with a brief greeting. Then, inclining his head dismissively toward the other two, he signaled her to follow him to his bedroom. When she set aside her spatula, Tony raised a brow and Andi winked. Lauren shrugged.

David closed the bedroom door behind them and wordlessly passed her something somewhat similar to the flip phones from the Y2K era. "A burner phone."

Stupefied, she eased down onto the bedside and stared at it. Sitting next to her, he took it from her and opened it up. "It doesn't offer app use or online browsing. Only calls and texts. I want you to keep it with you at all times. In case we become separated between now and the expiration of the temporary psychiatric hold order."

He ran through with her the burner phone's basic usage. His presence dominated the tiny room. His callused fingertips thrumming the burner's keypad evoked the memory of the photo below the bed of his strumming the guitar. Finished with the instruction, he stood, as if preparing to leave.

She touched his wrist, halting him. He looked down at her hand then into her eyes questioningly. Did he recall that brief but reassuring kiss he had bestowed in their flight from the rave?

"Do you mind if I play your guitar while I am cooped up here?" She nodded downward, beneath the bed. "It offers some normality of a routine life before . . . ," she gestured helplessly, "before I answered this bizarre call to adventure and moved here."

He rubbed the back of his neck, then nodded, and reached beneath the bed to draw out the vintage guitar. Naturally, the photo fell out again, fluttering to the floor. He scooped it up, staring down at it. "You asked about Pilar," he muttered and glanced down at Lauren. "She wasn't perfect. Far from it. But then neither was I. Yet over the years we learned that love wasn't something you look for. It's something you work at."

She wished she and Marty had been mature enough to practice that philosophy. "You were most fortunate to have had one another . . . even if it did not last forever."

He deposited the photo atop the bureau, and then settled onto the bed once more, one ankle crossed at his knee. He began to strum a mindless melody, then his shoulders cringed. "It's badly out of tune, isn't it?"

She chuckled. "Here, let me. I used to tune my husband's

guitars—and I need practice, anyway."

He passed her the guitar. She plucked an offending string, listened, and adjusted its peg.

"Was the music the initial allure between you two, you and your husband?"

Her fingers paused on the strings, and her head canted in recollection. "No, not really. Marty resented that I was more musically inclined. I think it annoyed him to have to ask my opinion or suggestion, especially when it came to composition. I would say the initial allure was simply the lust between two teenagers." She made a moue. "A lust that lapsed."

"What does that mean? Did he become impotent?"

"Oh, his virility was never in question."

"I cannot imagine a man losing interest in you."

She sensed herself blushing at the intimacy of the subject. Mindlessly, softly, she fingered the strings. "It wasn't that our sexual activity waned; just that Marty's sexual drive had always been about satisfying himself. It wasn't that he was self-centered, you understand. He just did not have a clue."

She struck a sweep of harsh, dissonant chords then set the guitar on the bed between her and David.

He stood, arms crossed, looking down at her. She felt the object of his sole focus. "Then you were most unfortunate."

She felt skittish under his heavy-lidded regard. "I should get back to fixing supper."

✻

Answering The Call

After supper, David and Tony isolated themselves in the kitchen, conversing in mumbles and murmurs. Andi had tumbled into bed early.

Lauren needed a respite. The stargazer in her beckoned her out onto the front patio with David's guitar in hand.

A beat-up motorcycle she suspected belonged to Tony rested on its kickstand next to a weathered bench. David had parked his Pathfinder outside, in front of the rusting wrought-iron *zagúan*.

She sat on the bench, her back against a peeling wall. Face tilted up to the night sky, she mindlessly scanned its twinkling gems while playing the riff from *Pretty Woman*. She admired the haunting songs Roy Orbison had written. If only she could compose that spectacularly.

A wedge of light from the opened front door spilled out onto the patio. When David strode from the light toward her, her strumming dwindled away. "Off key, I know. I'm way off."

He joined her on the bench. Easing the guitar from her, he began tuning the strings this time. He canted his head, analyzing. "It's been far too long since I picked up this baby."

She noted that the parentheses at either side of his mouth were as tight as the guitar strings. Her instinct whispered he and Tony had been discussing that third option to her plight that he had derailed discussing earlier in the Pathfinder.

She did not want to hear what that particular strategy was. She had neither the emotional nor mental fortitude right now. "Where did you learn to play the guitar?"

He smiled ruefully. "In college. After a hostile student tried to garrot me with his guitar string. Akin to the usual frat hazing. The ritual didn't seem fun to me. So, I took the string, the guitar, and one of his eyes—or at least its sight—with his guitar pick."

She shuddered. She recalled the many nicks and scars that laminated his back. "And this fresh scar?" Lightly her finger traced the short but shocking pale path beneath the high ridge of one cheekbone.

His smile completely disappeared. "Macho Nacho."

Intuiting where this would all too likely lead, to a subject she was not ready to discuss, she jumped in with, "And this old scar on your forearm?"

"Got winged in my youth by a happy-go-lucky border patrol."

"What about all the tats? How did you come by them?"

He plucked another string, the G note, and tuned it. "Here and there. Most of the tats were meant to add luster to my image as a gang member." His lips tugged in a half smile. "Professional accreditations."

She pointed at a tat she had noticed before. The tat, which inked in crimson only the word *Madre*, was sandwiched on his forearm between a Georgia O'Keeffe-styled bleached deer skull and a skeleton hand on a fretboard. "You must have loved your mother very much."

"I barely knew her." He glanced down at the tattooed word. "Just to remind me that birthing a child does not a mother make. My half-sister Irma has been a better mother to me."

"After we met, you emphasized one time that you were Mexican-American. Is the American half on your mother's side?"

"She was a green-eyed blonde from Akron, Ohio, who had headed 'South of the Border, Down Mexico Way' for fun and play. Naturally, she fell hard for my father, an older, debonair entrepreneur from Querétaro, may he burn in hell. Don Ricardo Escobar was encumbered with fantastic wealth—from his startup electric typewriter company, which he expanded by moving later into the budding computer and cell phone industries—and he was encumbered with a wife and daughter."

"Irma? Your half-sister?"

He nodded. "As *mala suerte* would have it, my father not only divorced his current wife and disinherited Irma, but also ditched his mistress, my mother, to take up with a celebrated French actress. And my mother ditched me when she scurried back to Akron."

"How did you end up in Laredo?"

"Irma—she was a teenager and I just out of grade school when our father gave us the heave-ho. She decamped to Laredo and I tagged along."

"That's why you bought the home for her and her son Pepe to live in."

He set aside the guitar. He looked pointedly at her. "Well, home may not always be where the heart is, Lauren. That's why I came out here to the patio."

So this was it. Her back straightened. Her lips managed a polite smile. "Overstayed our welcome in your home, have we? I understand, really." Her heart sank. "Andi's flight doesn't leave for several more days, but I imagine I could catch the next bus bound stateside."

Standing, he planted his fist on his hips. "And then what? You're no better off. In fact, you're worse off. Going from the frying pan into the fire."

Confusion furrowed her brows. "Then what do you suggest?"

"I've been giving it some thought." His hand scrubbed his jaw, he issued what sounded like a groan, then he peered at her from beneath his dense, curling lashes. "I marry you."

"Wh-what?"

"As the wife of a Mexican citizen, you would be under my protection." Hands clasped behind his back, he began slowly pacing off the small patio's perimeter, as if with each step he gleaned further clarity. "Plus, I do have sway in court over some subordinate legalities, should documents you sign over to me be challenged."

"Documents? That I sign?" Parroting him, she felt moronic, like she really was losing her mind.

He halted and came to stand before her, his thumbs thrust into his jeans front pockets. As he spoke, quietly, he did not take his eyes off her. They examined every flicker of her stunned expression. "That I am in control of your estate and all that entails—which would thereby negate prior control you had signed over to your daughter and extended family members should it go into litigation."

"Why?" she breathed. "Why would you do this—marry me?" But suspicion was already whispering an ugly question, to which she did not want to know the answer.

"I could tell you it's because I cannot stop thinking about you. And that would be true. But you would not believe me. So, I shall tell you that once Tony graduates next year I want him to have the opportunity for a better life in the United States. He means everything to me. He is my world."

So, this marriage would not be world meaningful, as well, to David in regards to his relationship with her.

"With my marriage to you," David continued, "Tony, as your stepson, could ultimately qualify for immigration to the States." He wrested a deprecating smile. "Simply put, I suppose what I am suggesting is one of those old-fashioned marriages of convenience."

She slumped back against the wall. Like atoms colliding with one another, thoughts and feelings bombarded her. She could not focus nor comprehend or chase any single one to its conclusion. She rubbed her forehead. "I don't understand. I don't know. This makes no sense. Nothing does."

He reached down and took her hand. She felt the instant heat of kinetic connection, unlike any she had ever experienced at such a mere touch. His thumb gently rubbed the hollow of her palm. "I have enough on my plate right now that . . . well, you already understand my circumstances. My prison record disqualifies me for immigration. I could not go to the States with Tony and you."

This was the height of insanity, surely. Marrying a man she had known less than a month. A man who had done time in prison. A man who up front acknowledged he was leveraging her security for his end needs. Essentially, this could be termed extortion. And in return, she was to give him complete control over her. With the right to her financial assets.

Oh, Jesus Christ, admit me now to the nearest nuthouse.

As if reading her thoughts, he said, "Avoiding asylum commitment is a priority right now for you. In fact, we are down to the wire. Most likely, a matter of hours at the most."

He lifted her trembling chin, angling it up toward him. She could only make out the dark hearts of his eyes. "I would suggest that a civil marriage would not preclude you—us—from seeking the contentment, uhh, the satisfaction elsewhere. . . should our relationship prove . . . untenable. We just have to sustain our marriage contract for five years in name only before agreeing to divorce, if that is the case."

Like her, he, too, seemed to be striving to make sense of a non-sensical situation. Was it wise to give him the benefit of the doubt? He glanced out into the stygian night, then returned his searching gaze to lock on her. "We may have little time to pull this off. Will you trust me, Lauren?"

CHAPTER 27

How ironic. Nuestra Señora de Perpetuo Socorro—Our Lady of Perpetual Help.

Disregarding his damnably nagging arthritis, Don Ricardo Escobar knelt alongside the confessional box of Nuestra Señora de Perpetuo Socorro, as he did each week for the past fifty years on behalf of a woman to whom he arrogantly, harshly, and selfishly had given no help.

He gave help when it directly or obliquely served his purpose. On occasion, he would give help solely on a whim, depending on his mood . . . not on legalities of right or wrong nor hypocritical religious teachings. He freely acknowledged he was without conscience.

But this was a rare occasion, indeed.

Ilene and he had shared that similarity—capriciousness. An eighteen-year old American from Ohio, she was of the *nouveau riche*. His family was from a branch of the House of Bourbon that descended from Philip V of Spain in 1700.

Like Ilene, he had been too young. Had not been able to recognize, or perhaps even wanted to take notice, anything outside his narrow twenty percent of life's 180° spectrum. He had carelessly been unaware of the pain he inflicted. Not that it would have changed anything. Still, something within him had insisted on keeping track of Ilene over the years.

Don Ricardo's aristocratic family would have nothing to do with her or the boy she had birthed. With her own parents threatening to disown her and she suicidal with her impoverished life in a Mexican slum barrio, she had abandoned the six-year-old David and jetted back to Ohio. At forty-one, she had died of cirrhosis of the liver. A slobbering alcoholic.

And their son? Through David's mother-in-law, Don Ricardo was keeping tabs on him and on Don Ricardo's grandson. Never once had David reached out, much less given due obeisance or even respectfulness.

That disregard, that slight, could be fatal, as evidenced by many of Don Ricardo's dearly departed foes. The nature of David Escobar's fate was yet to be determined.

Making the sign of the cross, Don Ricardo began his weekly ritual Sacrament of Confession. "Father, I have sinned. My latest mortal sin is—"

A dry clearing of the throat interrupted. "The usual, my son?"

My son? Don Ricardo was seventy-three. The good padre of Nuestra Señora de Perpetuo Socorro, the church for the *ricos* of Querétaro, was thirty-one and a pedophile, according to Don Ricardo's reliable sources, his falcons, *los halcones*—the eyes and ears of the streets.

"*Sí*, Father." He ran blunt fingers through slicked back hair, which had only a threading of gray. "This week, I deemed it expedient I send a *capo* his notice, my usual calling card."

Answering The Call

"Ahh, the Ace of Spades with the poor motherfucker's face in the center? God have mercy on his soul."

"He had been honing in on my cellular business in Guanajuato. This morning, his head hangs from one corner of Alhóndiga de Granaditas." The grain house was the same two-story building from which for ten years had hung the head of the man hailed as the Father of the Nation, the Catholic priest Miguel Hidalgo y Costilla.

As would the good padre's when either the caprice overtook Don Ricardo or when the information the priest gleaned at the confessional box no longer served Don Ricardo's purpose. ¡*Chinga de madre*! So true, there was no honor among thieves.

CHAPTER 28

Later that night, Andi and Tony sat side by side on the couch, opposite Lauren in the one pigskin-covered chair and David in the other, his interlaced fingers between outstretched legs. The three were attending a committee meeting called by him to address what looked to Lauren as a slow motion train wreck.

Andi's expression was one of stunned disbelief. "So, does this marriage proposal of yours sort of make Tony and me brother and sister?" Her attempted joke came off in a skeptical tone. Lauren could only agree. This solution, marriage, was off the wall preposterous.

David looked up from his clasped hands. His reaction to Andi's joking was anything but jovial. "If what I believe to be true—that Macho Lopez has tracked her down—we have little time before Lauren is served the temporary psychiatric order and authorities show up to take her into custody."

"Can she be bailed out?" Andi asked.

"Sooner or later, if she is lucky. She will be temporarily

incarcerated in a holding cell in a Mexican prison—and it is a prison, not a mere hoosegow—crawling with not only roaches and rats but the most depraved. A cavity search would be the least unpleasant of her experiences during her incarceration."

Shuddering, Lauren rubbed up and down her upper arms. Clearly, here and now was not a particularly pleasant experience either—this blasé discussion, like getting a marriage license was equivalent to getting a fishing license.

"Even if she is a citizen of the United States?" Andi asked.

"You'd be surprised the number of United States citizens I come across in Mexican prisons. Granted most of them are young, up to no-good mischief. But not all. Names and info can get conveniently lost in the mass of data."

Tony leaned forward, his forearms braced on his thighs and groused, "Yeah, a Canadian friend of mine was stopped last year outside a cantina for no reason. He hadn't been drinking. But, unluckily for him, he did not have his passport with him."

"Yes," Lauren said, "my inquiries when moving here stressed that you don't get caught anywhere without your all-important passport on you."

"Exactly," Tony said, "and he got arrested. In the prison, they took away his cell phone. He was in there almost two weeks before he got a call out to his family by way of a cell phone smuggled in to another inmate."

Mouth set in a grim line, David nodded. "Older men and women—let's say stopped for a mere driving infraction by a police officer who's having a bad day—can and do end up in prison. Marriage to a Mexican is Lauren's best option."

Her head was throbbing. Making clarity out of all this

was impossible. Her imagination was fertile ground right now. Could David's quid pro quo offer of marriage, indeed, be a calculated plan to take control of her funds? Instead of an Alzheimer's care facility in the United States could she end up ditched dead in a Mexican arroyo?

And she was concerned for Andi, too. She turned to the wild child. "I know your flight out isn't for three more days, but I think its best you leave Querétaro. Today."

"No way, José. Miss out on a hair-raising adventure like this? Something I can recount to little Vinny here?" Andi's hand patted the top of her stomach. "Nope, we three are a team, Ms. L."

"Then it appears I have run up against a dead-end street's adobe wall." She glanced from David to Tony to Andi and back to David. She smiled brilliantly at him. "I do declare, Señor Escobar—your marriage proposal surely ranks up there with the most romantic in history. I accept."

※

Since this was Sunday morning, the civil wedding ceremony could not be performed until Monday, and this inordinate expediency in itself was due only to David's nefarious governmental contacts. Lauren would need present only her birth certificate and passport.

Sleepily, she stirred in his embrace. Her spine was cradled by his encompassing chest; his hardened penis nestled in the crevice of her buttocks. Obviously, he was aroused but apparently he was in no hurry to gratify his lust; at least, not with her. She would give him that, over Marty, with whom a hole in the wall would have sufficed.

Answering The Call

David's hand released its anchorage at her hip to slide downward and graze the indenture of her waist before skimming across her belly to caress its fleshy mound and stroke lower. His head dipped into the curvature of her neck and shoulder, his stubbled jaw chaffing her tender flesh.

Impossible! That could not be her body's feminine dampness seeping from her! Not when she was quite possibly in bed with the enemy. Surely not. But then her traitorous body was incredibly evidencing youth. She had also noticed her legs now needed shaving, for the first time in she could not remember when.

"Wear your jeans and tennis shoes today," he ground out in a voice still raspy with sleep. "We are going biking."

"What?" her breathy question tumbled into her pillow. "You talking Schwinn or Harley?"

He chuckled. "We're talking Kawasaki. To a winery."

She half rolled to face him. "Why? Why a winery?"

He dropped a kiss on the top of her nose. "Because it's your birthday."

She gasped. In all this turmoil and chaos, she had forgotten. Yes, today she turned that dismal seventy years of age. "How did you know?"

"How could I not? My business is about details. All of your information is recorded on your application for the renter's policy."

"Won't it be dangerous? If we should be spotted?"

His lips nuzzled her temple. "The two of us won't be expected to be riding Tony's motorcycle. And, besides, it will get us to the winery via circuitous routes that a car tracking us cannot."

Later that morning, she found it mind blowing that at

her advanced age of seventy she was sitting astride a motorcycle zigzagging through back streets, her arms clasped around David's muscle-striated torso, her cheek pressed against his leather jacket.

Like all mornings on the high desert, the temperature was chilly, so she was wearing Tony's leather jacket, which swallowed her. By noon, the sun's ultraviolet rays would be decimating.

After close to an hour and unfamiliar sights had passed, she leaned forward and shouted against the wind, "Are we close yet to this winery?" The motorcycle's jarring was taking its toll on her bum. So much for the resiliency of youth.

"La Redonda Winery," he flung back. "*Si.*"

Surrounded by amethyst mountains, La Redonda Winery's lush green vineyards were fronted with private umbrellaed tables, widely separated and each on its own small terrace of terracotta-painted pavement.

He throttled down to park the motorcycle, helped her alight, and led her over to one of the vacant round tables, replete with menus. No sooner had she divested herself of helmet and jacket and taken the chair David pulled out for her next to his, than a white-shirted waiter arrived to take their order.

After the waiter left, she plowed her fingers through her mane, shaking out its wadded, perspiration-damp mess.

"Every weekend in July," David told her "a grape-stomping festival is held here in several circular tanks. Visitors purchase white t-shirts, and after finishing their stomping in the tank, they get out, planting their two purple feet on the t-shirts—and voila, the t-shirts are personalized."

Answering The Call

"That sounds like a lot of fun." Then, she grinned. "I have to wonder what happens to those grapes smashed by perhaps not the cleanest feet. Do you think the vineyard bottles and sells the grape juice later as the wine we are now getting ready to drink?"

His low laughter did a rollercoaster number on her stomach. "What I think is maybe I should have ordered us *cervezas*."

She laughed back, realizing that she was enthralled with him all this time because he made her laugh. She wondered what had happened to the compliant, apathetic Lauren Hillard, the aging one, indifferent if The End came sooner than later? She had answered this call to adventure, that's what. She felt alive, vibrant, eager to taste more of life.

And at the same time she was wary of taking that next precipitous step over the cliff, that Tarot's Fool step. Was she coming under David's spell? Could her nominally good sense counter the deception and deviousness practiced by a man with such glorious gifts as his? Old world charm, stunning good looks, high intelligence . . . all this could equate to her shattering.

The waiter arrived with a bottle of wine and a platter of various cheeses, for which Mexico's Central Highlands was famous. Popping the cork, he poured the wine then departed. David raised his glass. In his sensuous Spanish accent, he said, "To your light—I see it, Lauren, ever shining in the darkest nights."

She blinked back threatening moisture and managed a tremulous smile. He could have uttered some suave toast like, 'To a lovely lady' or a sappy 'To us.' She took a sip of the wine, savoring its rich, fruity flavor on her tongue.

Leaning across his chair arm, he said, "I know I will

make us both sorry for doing this." His hand cupped her neck. He drew her toward him. At the last second, she closed her lids. Gently, lingeringly, his mouth feathered across hers, back and forth as if to make sure it missed nothing about her lips.

Then the quality of his kiss altered. Hungrily, he nudged open her lips, until his spiced breath captured her own. His exploratory kiss alone was a grand seduction. Oh my god, could this man kiss. She tingled with all the feelings and longings of her youth that could not possibly be repeated within the diminishment of aging. And yet she was feeling all that and more.

It really was better, the second time around.

Sliding her arms up around his neck, her wine glass slipped from her fingers to splinter on the paved terrace.

CHAPTER 29

"**S**omething borrowed, something blue," Andi said. She laid aside her curling iron and began securing Lauren's mass of curls atop her crown with a blue sequined stretch band filched from Andi's hoard of grooming accessories she kept in her tote. For wedding attire, Lauren wore the same blue flowered skirt and white peasant blouse.

She studied the upper portion of her image in David's bathroom mirror, tarnished at its edges, and bit her lower lip. Was it true? That ardor amped up the body's serotonin? Her reflection would seem to verify that. Did she appear less beleaguered? Had the aging lines around her eyes and mouth lessened? Were her lips fuller, an aftereffect from that devastating kiss at the winery the day before? Did she detect a glow in her features?

Surely not infatuation. Infatuation with a man young enough to be her son? Stud handsome he might be. Highly intelligent, as well, with an admirable education. But opportunistic also? Enough to take advantage of her dire predicament?

All that morning, he had been working at his laptop on the dining room table. Every once in a while she would hear the whirr of his printer . . . and she knew he was preparing the legal documents on which she was about to sign away her life.

"So, this is crazy," Andi continued, oblivious to Lauren's turmoil. "Here you are marrying. While I came here to Mexico, thinking I might be marrying the father of my child."

She glanced in the mirror at Andi. The glow of pregnancy suffused the girl's face. "Love should be a factor in marriage. Or, at least, it makes marriage more . . . manageable."

The girl's mouth screwed up. "Love? My parents, like I doubt they even knew the definition of love. Not for themselves. Not for me, certainly. For scripture, maybe." Her fingers flurried here and there, rearranging Lauren's curls. "For control freaks—cults didn't have a thing on my parents. Growing up, like, I didn't have the foggiest what it felt like to be loved. My upbringing was psycho."

Lauren reached up to halt Andi's darting hand. "Then let me give you one of the better definitions of love—and lust has little to do with love. What it feels like to be deeply loved by someone . . . why, Andi, the feelings make you fall in love with yourself." Not that she had ever been loved so deeply by someone. "I am learning from life's experiences," she finished, "that we need others in our lives for growth. But we need ourselves for love. Does that make sense?"

Andi frowned into the mirror. "Is that what I am feeling right now?"

She narrowed her at eyes at the girl's reflection. "Are you coming to love this child you carry . . . or are you still carrying a torch for its father?"

"I . . . I don't know. Like, once here in Mexico, I feel like I am falling in love with everything and everyone. I know, cray-cray, isn't it?"

"No, it isn't. Because I am having the same crazy feelings."

"My turn, Ms. L."

"Your turn? To what?"

"To give advice."

She stared back at the girl's reflection. "Go ahead."

"Well, sometimes you do crazy things for love—but that doesn't mean you're crazy."

She gulped and turned around to hug her. "You are a very wise woman to be such a very young girl." Releasing her, she said, "Unfortunately, tomorrow you leave Querétaro—and right now we leave for its Antiguo Palacio Municipal."

To be marrying again, at seventy . . . she would have thought death would have claimed her first.

Tony and David awaited her and Andi at the front door. Stunned, Lauren could only stare at David. He had opted to wear a tie, dress shirt, and navy dinner jacket and trousers for the ceremony, so out of character with his usual edgy, grunge style. His hair was caught in a knot at his nape. He was breath-stealing handsome.

His warm gaze roamed over her face, taking in her upswept curls, and returning to linger on her eyes. He smiled and nodded slightly. That mere nod stirred her more than any suave, "Well, aren't you beautiful, doll!"

Or was just one of his ploys at which he excelled . . . subtle seduction?

The drive to the Historic District was as silent as inside a hearse. When they reached the Municipal Palace, a magnificent 18th century baroque building, he told Tony to escort Andi in.

Grasping Lauren's elbow, David steered her toward the plaza fronting the Moorish-influenced building. Topiary trees offered shade to the walkways, and an ornate fountain shared the center with an immense statue of some statesman.

David drew her off to sit at one of the wrought-iron benches, deserted at that time of afternoon. Arm braced on the bench's back, he angled his taut body toward her equally stiff one. "Look, this . . . it is not the way either of us would have it. But I need to know that this is what you want to go through with, this Faustian bargain of an open marriage."

Her eyes flared at the mention of both Faustian and open marriage in the same sentence. "What are you asking—explicitly? I need to know now. Before the 'I do's'."

His gaze was piercing. "All that we have is right now. And I cannot promise you that right now is forever." He shrugged. "At this moment, Macho Nacho could stroll across the plaza to serve you with the temporary hold order. Or even serve you after our marriage but before I can get the various documents filed on both sides of the border. And if not, there's always later. Up to a year from now your daughter's Mexican attorney can file a lawsuit to revoke our marriage."

"But you could contest it?"

"Sure, I could fight it—and maybe win. But I need you to fully comprehend that our marriage could end in a month—or we could end it in five years, finding we are totally unsuitable for one another."

Answering The Call

It would most certainly end within five years, she thought, because how could resentment not build?

As if reading her mind, he said, "Look, I don't want you to feel coerced in any way. This is to be solely at your discretion."

She turned the tables on him. "I need to know this is what *you* want, David. Specifically, is what you want an open marriage for us?"

He looked up to his right, as if searching within the shade of the trees for the exact response, then back to her. "What can I say . . . that is to be determined by what you want as much as what I want. *Que sera, sera.* As for now, I know only this, that I want you."

This she had to know—"Why me?"

His broad shoulders lifted. "Who can say for certain what causes a powerful wanting between a man and a woman?" He permitted a slight smile. "You caught my attention from the first. When you shot me the bird. I do know that I am drawn to you by your wit and humanity and warmth. No other woman has that look you do. Is that not enough for now?" He held out his palm, so much larger, longer than her own.

His response was so raw she had to swallow hard. She could not question further. "All right." She put her hand in his. "I'm ready for this farce of a marriage."

"It will be quite legal, I assure you—unless and until courts rule otherwise." He cast her a reckless grin. "Besides, I paid the requisite *mordida*."

From that point, he held her hand through the moment he slipped a simple band of braided silver on the third finger of her left hand, through the magistrate's pronouncement of husband-and-wife, when David bent to bestow a simple kiss, and through Andi and Tony's signatures as witnesses.

Their small wedding party of four then adjourned to a colonial boutique hotel a block away, where David checked in. Casa de la Marquesa was a first-class hotel but retaining all the charm of its historic past. She worried how he could afford this—or, if he indeed could, from what various means came his funds.

In the dining room, a waiter wafted napkins across their laps; another took their order. Only a few other tables, draped in white linen, were occupied. From the courtyard drifted the sound of a fountain's splashing water. And soon champagne was splashing into their flutes.

The conversation was light, if one discounted the tension brewing beneath. Andi and Tony did most of the chattering. "Before you leave, we should check out nearby Peña de Bernal," he was telling Andi. "It's the world's tallest monolith, and rumor mill has it that the area is energized with a mind-goggling vortex."

"I'm checking out that boujee guy in the tux," she said, nodding toward a distinguished older man entering the dining room.

Crossing to the grand piano, he flipped out his coattails and sat at its piano bench. Lightly his fingers danced over the keys before launching into *Last Dance*. Lauren's gaze flew to David. "You arranged for this, as well?"

He settled back in his chair and gave her his usual cryptic smile. "Like I told you, I paid the requisite *mordida*."

When after dinner cocktails were served, he also produced the pressing papers for her signature. She had been anticipating this. He made no excuses or justification for what he wanted her to do.

Answering The Call

He inclined his head toward Andi and Tony. "They will also need to sign—and witness— these documents. Then I'll file them, along with the marriage certificate, as soon as possible with the various agencies."

It was one of those 'live or die' moments. She took a gulp from her extra rich chocolate martini. After all, the seductive chocolate was born out of Mexico. The Olmecs had used it for medical purposes and rituals. Well, this, her wedding night most certainly could be considered a ritual.

She experienced a paroxysm of panic and broke into a cold sweat. So what if she lost everything in this adventure? Her senses were aflame. She felt alive for the first time in years. David Escobar was her sliver of salvation.

She scrawled her initials on each page and finished on the last page with a flourish of her signature.

CHAPTER 30

From their large bedroom with its towering wood-beam ceiling and heavy antique furniture, Lauren wandered through the double French doors out onto the private balcony. Flowers cascaded from its railing's boxes.

The balcony faced a quiet street—but for the accordion player below. He was softly playing a song she did not recognize. David followed, bracing forearms on the wrought-iron laced-work. With a teasing smile that belied her nervousness, she said, "I half expected to hear the guy rendering up *Last Dance*.

He cast her a sidewise, inquisitive glance. "What was your last dance, your last husband, like—outside of the bedroom—that is?"

She shrugged. "Marty was fun, clever, charismatic and . . . self-absorbed outside the bedroom, as well. We met in Spain. College-bound backpackers breaking loose for the summer. He also had an addictive personality." To drugs and love affairs. "We had been married almost twelve years, when he—"

Answering The Call

"Died of gastrointestinal bleeding—and left you a widow."

As if an ice cube had slithered down her spine, she shivered. "I forgot. You have built a dossier on me." She shrugged and managed a smile. "I seem to have a predilection for musicians, don't I?"

He straightened and began shrugging out of his suit jacket. He draped his jacket over her shoulders then, arms folded and facing her, buttressed himself against the railing. "I'm not Marty, Lauren."

She turned inquisitive eyes up to his and moistened her lips, dry from either the high desert clime or her present apprehension, she was not sure which. And, she noted, his eyes did not miss the gesture. "That's just it," she mumbled. "I don't know who you are, really. Oh, sure, you are a lawyer, an activist, an ex-con. But those are labels, and you are too complex for me to understand. At least, this soon."

"This soon? What's to understand? We are a man and woman drawn to each other. For now, for tonight even, is that not enough?"

"And it's scary as hell that you know me all too well." Better even than she knew herself, apparently. "Is tonight, this hotel . . . is its purpose for making use of the . . . advantages, as you deemed them . . . that we each bring by merely signing the marriage license?"

"And those advantages tonight would be—what?"

"You're goading me, damn't, David. The advantage that comes following a wedding ceremony with the usual mating ritual."

He grinned at her discomfiture. "You cannot find it conceivable that I view you not as an advantage I should make use of but as desirable, all on your own?"

Her breath corked. She could only stare back. Then the fear burst from her lungs in a low, anguished retort. "Hell no, I can't—seventeen years difference in our ages is inconceivable!"

"And I find it irrelevant. You are vastly different from the others."

"Should I ask how many others?"

"Does it matter? It is only you I want. Here and now. And as I told you, now is all we have, *mi alma*."

The romantic endearment weakened her resistance. She turned back toward the open French doors and the respite they offered from his arresting masculinity. "I would like a bath."

"You do know the bathroom tub is large enough for a baby elephant." She heard the amused challenge in his voice. Then the added gentle reassurance, "But you first."

She stopped, looked back at him. "Once again, since I wasn't aware we'd be staying overnight here, I don't have a change of clothing."

Those wide shoulders affected indifference with their slight shift. He moved to take her elbow, ushering her back into their bedroom. "There's a complimentary bathrobe hanging behind the bathroom door."

"You've stayed here before?" So many questions she could have, should have, asked, but, surprising her, prickling jealousy, unexpected and sharp, claimed her attention foremost.

"My work takes me everywhere. From the prisons to the governor's palace." He unknotted his tie, tugged his shirt tail from his trousers and began unbuttoning the white dress shirt.

Not wanting to foolishly ogle the broadening expanse of

Answering The Call

coppery skin, she pivoted and shrugged his dinner jacket off onto a brocaded chair. Grabbing her purse, she headed for the bathroom. Fleeing neither out of prudery nor modesty but out of uncertainty.

Like Abba's song, she did not know the name of the game. Whatever it was, she was too old to play it . . . this devilish game to make her thoughts solely of David, of wanting to experience his lips moving over hers again, to feel his fingers stroking her flesh, starved of human touch. Her church choir friends would likely be triggered into finger-wagging overdrive.

The large bathroom included a hot tub, separate from the bathtub that was, as he had claimed, large enough for a baby elephant. One entire wall of the bathroom was mirrored. An array of exotic oils, lotions, shampoos and soaps banked a long, Talavera-tiled counter.

She was too hyped to take a hot bath. She could not afford to succumb to the luxury of the laxness it bestowed. She showered and wrapped herself in the plush robe, of which David apparently was quite familiar.

One bedroom lamp was on, its low light setting aglow the handsome, fit man stretched the length of one side of the immense bed. He had shucked his tie, dress shirt, and shoes. His hands were locked behind his head, revealing his armpit hair. Dark hair curled across his swarthy chest, then arrowed downward. His narrow, bare feet were crossed at the ankles. She had not realized how sexy feet could be.

Self-consciously, she stood in the ankle-long robe at the foot of the regal four-poster bed. "There is something I have to know."

He looked her up and down, his lips edging into a slight smile. "There is a lot you could know."

217

"You went to all this trouble. This hotel room. Why all this? When we could have just as easily spent this night back in your house?"

Through half-masted lids he was watching her closely. "Then this is what you should know. Trusting this is the last marriage, last dance, for both you and me . . . and concerned that perhaps this could very well be the last night of freedom for us, I wanted it to be meaningful."

"Last night of freedom?" She shivered again. Not from fear but once more from that sickening suspicion. Following their marriage, was this now the Judas kiss? Hoping her voice did not come out shaky, she steadied her tone. "Surely that can't happen? That's why we married, right?"

"*One* of my reasons for marrying you. And as I explained to you this morning, anything can happen in Mexico. After this, I could be arrested and imprisoned as an accomplice, an accessory. That is why I feel tonight should be worthy of remembrance, something special, if this is all we have. And because I have said before, Lauren—age does not matter to me."

Oh God, she did not want to fall in love with him.

"But, *por favor*, do not stress about this . . . ," he gifted her with a faint smile, " . . . stress about this consummation, as you would term it. I learned a long time ago that sex is not pleasurable to either partner unless both want it."

He swung his legs down off the bed and standing, winked at her. "I'll catch a brisk shower—to dampen the ardor you are wary of. Meanwhile you can tuck yourself into bed." He looked her up and down, from her bare feet, up past where her pulse beat at her throat, to her damp hairline. "Although I would imagine that thick robe will prove uncomfortable for sleeping."

Damn't, he was right. While listening to the running of his shower, she shifted to her side, then to her spine, rolled over onto her stomach, and back to her other side. The robe was an encumbrance. And, damn't she was too old to play the coy maiden. Expelling an aggravated sigh at this ridiculous display of naïveté, she shed the worrisome garment.

Soon she heard him pad into the bedroom, heard the click as he turned off the lamp. Then she felt the rustling of the bedcovers and the give of the mattress as he stretched out beside her, causing her body to roll slightly toward the depression his weight created, near enough for her to feel the heat of his skin and smell its soapy cleanliness.

She had read in one of Renita's *Psychology Today* magazines, that skin-to-skin contact between adults could reduce stress levels and increase levels of oxytocin, the "love hormone," making one feel more connected to their partner.

What she was feeling was dizzying. A yearning that was disorienting. All rules, all propriety, all defenses were obliterated by this maelstrom of wanting. Yet she could not recollect ever feeling this vulnerable. God help her, it was now or never.

She rolled on her side toward his back. "I may be numbered among the elderly," she whispered, "but I do not want to miss out on this either."

He shifted to face her. "This . . . what?"

He was not making it easy for her. "This . . . " her psychedelic thoughts searched for her intended meaning. Her eyes were adjusting to the dark, and she could barely make out the angular contours of his face. "I . . . David. It's been so long. I don't know if . . . if my body will respond. I feel like a withered and dried-up piece of fruit."

His slow smile was like the evening's first star. "The benefits of my living beyond the half century mark have been claiming their dues, as well." His voice was lazy, sensual, and tinged with amusement. "You worry for naught. I'm not even sure I can sustain my passion throughout this night to the mutual satisfaction of us both."

"Please, pace yourself," she said, managing a tremulous smile in jest. "I don't want this night to end."

He chuckled. "I'm too old, Lauren, for some grand seduction. Only lovemaking. Simply put, love-making. This is what I am wanting for tonight."

He shifted, so that his thigh rode up over her hip and she was gently pressed onto her back. Lightly, he kissed her forehead, then each eyelid. His thumb traced the sweep of one cheekbone, then the other. "I want for you that most basic instinct . . . that can be the most fulfilling . . . meant for something I suspect in you has been neglected."

Only a second's hesitation. Then her arms of their own accord slipped up over his shoulders. She caressed them, her fingers feeling their muscles twitch at her touch. Next, her fingertips trailed down his spine, exploring the muscles ridging either side, and she felt their shudder response.

"By all that's holy, Lauren," he muttered, "you do have the siren's touch."

"And you have a lot of scars."

"We all have scars. Some you can see. Some you can't."

She wanted him to tell her about them, the where and the when and the why of each. In a sense they were beautiful in that they gave evidence of the inner and outer battles the warrior in him must have fought.

Answering The Call

She left off her investigation of his back to tunnel her fingers through the crisp hair on his chest. Then her palms cupped either side of his face, drawing his mouth down to hers. His long, shower-damp hair curtained her world. Tentatively, she brushed his lips with hers, savoring this long forgotten experience.

But then he took control and began his pleasuring of her with feathering kisses and light nips at her earlobe and throat. His lovemaking, both passionate and persuasive, was also laced with patience and infinite tenderness. Somewhere during it she lost the sense of time, of coherent thought, of her body as a separate, physical thing.

Indistinctly, she heard his urgent, "Move with me, Lauren." And later, when he filled her with himself, she heard his whispered, "*Mi amor.*"

As the night closed in, what transpired was like nothing she had known before . . . a taste of loving so sweet yet perversely a conflagration of her senses. A passion sanctified. As her rapture began to morph to an unbearable, insistent, and compelling need, as she crested the climax, tears surprisingly flooded from her lids.

Rolling off her and wrapping her in his arms to cradle her against his chest, he attended to her wracked emotions by simply stroking her shoulder, her arm, the hair back from her face. Marty would have said, "What the fuck are you crying for?!"

"I . . . I had no idea," she sniffled, trying to explain her ridiculous fit of weeping, made worse by saturating David's chest hair.

He chuckled softly and tipped his forehead to press against hers. "You still have no idea of the pleasure that awaits."

He was right. Much later, when she regained some sense of time and space, her body ravished beyond endurance, she lay with slack abandon in his arms. "I am astonished," she murmured, "and thrilled . . . and grateful."

All concern about her body's aridity was vanquished, proving medical authorities had no clue to the power that genuine lovemaking exerted. No oils or ointments had been needed. Her eyes felt weighted and her lips tingled. Her blood seemed vitalized by this most wonderful elixir, and her body felt inflamed.

Placing his head softly on her breasts, he murmured, "I would like to continue kissing you all over, wishing I could lay with you, loving you like this, for the entirety of this new day, *mi amor*."

Her gaze flew to the window's jalousie slats. Faint lavender light seeped through. Surely, an entire night had not passed.

He raised onto one forearm, staring down at her with an intensity that was unsettling. "However, I think a change of residence is of immediate importance."

She raised a sleepy brow. Tilting her head in perplexion, her hair rustled the pillowcase as if making audible her disappointment at being disturbed from the love nest. She inhaled the redolence of their lovemaking.

"We still have to elude Mexican authorities." He nodded at the folder on the rococo chest of drawers. The folder contained their marriage certificate and the document granting him her power of attorney. "At least, until I can file the signed papers. But tomorrow I'll see to having all the official documents recorded, stamped, and counter-stamped, although you understand this is on Mexico time. Meanwhile, the sooner we check out of here and into a safe house the better."

Shoving back her riotously mussed hair, she raised on one elbow, careful to tug the sheet over her bare breasts. Strange, her modesty, when throughout the night his hands and mouth had mapped every inch of her flesh. She braced her head on one palm and asked, "A what . . . a safe house? You're serious?"

He muscled up from the tangled sheets to stand and, arms angled outward, stretched his ropy length in a yawn. His body still shone with his sweat and seed. His silhouette evoked the memory of her fingertips exploring his body's tensile strength. She went weak with the knowledge she had fallen irrevocably in love with David Escobar. This could prove to be a bittersweet journey on which she was embarking.

"Uhh, colleagues use the safe house occasionally," he explained, "whenever Big Brother here in Mexico gets too nosey. When Tony and Andi join us for lunch, I'll have him drive us to the safe house."

She wanted to ask if this colleague was using the safe house for legal or illegal purposes. But at that idyllic moment she truly did not care. Her body felt rejuvenated. Her blood sang. She might have been a youthful eighteen-year-old again. She felt both soporific from their love-making and euphorically light of body. Incredibly, she also felt sexy.

He crossed to her, leaning over to plant his arms on either side of her waist. His eyes were smoky with lingering desire. His mouth was generous with its seductiveness.

Smiling languidly, she looked up at him. "What?"

"Only that you need to know this—that no matter what happens from here on—that this night your age did not matter."

"I can't imagine you find pleasure in pleasuring this aging body when you could be pleasuring a 40- or 50-year-old."

"To me, *mi amor*, you are the sky and the seas. Timeless, like they are. Does their beauty ever stop? Neither does yours."

CHAPTER 31

Rousing a sleeping Andi at six that next morning was no easy feat for Tony. The carrot-topped female burrowed even deeper in the covers. "Come on, Andi, we're going to Never-Never Land."

It truly was a magical place. He wanted to drive her up to see Peña de Bernal before they had to meet his father and Lauren for lunch. And after that . . . taking her to the airport was something he did not want to think about.

"I don't wanna go anywhere," she grumbled into her pillow. "It's still dark."

"That's when I always wake up." He grabbed her ankles and flipped her onto her back. "You're burning daylight." He tugged her to the edge of the bed and thrust his head between her knees.

She shot to a sitting position. "You chad!" She hurled a pillow at him.

He tumbled back onto his ass. Hands braced behind him on the floor, he grinned up at her. "I take it a chad is bad."

She scrambled to sit on her knees, her hands clasping her

225

belly, as if protecting the unborn child from the outside world. "A hyper-sexed dude." From her mattress's perch, her eyes narrowed down at him. "What's your donger's body count?"

"What?"

"You know, your cum gun. Come on, how many people have you slept with?"

"By people, I am assuming you mean both male and female."

"Quit stalling. You can't shock me."

He shoved to his feet. Fists jammed on his hipbones, he glared down at her. "Bet I can."

She smirked. "Try me."

He liked her too much to lie. "No one. None. Zero. *Zilch.*"

Her mouth dropped open. "Are you screwing with me?"

"No, I'm not screwing with you—or screwing anyone for that matter."

She slid off the bed onto her bare feet and, mirroring him, jammed her knotted hands at her thick waist. They stood inches apart, heads jutted forward like butting rams. "You're too damned good at making out to convince me you're a virgin."

His mouth pinched. He could only glare back.

When no answer issued forth, she breathed. "My God, you are!"

Mortified, he started to swing around for the bedroom door, but she latched onto either side of his head and spun him back to face her. "Not so fast, dude."

He groaned. "Listen, can we just drop the subject?"

Her fingertips scooted from the side of his head down to the earpieces of his eyeglasses. Slowly, tantalizingly, she

Answering The Call

removed his eyeglasses and flung them over her shoulder. He heard them thunk somewhere but instantly forgot his fear of their breaking—she was standing on tiptoe raising her lips toward his. "It's time we changed your virginal status," she murmured.

When she tugged him toward the rumpled bed, his feet balked. He tilted back his head, stared at the ceiling's age-spotted stains. "Uhh, this donger, as you term it, is not good at obeying on command."

She gave him that percolating smile of hers and rubbed her heavy breasts back and forth against his ribcage. Her enlarged stomach nudged his crotch. "I bet if I whisper sweet nothings to it, Tony, it will do anything and everything I tell it to." She drew him down on the bed to stretch out beside her. "Just call me the Donger Whisper-er."

She was right. It did, he did, anything and everything she told him. He never knew coming could be so euphoric. Any thought of touring Bernal was blown with the blow job she first gave him.

Three hours later, sprawled in replete lassitude, she moaned, "My lady bits send you to the head of the class."

That pleased him. But he could not help but blurt, "And how many lovers has your Lady Bits had?"

On her back, she linked her fingers atop her pregnancy bump. In contemplation, she eyed the ceiling, where a patch of stucco had fallen off. After a moment, she said, "Seventeen—if you count my brother."

"Your—your brother?"

She sighed. "Yup. I was just getting my breasts buds. At ten, puberty hit me like a Houston hurricane. And my sixteen-year-old brother, Peter . . . ," a grim smile tightened the corners of her mouth, "well, you might say he introduced my lady bits to his peter."

He tried to keep the dismay from his voice. "What did your parents do?"

"They talked smack. 'What will the people at our church say?' Told him never to do it again. And told me not to tell." She shrugged. "After that, he left my lady bits alone. And I didn't tell."

He saw the glistening in her eyes and reached for her hand, holding the back of it against his cheek. He did not care how many lovers she had before him; he wanted to be her last.

"We're sticky and icky," she said briskly and, withdrawing her hand from his, pushed herself up from the mattress. "A shower is in order before we head out to meet up with your father and Ms. L."

"Mrs. Escobar," he reminded her, tumbling from the other side of the bed. "They're married now."

Hurriedly they showered, the two of them—or three of them as it was—barely fitting into the stall. The thought of the *three* of them stuck in his mind. As he drove the Pathfinder back toward El Centro and Casa de la Marquesa, it hit him with the force of a sledge hammer that he was slam bang in love with Andi Lyons.

He nearly swerved out of his lane on the *autopista*. The remainder of the trip he ruminated on this epiphany. As usual for him, he analyzed the authenticity of his feelings. Sure, he was aware that the sharing of bodily fluids enhanced romantic and emotional feelings that in turn subsided dramatically, ironically coinciding, more or less, within the same nine-month period it took to birth a baby.

But on the practical side, he really liked her. He respect-ted her for striking out on her own so young. And could understand more fully now her need to ditch her past. He admired her spontaneity and spunk. Her responsible yet whimsical nature. She would be no clinging vine. She could take him on flights of fancy that freed up his methodical mind.

Without looking at her in the passenger seat, he said, "I don't think your baby should be born out of wedlock. I think we should get married. I want to be your husband, *amada mia*. And I want to be your baby's father."

Peripherally, he saw her gape. Equal parts intensity mixed with regret reflected in her eyes. Then she shook her head. "No way, *nada*, no how."

CHAPTER 32

In the Tikua Restaurant, just around the corner from the Hotel la Casa de la Marquesa, Lauren surreptitiously studied the expressions of the other three at their table.

David's expression, as always, impenetrable. This, despite the hallucinatory passion he had displayed throughout the night before.

Tony's placid features could not conceal a dissatisfaction that had nothing to do with the wheel of cheese and freshly baked *bolillos* just brought to the table. Behind his eyeglasses, his eyes mirrored something deeper within. An anguish perhaps?

And Andi? Her flippant expression contained the wealth of the universe. Her chartreuse and purple tote, hanging from the restaurant's adjacent purse stand, perfectly mimicked her defiantly free-spirited nature. The bag could hold all her worldly belongings, setting her free to flee at any moment of peril.

Behind the three, the brightly painted mural mocked the wedding party's charade.

Answering The Call

"I have decided it's best, for Lauren's safety, that she stay elsewhere," David was saying. His arm overlapped the top rail of her chair. "At least, until we are past this initial ten-day psychiatric hold order. I think it best we register our marriage certificate with the U.S. embassy, as well. And the sooner the better."

It was decided to take Andi to the airport first. This drive, like the previous one, was strained by unspoken, repressed feelings.

Querétaro's airport, although an international one, was small with three gates, only two of which were serviceable. David pulled into the parking lot and came around to open Lauren's door, as did Tony for Andi's. All four met in front of the Pathfinder. "We'll wait while you see Andi safely through to customs," David told Tony.

Lauren was only now realizing how much she would miss Andi. She hugged the girl. "Please take care of your beautiful self. And somehow keep me posted about our Vinny."

Her tote in her hand, Andi nodded, her mouth set in a glum line. "When he pops, I'll let you dudes know."

Lauren blinked back tears. David gave her shoulder a comforting squeeze.

With Tony, Andi set off in what was a pregnancy waddle. She took several steps, then halted abruptly, and turned around. "Yo guys, uhh . . . I, uhh," she glanced up at Tony. "I have changed my mind. I'm staying." Her voice held a questioning note. "That is, if you haven't, Tony—changed your mind?"

He was grinning widely.

"But no marriage," she qualified quickly. "I have to be free to be me."

He looked unfazed by her stipulation. "I can't promise I won't try to change your mind on this, as well."

Stupefied, Lauren glanced from Andi to Tony and back. "But you've only known each other a week."

"You and David have only known each other only a little longer," Andi pointed out.

Lauren looked up at David. His expression was no longer unprobeable. His features plainly communicated consternation. "Is it because of the child involved, *mijo*? I know growing up without a mother yourself, you could feel a sense of concern for—" his extended palm indicated Andi's obvious condition.

"Andi makes me happy."

"What about college?"

"I will find a way to finish it." He squeezed Andi's hand. She grinned up at him with puckish adoration.

David's narrowed eyes switched from his son to Andi and back. "You both are out-of-your-depths too young."

"Does love have an age limit?" Andi asked.

Out of the mouths of babes, Lauren thought.

"Forget the rigamarole. I say we crack on for better or best." She cut David a sidelong look. "That is if it's okay with you if I bunk with Tony."

Lauren held her breath, watching David scrutinize the two, as if he could plumb their minds—and hearts. She had to agree with him. Tony and Andi's lives were still new. At their age, they had no idea what life would require of them in the months and years to come. But then she could say the same for her present dilemma at her advanced age.

At last, David shrugged his consent. "Have at it."

"Hey, Papi," Tony said, "if you haven't checked out of your hotel room, can Andi and I have it for tonight?"

David rolled his eyes and growled, "The room but not the Pathfinder. You two are on your own getting home."

After slingshotting back to the boutique hotel to drop off the young sweethearts, he drove to the safe house. During this time, he grew steadily more taciturn. Lauren sensed he was internally transmuting from role of warm and tender lover to cool and distant professional.

All this unnerved her. She wanted the security she had felt last night, wrapped in his arms, the comforting squeeze of her shoulder at the airport today, or merely to feel his large hand reassuringly clasping hers there at the municipal palace.

Even more, she wanted him to know those affectionate gestures would continue, as well as the more ravishing love play demonstrated throughout last night. Never had she been kissed like that. From the light, tender kisses dropped on her temple or her palm to those long, exploratory kisses on her nape or the inside of her thigh. The kind of kiss that required no words . . . like does this pleasure you? Here? And there?

But then his murmured, "*Only that you need to know this—that no matter what happens from here on—that this night your age did not matter,*" haunted her. With their marriage had he not secured what he wanted from her? Entry to the United States for Tony? There only remained the filing of the papers—and keeping out of reach of Kramer, the process server Macho—and her daughter.

Renita's relentless persecution gutted Lauren. Obviously, her daughter was beginning to suffer the ravages of dementia while continuing to harbor in her heart the hurt from childhood—and she was projecting it on Lauren. She told herself that she had to let this hurt go. She was here on earth with her hopes and dreams long before she had birthed Renita. These were still Lauren's to claim.

David turned into an upscale community near the *autopista's* intersection with Querétaro's historic pink-stone aqueduct. She had expected the safe house to be one of those roach hovels in a down-and-out barrio, but the two-story house halfway up the hill looked like a sprawling Mediterranean villa.

"Wow," she murmured. "How big is this place?"

"Six bedrooms and seven baths. To be more precise, 11,248 square feet."

"What a perfect place to foster homeless children," she blurted.

He glanced askance at her. "Tell me, do you always work this tirelessly on behalf of others?"

"What makes you ask that?"

"Think about it. You've taken Andi and her unborn child under your wing. And you shared how all those years you worked to keep your daughter's psychiatric practice afloat. Now you're seriously contemplating care for homeless children."

"Well, you did say if I wanted to see changes, I would have to begin with —"

"I know, I know. But for one, the place is not mine, and for another you do not even have permanent residence status in Mexico yet."

She slid him a sidewise smirk. "If I did need legal service in carrying this through . . . would you give me a discount?"

His groan was accompanied by a rueful curve of his lips. "At this rate, this marital union of ours may not make it the full five years."

She did not know what to say and could only nod self-consciously. What had happened to the easy camaraderie they had shared when making breakfast that first morning? A night of lovemaking that had left her heart vulnerable, that's what had happened.

A high, spiked gate permitted them entry into the courtyard's terra-cotta walls, topped by rolled barbed wire. Even the Moorish arched windows were ornately barred. He fished a key ring from his jeans pocket and by remote opened first the high gate and then the front door, as heavy as cast iron.

Surprisingly, the spacious interior was a charming rustic urban chic, not overly curated but contemporary with a white leather Italianate sofa and chairs banking a beehive corner fireplace. A large television screen occupied nearly the entirety of another wall. Off to one side of another wall stood an upright piano.

Immediately, Lauren crossed to it. Her fingertips trailing over the ivory keys, she noted the piano was a Bechstein, one of the world's best piano makers. *I could lose myself here easily.*

David gestured carelessly in the opposite direction, toward an open kitchen. Its red-bricked island separated the kitchen from the dining room. "The fridge and pantry need to be restocked. I'll see to that."

She wandered on past an expanse of glass. It showcased outside a palm-fringed swimming pool. "Children could be happy here," she murmured

Hands on hips, he tilted his head, as if to eye her with better prospective. "I could see you as an Audrey Hepburn-child advocate type."

Continuing her tour took her to a wide staircase that beckoned exploration of the floor above. He followed her up as she climbed. She could feel the heat of his eyes on her.

Midway up the stairs, at the first landing, was a guest half-bathroom. She gave it a once over and continued on up. The master bedroom featured a massive, canopied bed—and a floor to ceiling glass window that provided a magnificent view of the famed aqueduct.

As she drew closer to the window, she could make out where the stone canal, channeling down from the mountain, fed into the aqueduct at the bottom of the hill. From there, the aqueduct's arches steadily graduated to an enormous height. Evening was gradually closing in, and lights illuminated the pink arches.

"Lovely," she commented, when what she wanted to say was, I want to feel the closeness that bonded us last night. And I want to trust you.

He came up to stand behind her, so close she could feel the thousand-watt energy arcing between them. "Forlorn lovers often attempted suicide from its highest point, seventy-five feet, so the city has erected a wrought-iron barrier where the canal feeds into the aqueduct's lowest point."

"Forlorn lovers," she murmured. "Not exactly one of those happy-ever-after fairy tales."

"Aww, but the story behind the aqueduct is just that," he said. "The love between a Basque man from Spain and a Capuchin nun."

She almost turned to glance up at him, then restrained herself, for fear he would see the weakness of her wanting in her eyes.

His hands clasped her shoulders, gently kneading them. "This legend speaks of the Marquis of the Villa del Villar del Aguila and one of the most beautiful nuns in Mexico, young Sister Marcela. According to the story, when first the much older Marquis saw Sister Marcela, the love between both arose immediately. Their difference in ages mattered not. Love is love."

To better catch his murmured words, she had had to angle her head up closer to his.

"However, due to obvious complications," he continued, "Sister Marcela being not only a nun but also his wife's niece, he and Sister Marcela could never have consecrated their love. So, they made a pact. Her heart's eternal love, asking him in exchange only to build this majestic aqueduct to carry water to the convent of the Capuchinas and from there to Querétaro's dozen fountains for public use. It was completed almost five-hundred years ago. He kept his word."

Dispirited, Lauren pivoted within his arms. She had to tilt her head to look up into his eyes. "Therein lies the ending to the tale. Two lovers mismatched."

"Ahh, but you are no nun—and I, I am married not to another. I am married to you."

"This . . . this marriage of convenience is ludicrous, David!"

"Is it? By whose judgment? Not mine." His forehead lowered against hers. "My people, the tall ones, the Yaqui, would say what matters is how our spirits were placed in relation to each other. How they were aligned with the stars and moon and sun, nothing more."

Later, as she lay enwreathed by his arm and legs on the canopied bed, he muttered drowsily, "Why do you bury your heart and say the fires of womanhood are spent, *mi amor*? I don't understand this. If you burn a little, it is not a bad thing. There is always some deadwood within us that needs to be consumed, *sí?*"

"There should be a *Growing Old for Dummies* manual," she sighed, arms flung to either side of her in languorous abandon.

"You must understand you have a beauty far better than that of youth. Your gringa's eternal femininity and strength is one of the few things that that have brightened lately tortuous days. Now kiss me."

She opened her mouth to his. He tasted like domination, desperation, and damnation.

CHAPTER 33

"¡*Mierda!*" David was prowling through his shaving kit.

Brushing her teeth with the hotel's complimentary toothbrush and toothpaste she had purloined, she halted over one of the safe house bathroom's two basins, and glanced up at his reflection in the steamed mirror. A towel wrapped his muscular midriff. His hair plastered his neck and bridge of his shoulders. "What?" she asked.

"I could have sworn I brought my razor with me."

She made a rueful face. "I'm sorry. I haven't had the opportunity to shave my legs in a while, and this morning I took advantage of . . . your razor's in the shower."

His head tipped backward, his eyes closed. She could make out the muscles knotting in his neck and the deep inhalation of his broad chest.

She went to slide open the shower stall's opaque glass door, and his hand captured her wrist, and his other reached around her. "I got it." His voice was monotone, betraying no anger. But the entire bathroom was steamed with a tension that sizzled the skin . . . and the nerves.

It mattered not that the previous hours of the night spent ensconced within the maelstrom of David's Latino passion were blissful. This morning, his broodiness reduced all intimate inclinations into this heated argument. It was risible, all over a razor.

But she was fed up with kowtowing to other people all her life, to placating their rages, to pacifying their petty demands. From her father to Marty to Renita, and now, David.

She jerked her wrist loose to fist her hands at her sides. "Damn't, David! Now that I am your wife, is your Mexican machismo finally surfacing? Over a goddamn razor? Am I next to be relegated to the kitchen?"

His eyes burned a molten moss. "To the dump of *my* kitchen, you mean? Clearly, you feel you are too good for my Mexican hovel."

He flung the safety razor in the sink and began to dress. She stormed past him to the bedroom to grab her own clothing, her ridiculous wedding duds. Dressing, she felt crummy, blowing up like that. Spitting her waspish words. But she could not bring herself to apologize. Instead, she followed him into the living room. "Where are you going?"

Attired in his customary grunge-street clothes, he half-turned, his hand on the knob of the front door. "I've business to attend to."

The dangerous look on his face gave her pause. Then, mistrust reared its ugly head. "Surely, the day after a wedding even the average Mexican couple would be spending it together?"

He lifted a brow. "We are not your average Mexican couple are we? I could be late getting home tonight. I'm leaving a skeleton key to the house on the counter. But unless the house is afire, don't leave it. Surely, you'll find its opulence more accommodating than mine."

"About as accommodating as you are with your razor."

"You can slit your throat with it if you are not happy with our marital arrangement."

"Or I can slit yours if you are not happy with my financial assets!"

"I would have expected better from a woman your age," he said with astonishing and infuriating calmness, then slammed the door behind him.

"Good riddance," she muttered.

His last remark stung deeply. How did this fall out happen? She knew an incoming text on his cell phone very early that morning had awakened them while they were still abed. Rolling naked from the bed, he had leaned over, planting his hands at either side of her pillow and dropped a light kiss on her lips. "I'm in need of a shower, *mi amore*." Then, grabbing his cell phone, he had strode from the bedroom.

Whatever the message, it was brief—and it had altered his tender mood to a dispassionate professional one and now to an adversarial one.

Admittedly, David and she were both strained to the max. He had that hit man Macho—or Nacho, whatever his name was—to ward off. She had her daughter-gone-berserk to deal with. And together she and David had a parody of a marriage with which to contend.

But the worst of this was his departing dart. It poisoned her belief that at her age she was worthy of love. Devastated, she buried her face in her palms and wept. When at last her soul was drained, she swiped the tears away. Her palms dropped to overlap her heart, with its faint, sluggish beating. Her chest actually hurt there.

Despair numbed her. She could summon no interest in watching television. She grew bored . . . but not bored enough to venture outside the safe house. She considered going for a midmorning swim, which would perforce be in the raw. But lethargy mired her vitality. By noon, depression overtook her. She curled in a fetal position to doze on the white leather sofa, as soft as marshmallows.

She awakened an hour later, tears gathering in her eyes again. How could she have let herself be so misguided? What had happened to the wisdom that was supposed to come with aging? She was bitter and furious with herself. Over the years, when faced with adversity, like lack of funds to fill her gas tank or come up with the fee for a daughter's ER visit, she had sucked it up and found the wherewithal.

Later that day, as she puttered around the kitchen, half-heartedly perusing the refrigerator and pantry for something to mollify her growling stomach, she made up her mind. She was being used. She needed to put a stop to her inanity right now. Except she could do nothing until David returned. And then . . . then tonight she would confront him. Somehow convince him his farce of love and marriage did not go together like a horse and carriage. Somehow convince him to forego filing the marriage papers. And somehow find a way to elude Renita.

With a goal finally in mind, her energy, her old self's reliance, gradually began to rebuild. She scoured up enough ingredients for a casserole—and located a single bottle of chardonnay remaining on the wine rack. Then, she found a linen tablecloth for the long glass dining table. She would lull David into agreement, as he had been lulling her all along.

Answering The Call

When dinner time came and went and he did not show, she stored the casserole in the refrigerator. He had said he might be late, but she felt frustrated now. Anxious to go through with her plan.

She poured herself a glass of the chardonnay and drifted over to the piano. After marrying Marty, his cavalier regard for her composing had shriveled her musical creativity. For five decades she had avoided playing a piano or songwriting. Sang, yes, she had. That she had continued off and on over the years, mostly with choirs, never solo.

Well, there was that one time she had sung at a karaoke. After two margaritas, she had gathered the courage to climb the stage steps. After her rendition of The Pointer Sisters, *I'm so Excited*, the resounding applause had astounded her. For that ecstatic moment . . . quite probably it was her light inebriation . . . that permitted her to believe she still had talent.

For more than an hour, she rummaged through her memory of songs, idly playing them. She had forgotten and neglected that pleasure. She glanced up at the shabby chic clock on the balcony wall. With a start, she realized it was past midnight. Another day. Three more days and she was home safe, safe from the ten-day court order, which by then should expire. If so, she would be her own person again without Renita's pernicious control.

Discounting she had only exchanged the control of her future by one person for another. Financially, physically, as Mrs. Lauren Escobar she was now under the more assertive control of a Mexican husband, a man she had known for little more than a couple of weeks.

She had fallen under David's seductive spell, totally willing to feel his strong arms around her, his romantic avowals mastering her runaway heart, and his lips restoring hers to incandescent youth again . . . all in exchange for her financial surrender. How could she have been so stupid? Despite his endearment of *mi amor*, my love, to his credit, he had never actually professed he loved her; she had to give him that.

She crossed to the counter, where David had left the spare safe house key. Also on the counter was the folder containing not only their marriage certificate but also the document granting him her financial power of attorney. In his foul mood, he had left without it.

History could testify she was not the first susceptible woman to barter away her finances for flattery. She could shred that particular document before he returned. Dared she trust him?

No, this was her opportunity. She grabbed the folder and set off for the staircase and the guest bath. There she could flush the confetti of the damning document.

Midway up, at the insistent ringing of the gate's doorbell, she stopped short. She swiveled on the landing. The ringing was followed by banging against the gate's wrought iron. She frowned. That would not be David. He had the keys.

She descended several steps, where she was able to see through the door's overhead fan window. The front patio's timer light had switched on. Below, an agitated Andi and Tony were the culprits. Behind them was parked Tony's motorcycle. Something had to be amiss. Could Andi be going into labor this early? Surely, Tony would have first taken her to an ER clinic or hospital.

Rapidly, Lauren descended the remainder of the stairs, dropped the folder back onto the counter, and collected the skeleton key. Unlocking the front door, she hurried across

Answering The Call

the enclosed patio to the gate. "What is it? What's wrong?"

Tony caught her elbow and pivoted her back toward the front door. "Kramer's service processor may be on his way here, with your daughter."

"Renita? She's on her way here?"

Andi sputtered, "Ms. S—Sylvie—she phoned me about an hour ago to warn that Renita had booked a flight this morning to call on that law firm in Mexico City." She had the grace to look sheepish. "I panicked and called your burner phone to warn you but hung up before I heard it ring through."

Tony wrapped a supportive arm around Andi's expanded waist. "That does not mean Kramer's tech staff could not pick up on the ping connecting through to Andi's phone. Best we relocate. *Pronto!*"

She gestured helplessly toward the motorcycle. "We can't all three ride—"

"I'll stay," Andi said. "They don't want me. It's you your daughter wants."

Lauren squeezed the girl's shoulder. "You are one badass young woman. Let me get my purse and passport."

She whirled, running back into the safe house. Upstairs, she grabbed her purse with its precious passport and headed back downstairs. As she ran across the patio to the front gate, a dark sedan screeched to a halt alongside the motorcycle.

A mammoth of a man, one shoulder hunched significantly lower than the other, ejected from the driver's side. This could only be Macho Nacho. He jammed a pistol inches from Andi's temple and yelled, *"No muevas ni un dedo."*

"Don't move" and "finger"—those words Lauren could translate. As if anyone in their right mind would move a single finger with a death-dealing weapon aimed at their head.

A dark suited, older man with blah-blond hair exited the passenger side. Papers in hand, he strolled toward Lauren. Simultaneously, a robust figure of about the same height but that of a female, opened the car's rear door—Renita!

Like the instantaneous passing of one's entire life before the eyes at that exact moment of death, Lauren's only option presented itself: to divert both Macho and the other man's attention to her solely, away from Tony and Andi—by surrendering, acquiescing to the psychiatric hold, and returning with Renita to the United States. Dear God!

Lauren swallowed, then nodded toward her daughter who joined the flamboyantly dressed man. "No need for whatever executed orders you have, Renita. I'll willingly go with you."

Renita flashed a patronizing smile. "Glad you see that this is the best way, Mother. Electrotherapy can help your poor brain. Some patients of mine have returned to live normal lives."

"We have hospitals here for the deranged," the man with her said in a suave tone. "Let me introduce myself."

She could feel the bitter bile rising in her throat. "I know who you are. Abogado Jürgen Kramer."

He held up what looked to be a sheaf of documents. "Then you know I represent your daughter in executing your confinement and treatment."

He nodded toward Renita. She went to seize Lauren's wrist, and Andi swung her huge tote bag at Renita's chest. She stumbled back into the attorney. The papers went flying.

"Run, Ms. L!"

CHAPTER 34

Reining in his anger, David focused on navigating the Pathfinder at hypersonic speeds along the superhighway, nearly empty at one o'clock in the morning. Carretera Estatal 200 led from Querétaro's outlying international airport to the city proper.

That morning on a tip that Macho Lopez was on the move, David had made a furious dash to Mexico City, an hour's flight away, to track down the known haunts of the enforcer. He was determined to exterminate Macho, here and now, before he could harm a single hair on Tony's head —or Lauren's.

This, despite David's overwhelming compulsion to walk away from her, dump her at the border to make her way on her own . . . or break through to her heart, keep her with him as long as she would willingly stay. But his vile mood and spiteful words this morning had nixed the latter option without a doubt.

She did not fully trust him yet, much less love him, and he could not blame her. Their marriage was one-sided in his favor. She stood to lose everything; he, nothing.

He had been so wired, edgy beyond caution, beyond prudence, about Kramer and Company coming for Lauren that he had gone off and left the folder with its marriage certificate and financial instrument he had been determined to file today.

Only, Kramer stood in the way of finalizing Lauren's protection. David knew he was the better man. Kramer huffed and puffed his way through shady deals like a bull charging a red cape. And he had no scruples. Which gave him more leverage. Thus, he was more powerful . . . and more dangerous.

Mexico City's street informants, the falcons—*los halcones*, whispered Macho had only that day, that very evening, quit the city. But no one knew to where he had vamoosed. David had an awful suspicion that ruffled his hackles.

A check with his connections at the capital's international airport confirmed that Kramer and Company had caught an earlier flight out of Mexico City, just ahead of David's, and it was also bound for Querétaro.

Immediately after landing, he switched on his cell phone to find the message from Tony: Papi—Ms. L's daughter has flown to Mexico City to meet with Kramer. Fear they know safe house location. On my way there now with Andi to get Ms. L.

David coldly calculated the possible scenarios should he not arrive in time. Any one of them was intolerable. He had not protected Pilar. He had to Lauren.

He pressed harder on the accelerator. At the Bernardo Quintana exit, he swerved off, shot down it to the safe house's street, and sped up the hill. Half-way up to the safe house, he shut off his headlights and slow rolled the car to

Answering The Call

within fifty yards, two houses away from the safe house. It was lit up like a Las Vegas casino at that ungodly hour of the morning.

Heedful the Pathfinder's door hinge did not protest too loudly, he eased out. He crept to the front of the auto and, sliding beneath, groped the forward axel for his Sig Sauer P365. He jammed the handgun into his jeans back pocket.

From the driveway's shrubbery abutting the safe house patio, he knelt and surveyed the scene. Macho was aiming a handgun at Andi and Tony, backed up against the motorcycle. Quasimodo was muttering something. Off to one side, Kramer stood amidst a littering of papers. A smarmy smile plastered his handsome face.

Simultaneously, both hyper rage and equal relief that Tony was unharmed shot through David's veins like a super boosted steroid injection. He had never wanted Tony to be caught up in the underworld his father had to navigate. And where was Lauren?

He stepped out into the patio's bright timer light. In two rapid strides, as Macho's head whirled toward him, David jammed his pistol barrel against the hunchback's ear. With soft menace, he said in Spanish, "Drop your gun—and save one." The henchman tensed, and David ordered, "¡*Tira tu arma! ¡Hazlo!*"

Macho's narrowed-eyed gaze sidled past David to Jürgen Kramer. The pompous man smiled congenially. "Well, well, well."

David jerked his chin toward Macho and ordered in English. "Call off Macho Nacho here, Kramer. He knows—and you know—I'll kill him if I have to."

"Or he could kill your dearly beloved son first. What it looks like we have here is a standoff, wouldn't you say,

Escobar? Meanwhile, my client is bringing back her mother, your pseudo-wife Lauren, who tried to fly the coop."

There was a roaring in his ears. "Or I could kill *you*, Kramer."

"No need to have all this bloody and brutal kind of brawl." He snapped his fingers at Macho and nodded for him to drop the gun.

Macho scowled but let it clatter at his feet.

"Look," Kramer continued in a reasonable tone, "my firm likes to keep everything above board. So, I have also hedged my bets. I have here that exoneration of your prison record you wanted."

He went to reached inside his jacket, and David growled, "Don't—or you're dead."

Kramer's palms went up in a placating gesture. "Easy there." He nodded at Andi, standing closest to him. "If you like, the girl here can retrieve it from my inside jacket pocket."

David raised a brow at Andi. She grinned. "Always wanted to frisk a gangsta." She stepped to Kramer and cautiously reached inside the unbuttoned jacket to withdraw an oblong folded paper.

"So, here is my offer," Kramer continued. "In trade for the cancellation of your, uhh, quasi-Mexican marriage, I'll have the Texas governor sign the exoneration in order for you to obtain your pardon. Cleared, you'll be able to file for Tony's U.S. citizenship and accompany him north of the border, both of you happy campers. My client, with her demented mother, returns home, north of the border, a happy camper."

David's blood pulsed in his ears. Sweat beaded his temples. Considering all the ponderous aspects, he saw everything stood to reason that Kramer's offer made sense. After all, Lauren would never have committed to wed a poverty-stricken Mexican such as he had she not been cornered into their marriage of convenience. She would be free of him.

She deserved a home, and life, of comfort. Not his hovel. Not living on the pesos he eked out. And, too, the silly age-difference mattered to her. She and he both had undergone this farce of a marriage most reluctantly. And while she was certainly not crazy, that was a family affair to be sorted out—one in which he had no business interfering.

Yet for him, this had become much more than a mere marriage of convenience. What a fool for romantic gestures he was. "Fuck off," he told Kramer.

The arrogant attorney puffed up like a blowfish and in the artificial light his fair skin reddened. "You low-life scum, you have no idea what kind of painful pressure I can bring to bear on you and your—"

"Cover these two for me," David told Tony and passed him the Sig Sauer. "I'm going after my wife."

But after he swerved away and set off in a sprint down the cobblestone street, the safe house's timer light went off, putting the street ahead in the dark. Behind him he heard sudden scuffling and Tony's enraged howl.

CHAPTER 35

Kicking off her *huaraches*, Lauren reached the bottom of the steeply sloping, cobblestoned street, expecting any moment to twist an ankle and go splaying. She did not risk looking over her shoulder. The hill's descent had gained her speed—but that, too, of her pursuer. The briskly amplifying sound of footfalls, those of her daughter, the athlete, screamed that Renita possessed the advantage.

The intersection of Bernardo Quintana Boulevard with the spotlit aqueduct, by day highly trafficked, was at that early hour of morning deathly quiet. No cars immediately in sight to hail for help. No businesses open in which to take refuge. Her eyes skimmed the area for some sort of concealment.

"Stop now, Mother! You can't outrun me!"

Panting, Lauren darted behind the aqueduct's first arch, leading off the stone canal. Her daughter was younger and in a lot better condition. Lauren scoured the other side of the aqueduct's boulevard for concealment. Nothing—all the shops' galvanized doors were drawn down over their fronts securely.

And she was not secure. She had not the lung capacity to outrun her daughter. But climb she could—and the nearby, purple-flowered jacaranda tree offered her only retreat.

The tree clung to the aqueduct not far from where it connected with the canal, at that point no more than twenty feet or so high, she guessed. She was counting on Renita to take stock and realize her heavier, muscled body would have a tougher go of it.

Lauren began to haul herself up the trunk. She had once, for fun, taken pole dancing lesson. She had been abysmal. As testified now by her upper arms' lack of strength. She slid back down the few feet she had gained and tumbled backward onto her butt. She scrambled to her feet and tried again. Ignoring the bark scraping her arms and shins, she managed to scale the trunk to a point where she could latch onto a lower limb.

When a hand seized her ankle, seismic fear shuddered through her. Adrenaline must have taken over, because she kicked loose the grip and shinnied upwards. Then her skirt's long flounce snagged on a branch. She was wrenched to a halt. *Shit!*

Without looking down, she yanked violently. The ripped flounce gave way. Blindly, she grasped through the sparser latticework of upper boughs to yank herself ever higher. Twigs lacerated her face and hands.

The headlights of a lone, passing car briefly lit the street below. Obviously, the driver could not see the struggle occurring in the branches above. Terrified of heights, she could not look down. But she heard the cracking of branches below her. Surely, her daughter's weight was too heavy for her to pursue where the limbs grew more slender.

There, the advantage would be Lauren's.

She scaled as high as she dared. Here the slender trunk swayed with her weight. A yard above her, within reach now, the canal's ledge offered blessed refuge. Her fingers scraped its rough edge, then gripped as if doing a high school chin-up. Her fatigued arms lacked the strength to leverage her up even those last few feet.

She risked a glance below. Among the thrashing branches, her daughter was within a yard's reach of her. "Renita! Stop! We'll both fall!"

In the aqueduct's illusory spotlight, Renita's eyes looked saucer-size. "It's for your own good, Mother." One arm snaked upward. This time, she just missed grabbing Lauren's foot. The tree's insubstantial limb swayed violently with the motion. "You're crazy, don't you understand?"

God almighty. Below, another car idled by and was lost from sight. She considered jumping, trying to encounter another car for help—and knew if perchance she survived the jump, she would be a paraplegic, at best, if not comatose the remainder of her life. Comatose would compete with dementia for her most abhorrent expectancy of life's finality.

Nowhere to go but up. She swung her right leg up and over, felt her shin slam painfully against stone. But her foot caught a perch. With a herculean effort she had no clue she possessed, she hauled herself inch by scrappy inch up and over. Huffing, she rolled over onto her back.

A hand grasped a fistful of her sweaty, straggling hair. She jerked her head loose and pain ripped through her scalp. She bounded to her hands and knees and inadvertently looked down, down—and wobbled with dizziness. And just below the ledge, Renita was hauling herself up.

Lauren pushed herself erect. Felt the wind swirling around her. She struck out along the canal's yard-wide stone top. Nine strides farther, she came up short. Ahead rose the wrought-iron arc David had described that blocked suicide attempts. Like a setting sun, it prevented access to the aqueduct's escape path, arching higher and higher on its traversing path through to the city's center.

She spun. Faced her oncoming daughter.

"You lost it when Daddy died," Renita said, advancing on her. "You fucked other men afterwards." She was whipping herself into a froth. "And now this, this schizoid betrayal with a common Mexican."

Lauren held up placating palms. "I loved your father. I never was unfaithful."

Renita lunged for her. Lauren sidestepped. Her arms flung wildly to counteract her lopsidedness. After a panicky teetering, she regained her footing.

Missing the intended target, her daughter's impetus crashed her headlong into the wrought-iron arc of a barrier. In shock, Lauren watched Renita's arms windmill.

"Renita!" Lauren shouted.

Her daughter lost her balance. She lunged and seized the wrought-iron spikes. Her chest slammed against the sharp ridge of the stone canal. Her legs swung precariously over the yawning space. Her feet clawed to regain a toehold in the stone's grouted wall.

Lauren's blood turned to ice water. "Renita! Give me your other hand!"

Her daughter shook her head vehemently.

"Trust me!" Dropping to hands and knees, she scooted closer gradually, not wanting to panic Renita. "Give me your free hand so I can help you pull up."

Eyes glaring as brightly as the spotlights pinned Lauren. "No, you'll let me fall! Like you left Daddy to die."

Jesus Christ! "Renita, I'll go back with you to Houston. I swear. Only let me help you back up. I love you—no matter what, babe."

"Babe?" Renita's eyes seemed to lose their madness, uncannily replaced by a reasoning focus on Lauren.

"Yes, you are my babe. Always have been and always will. Just let me help you." She leaned farther over toward Renita. "We'll get help back in Houston, all right? Everything will be okay, I promise."

Renita grimaced, as if pondering. At last, came a tight smile. "Yes. Yes. It will be all right, Mother." She held out her free hand, as if to caress Lauren's face—then flung herself backwards.

Lauren's engulfing horror welled from her core and peeled out in a curdling scream. "Nooooo!" Gasping tears choked Lauren's throat. Pain pumped her stuttering heart erratically. Her body heaved in spasms.

Far below, Renita's body lay crumpled half on-half off the boulevard's curb. Lauren's daughter, her first born she had nursed at her breast, the light of her life when there had been so little those first years of marriage, was no more.

A swirling purple haze of pain blotted her vision. She closed her eyes. The wind howled around her. She felt herself swaying. Tremulous weakness was wobbling her supporting wrists and knees.

No, she had to pull herself together. She had to get down to Renita. Eyes snapping open, she went to reverse her direction, back toward the direction of the tree. The wind had picked up, whipping her hair. Blinking at the blinding strands, she misjudged the width of the ledge. Her left palm, bracing her intended rotation, slipped on the rim's debris and twisted. Pain shot from her wrist up her arm, and her grip gave way. Terror paralyzed her lungs. Balanced solely now on one palm and her knees, she froze.

"Lauren. Ease backward toward the tree."

David! At the shouted order, she risked a glance over her shoulder. The wind lashed the tree's upper branches crazily against the stone. Yet, he somehow catapulted up onto the ledge. Hunkered low, he began edging toward her.

Sudden horror registered in her mind. With her dead, absolutely nothing stood between David and her assets. "Get away from me!"

He eased closer, coming up on her from behind. "I know what you're thinking. But it's not your money I want. It's you. You and only you."

She shook her head. A lone, slight movement. She could not even eke out a sound. She gritted her teeth until her jaw hurt, then managed, "How touching . . . when this morning you suggested slitting my throat."

Her heart was pounding like a jackhammer. From the corner of her eye, she could see below what appeared to be a homeless street person. From his pallet sheltered within a tienda's alcove, he scuttled to the curb to gawk at Renita's contorted body. Lauren doubted if she called out to the vagrant, he would summon help.

"It has always been you I wanted, Lauren." David was creeping closer. "Now, listen to me," he called out, "I am going to wrap my arm around your waist. We'll move as one, crawling on all fours backwards."

She opened her mouth to protest, but his body overlapped her own, and his arm ensnared her waist. She screamed.

He held fast. "Be still. Hush, *mi amor*. We are going to inch toward the tree."

The wind tousled her hair. Still, she broke out in a cold sweat. Her fingernails dug into the mortared stone. "I can't."

"Yes, you can," he said against her ear. "In many ways you have been acting dead. A tree fallen to the ground, losing your substance into the earth. I would have you stand tall again, like this tree that will offer its branches for us to descend."

His sedative tone soothed her nerves that were hot wires and knotted muscles vibrating like guitar strings struck too hard. She nodded her acquiescence. She could do this.

"I would have you put down fresh roots and your trunk run with your sap again." His words lulled her, as he inched her steadily rearwards.

She kept her gaze and attention on the stones, concentrating on counting each one she scooted past. *Seven . . . eight . . . nine.* She let him tow her backwards ever so cautiously several more feet. *Twenty-one . . . twenty two.* Then, something brushed her bare arm, and she squealed.

"Sshhh," he coaxed. It's only the leaves, eager to cradle us. So here's what we are going to do. I am going to let go of you."

"No!" she gasped.

He chuckled. "And before you did not want me to hold you. I will be right below you the entire way down—and my arms, like the branches, will be ready to support you."

The security his arms offered was withdrawn. She went rigid, afraid even to draw a breath. She heard the thrashing of tree limbs, shifting with his weight.

Answering The Call

Next, he was gently exhorting her, "Just below the ledge, there is a limb sturdy enough to support your right foot. Feel around for it."

I can do this. I can do this. She repeated mindlessly the words as she edged her right foot inch-by-inch downward. *I climbed up this way, I can climb down this way.* Then she felt a toe-hold. Her pent-up breath escaped in a relieved sigh. Next, she felt his warm palm bracing the quivering muscles of her right calf.

"Now your left foot." His hand guided it down to the limb below.

Glacier-like, it seemed, she was descending, branch by swooshing branch.

"You've got this," he reassured her. "We're almost there, home base."

But then her searching foot failed to find purchase. Suddenly, she was dangling, sustained from falling only by her grip on a limb. Her hands gave way. Next, she felt her palms sliding down rough bark. Screaming, she fell, ping-ponging against branches. Friction burned her flesh. She crash landed with a jarring thud.

"Bagged you," he gusted.

Her squinched lids fluttered open to an umbrella of green. She was cradled against his chest. He sat ensconced in the lowest web of the jacaranda's sturdier branches, his outstretched legs wedged against them for balance.

Drained of adrenaline, her body went limp. Tears pooling in her eyes, she wheezed, "I'm too old for this."

"So am I," he panted. "Hold on." Shifting his weight, anchoring her with one arm, he dropped to the pavement with an impact that shook. And at the unexpectedly jolting landing, she yelped.

"Papi!"

The shout belonged to Tony. Caught up in David's arms, she craned her neck in the direction of Tony's voice. Her vision coalesced the large approaching shadows into four figures.

Macho, followed by the attorney Kramer, was herding Tony and a lumbering Andi down the street's slope and across the boulevard toward them. As they drew closer, the aqueduct's spotlight illuminated the pistol Macho held and the bloody mess that was Tony's face.

David's voice rumbled with a quiet fury. "Jesus Harold Christ!"

Abruptly, Andi halted and gaped at Renita's battered corpse splayed awkwardly like a puppet with broken strings. Then, Andi bent over, hands braced on her knees, and began vomiting.

A sob burbled in Lauren's throat. David eased her to her feet but kept his grip forcefully around her waist, preventing her from running to her daughter's body. From somewhere farther along the double-laned street a siren wailed closer. He swung toward the hunchback gunman. "You cannot possibly kill all four of us before the police get here, Macho Nacho."

At the insulting epithet, Macho bristled. "Saw you up there dick-to-ass, Escobar." He sniffed and shifted his handgun's barrel toward David. "Last time you'll ever get near a piece of ass. Nor your son. The black market will pay for your body parts."

Kramer, drawing up alongside him, said, "'Easy there, Macho." Then, to David, "Killing is so sloppy. No, I'll have both you and Lauren Hillard charged with her daughter's murder."

Answering The Call

"The woman fell on her own," David spat. "You know it was an accident." He nodded at his son and Andi. "We have witnesses."

The attorney's smile was as cordial as a sucker punch. "Lo siento, but with your prison record and Lauren Hillard's certified mental instability in my keeping, neither you two nor your two accomplices here—your son and the girl there—stand a chance in hell of seeing the light of day again."

Lauren felt the anger flexing the muscles in David's arm around her waist. "Then bring it on, asshole. I welcome dueling with you in the courtroom. Attorney against attorney."

Kramer gave a grating laugh. "I've waited a long time for this, Escobar. You'll be disqualified from the bar—and you three will be on the wrong side of the bars. You, your son, and his slut conveniently lost among a mass of prison records, with Mrs. Hillard here confined in a mental institution. And I in charge of her funds disbursement."

Her skin shriveled.

CHAPTER 36

Shod in flapping *huaraches*, the homeless man shuffled forward from his pallet into the pool of the aqueduct's glaring lights to view the brouhaha. His episodic mobility problems might be an indication of weakness. Not so the eye patch he wore, along with his Grim Reaper grin that trumped any and all *Día de los Muertos* fiesta skulls. "Don Ricardo has something to say about that," issued his gravelly voice.

With a scowl, David Escobar jerked to attention. Like an owl, his head swiveled toward him, the perceived interloper.

"Don Ricardo's calling card, if I may." From the filthy folds of his serape, his dirt-crusted hand extended to Macho Lopez not the dark gleam of metal but the playing card, the Ace of Spades.

Sniffing, the man took the playing card without glancing at it. With a belligerent roll of his shoulders, he answered testily, "So?"

He clicked his tongue in mocking disapproval. "It is Don Ricardo's desire that your life is spared—because your cornea donations on the black market will be a God-given blessing to the sightless such as myself."

Lopez looked down at the playing card and, obviously, realized this time it was a photo of his own face framed within the black heart, because he dropped the card and the pistol. Clearly, Lopez knew there was nowhere he could run, no escape from Don Ricardo's long-reaching tentacles. He fell to his knees, his clasped hands imploring. "No, *por favor!*"

The homeless man's head canted toward the oncoming source of the shrill sirens. "One of Don Ricardo's capos—along with an ophthalmologist—will be in that ambulance to attend to you."

Next, he nailed Jürgen Kramer with a glare worthy of the Evil Eye. "With Don Ricardo's benediction—" he nodded toward Renita's body, "this will be deemed a most unfortunate accident. Your fault, *si*. But Don Ricardo assures you the ultimate penalty the authorities extract for such negligence will be no more than ten years in the San Miguel Prison."

Kramer's Aryan blue eyes widened. He pivoted to run.

This time from the folds of his serape, the homeless man produced not another of Don Ricardo's calling cards but a Welrod. The pistol's silencer made the sound of a puff, like that of an encyclopedia thudding on a desk. Kramer pitched forward on the asphalt.

The homeless man ignored the gasps from the older *gringa* and the pregnant one. Flashing headlights flooded the area. "Ahhh, here they are now, Don Ricardo's enforcers."

He spared a glance for the tall man, clutching the older woman's trembling frame to him. "I propose you and your wife—and those two," he nodded at the potbellied, carrot-headed *gringa* hovering within the *joven's* embrace, "retreat to the safe house at once."

"But my daughter," the older woman pleaded, stretching her arms out in the direction of the corpse.

He tossed his Welrod next to the corpse on the curve. A ghastly sight it was. As ghastly as the smile he gave the couple. "Don Ricardo will see to recovery of the remains. You will be notified when to reclaim them. And before I forget, Don Ricardo suggests you check the safe house kitchen's knife block. There you will locate what cuts all ties that bind."

The homeless man skulked back to the *tienda* alcove and watched his son David, still holding the *gringa* at his side, turn in the direction of the darkened cobblestone side street. Antonio, hampered by the pregnant girl, followed with a shortened stride.

The police and ambulance rolled up, one after the other. Reclaiming his pallet, the old man disappeared as quietly as a bat into the obscurity of darkness. He could have dispatched a couple of his capos to terminate all this unpleasantness singlehandedly. But this time he took perverse pleasure in doing the dirty work himself.

He chuckled, reflecting how he must be getting bored with his life of the rich and famous to venture out in such a disguise merely for amusement. Well, also, for dispensing his own stamp of due justice . . . and for rectifying regrets, finally.

CHAPTER 37

Straining to look back at the murder site to find her daughter's body, Lauren spotted, hurtling down the far lane of the boulevard, two police units and an ambulance, lights whirling and sirens blaring. The cruisers braked where a weeping Macho knelt in the aqueduct's flood lights.

"Let her go," David said softly from the shadows. "Let your daughter go, *mi amor*."

That was not so easily done, but Lauren had inwardly wept so much lately over the estrangement from her daughter that she was numb. The entire gruesome episode that night had physically and emotionally drained her.

Following a trudging Andi and Tony, David urged her onward, up the hill to the safe house. Inside, he pulled her down with him to collapse onto the white leather sofa, his long legs shoved beneath the glass coffee table.

She looked down at her branch-embattled body. Already faint bruises were pooling around her calves and forearms, and grime and blood speckled her feet. "I must say," she murmured tiredly, "your underworld compadres provide quite the diversion. From a hunchback to a homeless man in your father's employ."

He flung a weary arm across his forehead and muttered, "¡*Pinche pendejos!* One and all."

She tilted up her face, the better to see his hatchet profile. "You risked your life for me—when all you had to do was to file those documents and Tony could legally immigrate to the States regardless."

His arm dropped to the back of the sofa, as if to shelter her, as he had been doing all along. "Admittedly, I have the Latino's foolish and failing temperament for adventure," he said, his tone derisive.

She uttered a shuddering sigh. "I think I have had enough of adventure."

Tension darkened the green of his eyes, searching hers. "And enough of our marriage of convenience? It's no longer necessary, you understand."

How to answer? Was he hinting he was ready to call it quits? After all, he had never told her he loved her. She hedged. "I understand that this is a convenience, an adventure of ours, I am not ready to give up."

As if her answer had somewhat appeased him, a slight smile tempered his tension.

"Hey, Papi!"

Both she and David swerved their faces toward Tony. He stood with Andi behind the kitchen counter, in his upheld hand what looked to be a couple of documents. "Look what I found."

David leaned forward better to see. "What? What are they?"

"That homeless old man—remember? He said to look beneath the knife block." With Andi peering over his shoulder, Tony flipped through some pages then glanced over at his father. "Looks like you scratched off the lucky number."

David's brow furrowed. "What do you mean?"

"According to this one document, you have been awarded the deed to this mansion—to this safe house, free and clear."

"Impossible," David scoffed. "A prank. Whose signature is on it."

Tony thumbed through the document to the back page, then his expression turned disbelieving. "Your father's, my grandfather—Don Ricardo Escobar."

"Holy shit," David breathed.

"And then there's this one." As Tony perused the other document, his expression metamorphosed from elation to astonishment. "*Dios mio*—I have a four-year scholarship, fully paid. To—to Oxford," he stuttered. "In—in England."

"Yo, Ms. L!" Andi squealed, flinging an arm up around Tony's neck, "We're going international!"

David captured Lauren's hand and, standing, tugged her up alongside him. "And, we're going to bed, children." He threw back over his shoulder. "Make yourselves scarce."

She was grateful for his arm around her waist, supporting her. She was at once exhausted, drained—and paradoxically hyper charged.

After he closed the bedroom door, he backed her against it. His knuckles gently nudged aside the windblown hair stuck to her scratched, blood-crusted cheekbone. "You need to know this—*te adoro, te amo*. If I could, I would love you with such a fire and intensity that would give you back your notions of youth. But I need to know this is no longer merely a marriage of convenience for *you*. I need to know you need me. That you love me."

She stood on tiptoe to slip her arms up around his shoulders. "As Donna Summer would say, I need you to hold me, to goad me . . . ," she brushed his lips with a slow burn kiss, then finished, "'cause, when I love, I love you solely—so come on, babe, let's dance!"

ABOUT THE AUTHOR

Parris Afton Bonds is the mother of five sons and the author of over fifty published novels. She is co-founder and first vice president of Romance Writers of America, as well as co-founder of Southwest Writers Workshop.

Declared by ABC's Nightline as one of three best-selling authors of romantic fiction, the New York Times best seller Parris Afton Bonds has been featured in major newspapers and magazines and published in more than a dozen languages.

The Parris Award was established in her name by the Southwest Writers Workshop to honor a published writer who has given outstandingly of time and talent to other writers. Prestigious recipients of the Parris Award include Tony Hillerman and the Pulitzer nominee Norman Zollinger.

She donates spare time to teaching creative writing to both grade school children and female inmates, both whom she considers her captive audiences.

CPSIA information can be obtained
at www.ICGtesting.com
Printed in the USA
BVHW041055080523
663767BV00001B/35